the Beauty

A NOVEL BY

GLORIA NAGY

THE OVERLOOK PRESS
WOODSTOCK & NEW YORK

First published in the United States in 2001 by
The Overlook Press, Peter Mayer Publishers, Inc.
Woodstock & New York

WOODSTOCK:
One Overlook Drive
Woodstock, NY 12498
www.overlookpress.com
[for individual orders, bulk and special sales, contact our Woodstock office]

NEW YORK:
386 West Broadway
New York, NY 10012

Library of Congress Cataloging-in-Publication Data

Nagy, Gloria.
The beauty / Gloria Nagy.
p. cm.
1. Brothers and sisters—Fiction. 2. Cape Cod (Mass)—Fiction. 3. Beauty,
Personal—Fiction. 4. Hotelkeepers—Fiction. 5. Hotels—Fiction. I. Title
PS3564.A36 B4 2001   813'.54—dc21   2001021836

Manufactured in the United States of America
FIRST EDITION
1 3 5 7 9 8 6 4 2
ISBN 1-58567-149-5

To Frank W. Sullivan

Acknowledgments

For their support, help, and advice, I wish to thank
Peter Mayer, David Chestnut and The Overlook Press,
Ken Starr, Bob Bookman, Dan Adler, Patricia Soliman, Paul
Fedorko, Raphael Boguslav, David Sume, Loren Barnett
Appel, Michele Corbeil and Stefanie Burns.

and always
Richard, Vanessa, Tony, Josh, Ling, Reven, Ilana,
Rosie, Misha, Farrah, Max and Ollie.

Who is she that looketh forth as the morning, fair as the moon, clear as the sun, and terrible as an army with banners?

—The Song of Solomon 6:10

"You will come to a place where the streets are not marked.
Some windows are lighted. But mostly they're darked.
A place you could sprain both your elbow and chin!
Do you dare to stay out? Do you dare to go in?
How much can you lose? How much can you win?"

—Dr. Seuss
Oh, the Places You'll Go

Prologue

She never saw anyone and she never heard anything, but she knew. She felt danger where she had always imagined her soul was, if she had one, which she doubted. She was nothing if not calm.

Silent and slick as a pond eel, someone entered, slithered by, brushing her calves.

She turned and hit the light switch, arrogance masking her terror. Being seen was always her power. "You've got to be kidding," she said, sarcasm oiling her laugh, making it trill.

The laugh was a mistake. She had misjudged. She knew it instantly, saw the force of the rage it unleashed. She took a step back, bracing as the bullet invaded. Her fingers fanned, trying to cover that place where her soul could have been.

Time passed. Lying there, leaking life, hearing the flow of her blood, she had no sense of it. She opened her eyes. "Please," she whispered, honest now that the game was almost over. She raised her wounded arms, trying to protect her beauty as the gun came closer. "Please, not my face."

PART ONE
Us

CHAPTER ONE

One week last spring in New York City, two women died. This in itself was not unusual. What was unusual, even in a city such as New York, and even in the twenty-first century, was who they were and how they died.

One, unmarried and living alone in an expensive rental on the Upper East Side, was brutally murdered, her face shattered and her fingertips sliced off.

The other, a Park Avenue socialite married to a prominent businessman and mother of a ten year old daughter, committed suicide. She did this by crawling down onto the tracks at the Lexington Avenue and East 59th Street subway station during the height of the morning rush hour and allowing the Number Six train to tear her apart.

I was her brother.

To the follower of such news stories, these deaths might be shocking but wouldn't seem in any way related. But they were.

And that's the story I'm going to tell.

* * *

On a bright April morning, the first after a long New York winter, I was walking back to my apartment on West 72nd Street mulling over my first session with a well-reputed "grief therapist." My sister had killed herself one week earlier, and I wasn't doing so well.

I had been to see many doctors about her and with her over the years—it was very *Prince of Tides*—but I loved her and found her pain to be unbearable. For myself, that is; up until the moment she lay down in front of the train and gave up, she bore it with an enormous amount of grace.

Dr. Hofbrau, the therapist, was of the Upper West Side school of psychotherapists. Upper East Side shrinks looked and acted more like lawyers or bankers, well dressed, conservative, giving the patient an illusion of corporate acceptability. The Upper West Side favored sweater vests, Earth shoes, bow ties, and wrinkled corduroy suits that carried an anti-glitz professorial air. The females, even the young ones, hunched forward in a kind of osteoporotic expectation and were fond of large dangling earrings and pounded silver necklaces studded with large chunks of minerals mined by various tribesmen in remote Third World provinces.

Their apartment offices were clustered in cavernous pre–World War II co-ops, guarded by emaciated doormen left over from WPA days. The decor was invariably a kind of moldy "nature is good" motif and smelled of kitty litter, tobacco, and air freshener.

Dr. Hofbrau was an elderly, gnomish German woman with bright mischievous blue eyes and a club foot shod in an orthopedic shoe.

"What seems to be your problem, Mr. Duckworth?"

"What seems to be your problem, Dr. Hofbrau?"

"Is that supposed to be funny, Mr. Duckworth?"

"Apparently not, Dr. Hofbrau. I suppose it's a reflex. I'm a reporter, I usually ask the questions."

"Is there a question you'd like to ask me?"

"Well, actually, yes, Dr. Hofbrau. When was the last time someone butt-fucked you on the back of a Harley?"

"Last night, actually. I'm still a bit sore."

What had I said? What had *she* said? The words had spewed forth from my numb and battered brain as if an alien force had taken me over. I had gone there because I was frozen, unable to feel any grief, but something happened when she gave it right back to me like that; she thawed me out. The hands that had been squeezing me shut—clutching my throat, suffocating the blood struggling to reach my heart—let go. I began to sob. The last good cry I could remember was when my niece, Penelope, my sister's only child, was born some ten years before.

When I regained my composure the doctor reached into a small mollusk-covered box beside her, removed two unfiltered French cigarettes, placed them both in her wide unlipsticked mouth, and lit them.

Granted it was not Paul Henreid and Bette Davis, but I was impressed. She hobbled across her vast crown-molded living room and handed me one. Smokers are like drug addicts; they can always tell their own kind. I inhaled deeply, the first real cigarette I'd had in years, and watched her hobble back.

I thought of my sister and how she always ended up feeling sorry for her doctors, denying her own suffering in some semi-solipsistic effort to fix them up by altering her own truth. She would have liked Dr. Hofbrau.

The doctor inhaled deeply and swallowed. I was transfixed, imagining the smoke pouring out of her ears, floating around inside her, coating her frail innards with toxic ash.

"So now, Mr. Duckworth, would you like to start again?"

"I'm sorry. I apologize. I've never talked to anyone that way. I—"

Dr. Hofbrau exhaled and waved her free hand. "No, no, enough. Actually, I rather enjoyed it. A provocateur is quite refreshing. Everyone is so PC nowadays, no one takes any emotional risks. Shall I rephrase my original question?"

The cigarette on an empty stomach and all the unexpected emotion made me dizzy. I stubbed it out in a small conch shell that I assumed was an ashtray, since I doubted many pearl divers or conchologists had been to see her lately. I tried to take a deep breath, but the squeezing was back.

She waited, puffing away, her little legs barely reaching the floor under her bamboo chair.

"I can't seem to say it."

"Very well. How about starting elsewhere? What do you report on, Mr. Duckworth?"

"Actually, I haven't used Duckworth for a long time. My byline is Jonny Duck; it's what everyone outside of Newport calls me."

"Oh, yes. I've seen that name in the *Times*."

"Not lately. I was a crime reporter for the *Times*, but I quit, went up to the Cape for a while to edit a local paper, and now I'm mostly doing freelance white-collar-crime pieces for magazines."

"And why did you leave?"

"Let's just say I got tired of having bloody dead people all over my life and I needed to smell the sea again. New Englanders are like that. But now, thanks to the Menendez boys and O.J. and the rest, the bloody dead people have moved over onto the lifestyle pages, the travel and business sections, even the fashion news, so I'm seriously considering going back to violent crime writing to get some peace and quiet."

The sides of her mouth twitched, and I interpreted this to be a smile. There was a kindness, even empathy, in her eyes that was familiar. My grandmother's face replaced hers: wise bright-blue eyes that had seen just about everything. Longing roiled through me. One more minute of Granny O's love and I'd be fine.

The invisible squeezing hands were making it hard to continue. My dizziness seemed to make Dr. Hofbrau wiggle, giving her a cartoonish look. I was strangling. "My sister Faith—Faith

Hope was her name—but Faith lost her hope and she sat down on the subway track and the brakeman couldn't stop. Four cars of the Number Six train ran over her. Her legs were severed. She bled to death before the paramedics got there. She was so composed no one even noticed her. She climbed down, folded her arms, and waited for the train. Out like a lamb.... Jesus, she's fucking dead!"

The hands let go again. This time the doctor sat and waited until I stopped. My nose was running and I pulled one of my father's white-silk monogrammed handkerchiefs, which I carried in some sort of perennial prep school rebellion. Honking my snooter into it was like power or payback. And now here was his namesake bawling away in front of a stranger in the heart of socialist Urbania.

"Do you know why she did this, Mr. Duckworth?"

"Why does anyone do it? She certainly had the ingredients: lousy childhood, betrayals, fragile nerves. But people go through all kinds of unbelievable shit and forge ahead, and she had everything to live for; so, yes and no. I do and I don't. Maybe it's just a heightened moment of what we all struggle with every day, only one morning you wake up and you've utterly lost the courage to live. Whatever you need to believe in to get out of bed and brush those incisors and do that loofah shower act and perk the java, gulp down that multiple-with-iron, and go on. Great line in the epigram of *Portrait of the Artist*: 'Welcome, O life!' Well, maybe you just can't remember why the hell you should welcome life. Maybe that moment we've all had, when that courage just dies, it just didn't come back for her. She just lost it."

"But this was also an act of some very powerful rage. It was a violent, self-mutilating act. Is this familiar to you or in your family?"

"My mother killed herself and my sister found her. My mother was fifth ward Irish and beautiful; my father was Newport society, the only son of one of the old-money WASP families who chugged up to Rhode Island from Wall Street on the weekend steamers. He was a sadistic bastard, and the only good thing about her death was that he went away and my mother's mother raised us."

The doctor pushed herself forward with her tiny liver-spotted hands. Faith would have brought her some of that special cream she found in France for Granny O.

"Mr. Duckworth, we must stop now. Would you like to meet again?"

So walking home I was preoccupied with all the nuances of my extraordinary encounter with Dr. Hofbrau. I had insulted a crippled old woman in a hostile and pugnacious way, I had wept like a sissy in her presence. And why had I—who never talked about myself or my family to anyone but them and had never even thought of therapy for any Duckworth but my sister—decided to go there in the first place?

Our grandmother had raised us to rely on ourselves and keep it simple. And now I had gone over to the enemy and displayed self-pity and a whiny breast-beating sort of grief (her death is nothing compared to my loss). All this was enough to keep me from noticing the two fellows waiting for me in the lobby of my building.

"Jonny Duck?" said one. I turned, taking in the bad haircuts, cheap suits, and peacock posture required of all NYPD homicide detectives worth their salt. I thought I knew all of them, but I'd been away longer than I wanted to admit.

Badges flashed. "NYPD, Detectives Pacci and Dinelli. We'd like to ask you a few questions."

"Do I win anything?"

"This is not funny, sir. We've got a murder here."

"Here? In the lobby?"

"Figure of speech. You can talk to us upstairs or we can take a little ride downtown."

Upstairs we went, to the privacy of my bachelor quaters. I could see my apartment through the paranoid peepers of the "cop compass" as my friends in the DA's office would say.

I'd barely unpacked since I left the Cape, and my apartment looked exactly like what it was: the barren but cluttered waiting rooms of a man with no roots, no wife or children, no pets, plants, passions, or hobbies. A place where an unlived life went on as if the inhabitant were ever on alert, waiting for the call to drop everything and take off. But there was nowhere left to go. Wherever it was, I had been there. I did it, guys. Whatever the fuck it is, I did it; I must have to feel this guilty.

I didn't offer anything or ask them to sit down. I had hung out with enough cops to know that anything you did to be human only made them suspect you more.

Dinelli, the taller of the two, who had an excess of wavy black hair and sad hound-dog eyes, pulled out one of my business cards. "Is this yours?"

"Yes."

"Do you know a Madeline James who resides at 121 East Eighty-second Street?"

"No."

"Do you know how your card came to be in her apartment?"

"No."

He pulled out three other business cards. "Do you know any of these people?"

"Yes."

They made eye contact, which I took to mean this was a big deal.

"I'm afraid we're going to have to ask you to come down to the station with us."

"May I ask why?"

"Do you own a gun, sir?"

"No. And I've already told you I don't know anyone named Marilyn ..."

"Madeline James."

"—Whatever. I have absolutely no idea how my business card came to be in her apartment, but I'm a journalist and I give out cards to dozens of people every week."

They were not impressed.

Pacci, the smaller one, who was clearly the nervous caffeine-crazed crime buster of the two, was chewing gum so fast it looked like his jaw ran on batteries.

"Our lieutenant wants to ask you some questions. She said you're a good guy, so *be* a good guy, okay? We've got a Jane Doe who's been in the morgue for awhile and wasn't in such good shape when she got there, and we'd like you to take a look and see if anything comes to mind."

"Look, gentlemen, maybe I'm a tad slow, this hasn't been one of my best weeks—"

"Yeah, your sister. The lieutenant mentioned it."

"Well, then. If the victim has a name and an apartment, she's hardly a Jane Doe, so why do you need me?"

"Good point." Dinelli sighed, trying to figure how much it was safe to tell me.

"Let's just say she was—altered. Her name is phony and the apartment was leased through an intermediary in Geneva. The rent's been paid for a year in advance by wire transfer from a Swiss bank, and no one—and I mean no one—seems to know a single thing about this lady.

"She was like some ghost or vampire or somethin', never talked to anyone in the building, always wore purple—head to toe. Suits with matching gloves and big hats and sunglasses. No job, no visitors, and she followed the same routine every day. Bought exactly the same food at the market, ate the same breakfast at the Greek's on the corner, and always went out at night. No checking account, no credit cards so far, no family photos, no bills or letters. Just a lot of purple clothes and the business cards hidden in a drawer by her bed. *Capisce?* You're not a suspect at this time; we just need a little help here."

This was, of course, an old crime reporter's wet dream. There is nothing close to the rush, not to mention the distraction from my grief and Dr. Hofbrau, of a mysterious faceless female waiting in the deadhouse darkness to be reclaimed.

When Daisy Mae Decker was not storming around the Nineteenth Precinct ripping perpetrator and police egos apart with equal demonic glee, she was really a nifty broad, all 220 or so pounds of her, which of course gave her a provocative edge in itself. Being a big heavy blonde was even better than being black, in terms of nobody daring to mess with you at City Hall or the DA's office. I had known her for twenty years, ever since she was a rookie giving inspirational talks to battered wives and rape victims. Because she was both, she could take an audience of spiritually emptied women and pump hope back in with just the fervent zeal of her honesty.

We had walked a few crooked miles together over the years, and I considered her, as much as anyone, to be my friend. She had spent the last ten Thanksgivings with my family at my grandmother's house, and she had a special fondness for my niece, based, among other things, on the fact that Penelope was also chubby.

As long as Daisy Mae Decker was in charge of this case, I reassured myself as the gang of two drove me across town, I had nothing to worry about.

My escorts sat me down, brought me coffee and one of those greasy and irresistible doughnuts police stations are famous for, and left me alone with my new and surprisingly welcome thoughts. Who was she and who had killed her so brutally?

Swiss bank transfers and aliases meant someone seriously did not want to be connected to this woman. Married would fit. Married and maybe afraid of blackmail by a vengeful mistress? Discarded was possible, the free rent a payoff when the romance became nothing but butts and empty Beaujolais bottles.

I looked up to see the lieutenant herself waddling toward me, parachute wings of black fabric blowing beside her, gold balls swinging from her chest and ears, frizzy blond mane bouncing around her voluminous white shoulders. Everything about Daisy Mae screamed for attention; she could handle anything but being ignored. A massive virago, always in motion even when standing still, her voice now boomed across the room, a loud needy instrument. "Jonny Duck, you old preppy dick! I've missed your little Kennedy mug. Where ya been, boy? Heard you was back, no more hidin' out on the Cape, writin' restaurant reviews and home decor tips for the homos. Knew it couldn't last. You're a lifer like *moi*."

"Even lifers need a little break now and then."

"Naw. Not the real ones. One day without doughnuts and we're toast." Dinelli and Pacci swaggered over, waiting for directions. "So, my babies treat ya okay?"

"A couple of sweethearts. I was kind of disappointed we didn't have time to share some past life experiences, but otherwise they were swell."

Daisy Mae laughed, causing all her various gold baubles to jingle and her massive breasts to heave. "Oh, Ducky, ya always could make me laugh. It's that black-Irish heart of yours. You got your Granny O's ticker; it's what saves your sorry skinny ass."

The detectives were not enjoying this spasm of warmth toward an outsider and a rival for the lieutenant's attention.

Daisy Mae put her pudgy ring-covered fingers on her wide hips.

"So, Ducky, ya gonna help your old gal pal out here?"

"I'll do my best."

"Fabuloso! Let's hit the morgue."

She took off, hair flying and caftan billowing. She looked like a figure on the prow of some Disney Viking ship, her leonine head up high, as she led us, three spindly, surly members of the real second sex, down the bleak echoing hallways to her warship.

I had always found it interesting that the word *morgue* is used to describe both where dead bodies are held for identification and where old newspaper files are kept. Dead people and dead information, both languishing and hoping to be reclaimed: a perfect combination for a fool like me.

I had been in more than my share of both kinds of repositories over the years, and they basically had the same effect on me: anxiety and anticipation. The difference was in degree. Dusty jaundiced newspapers or reams of microfiche and computer data did not make me heave with revulsion or contemplate my own dicey mortality. At the same time I never dozed off while looking at a corpse. Both places had their pluses and minuses.

Police morgues are cold and somber and so, for the most part, are the folks who work in them, and this also applies to newspaper morgues. This is as it should be, since both places are about the past, the finished, the discarded, the of-no-further-use-to-anyone-but-the-seeker-of-memory, the resolvers of the unresolved. Daisy Mae Decker was a highly unlikely morgue visitor, since there was not a cold, somber corpuscle in her.

"Hey, Theo, shuck the oyster." This was Daisy Mae—speak for removing the body from the refrigerated box that held it.

Theo was a tall slim black man who would have been handsome if not for the unfortunate fact that he sported several large pinkish gray growths on his face and neck. Rumor had it that Daisy Mae and Theo had forayed together in the land of Eros, but the concept was too visually unnerving to pursue. What made it credible was the sexual bantering that went on between them.

"So, Theo, how's the fungus fucking? Any new porno? Did ya

know, Ducky, that Theo's been studyin up on this Valley Fever fungus makin' people sick, and some group of biologists investigatin' it found out that lo and behold, funguses fuck! Goin' at it like rabbits. Maybe that's not the right comparison. But this is big science news, right, Theo?"

Theo smiled, which caused the growth on the side of his jaw to shift. "Saprophytcs do seem to have their passions."

Theo was from Dallas and had the southern black man's laconic facade, which barely concealed the bitter victim's rage beneath. The only subject Theo ever talked about without an edge was barbecue. Concerning the fine points of Texas versus Carolina barbecue, he was beatific.

Theo pulled out the drawer and we all moved closer. The moment when the corpse comes forward is hard to describe. The gelid shrouded thing slides out into a room of viable life forms, its privacy violated, ripped from peace into confusion to be judged by its wounds, a vacated soul-departed object of pity. It is, of course, one thing to stand there as professionals and outsiders and quite another if the purpose of the visit is to identify a loved one. This was an experience Faith's husband, Benjamin, had spared me.

The hairs in my ears tickled for some reason and my whole body shifted into the kind of hyper-awareness you can feel in church or at a stuffy formal dinner. Before Theo unzipped the body bag, before I had moved close enough to feel the tingles of projection crossing the line between who I was and what I would someday become, my body knew a darker reality. The squeezing was back, only now it was accompanied by nausea and a pounding fear, pattering in my chest, making me gasp for breath. My most primal instincts, the Darwinian creature I harbored, knew that what waited in the zip-locked coffin would lead me to a truth that would buckle me, force me back through the maze of memory into myself.

Theo pulled the zipper, and the decomposing remains of a

woman appeared, a sick joke, like Theo himself, one cheated by some cellular folly, the other by an act of vengeance.

It was clear from the hair and the graceful fine-boned shape that this had been a beautiful woman. As she was now—the center of her face macerated, eyes, nose, and mouth, her hands broken like Christ's hands, holes splashed with tissue and fingers chopped into grotesque stumps—she was horrible, witchlike and perverse. Her full brown-nippled breasts and flat stomach, her mound of Venus, still enticing, created a tangle of inappropriate emotions, lust and revulsion twined together. And there was that apprehension, the pounding in my heart, the vomit pushing against my throat. Daisy Mae caught it, quick as a whiplash.

"So, talk to me, Ducky. Ya know her?"

I tried to swallow. I tried to breathe. Neither function seemed to be working very well. I must have been staring at her pubis.

"She look familiar or what?"

I found the breath I needed. "Could you ... could I see her feet?"

Daisy Mae and the Italian bookends did that subtle twitchy cop eye signal among themselves. "Her feet? Ducky, I never figured ya for one of those sniffer types. Theo, let the man see the feet."

Long slender legs, elegantly formed. Ankles like cut crystal, high arches, dancer's insteps. The toes slanting down, biggest to smallest, perfectly proportioned. I swallowed, trying to unsqueeze. I had to be sure.

"Is there a tattoo on the outside of the left heel?"

Daisy Mae nodded, and Theo reached down and turned the pale white foot as if it were part of his Sunday barbecue.

Daisy Mae leaned over. "Didn't see this on the autopsy report. You slippin', Theo? All that smoked meat foggin' your brain?"

She looked over at me, harder now. They were all poised, bloodhounds before the hunt. I closed my eyes.

"Is it a small purple heart?"

"Say the secret woid, and the duck pays off!"

I was not going to pass out in the Manhattan morgue, and I was not going to puke either. For a second, I almost envied her, envied the fact that soon they would cover her up and let her slip back into darkness, to arctic sleep. No more terror and regret and grappling with demons. No more desperate journey toward that elusive North Star I had learned to aim at in Narragansett Bay, a beacon you always knew was unreachable and mostly unseeable, except on the clearest fall nights. She was beyond all that and probably lolling below us, that caustic curl at the corners of her beautiful mouth. "I know her," I said, in a voice that seemed to be coming from someone else, someone much smaller and really scared.

CHAPTER TWO

*A*nd so you have the who, what, when, and where, the sine qua non of all traditionally trained journalists. The why will take somewhat longer, being part of the storyteller's job.

There are many places to start. I could begin all the way back with my ancestors. My Irish maternal side, "wharf rat riff-raff" as my paternal grandmother the Hydra dowager of Bellevue Avenue would say, or with my illustrious paternal side, the strain who arrived in relative style on the *Mayflower*, not too far from where what's left of them still reside.

I could tell a tale of robber barons and greed, of snobbery and ritual so stifling it led many of the coquettes and coxcombs to madness and despair. Or, I could begin later still, with the births of my sister and me and the confusion that marked our early years. Were we royalty or trash, rich or poor, deserving of kindness or wrath? Often an average day incorporated all these conflicts, all roads inevitably leading to a dead end. The Duckworths put their reedy little rumps in a row, my mother folded, my father decamped, and our Irish granny took us under her swan wing and held tight. But that's another story.

I could start many places in my past or even, though I have less information, in the past of the mutilated beauty on the cold metal tray, once human—though those who knew her well might quibble over that word—and now reduced to some sort of perverse essence. But I won't. I'll save her for later. I will instead begin where it really began for me: a year ago last January in the lobby of the Baumont Hotel in New York City.

A hundred years from now, if we haven't blown ourselves away in some spasmodic chain reaction of terrorist bombings and civil wars or plagued the planet with ravenous microbes, some cultural anthropologist will produce a work in whatever form has replaced books, newspapers, and slide-show presentations in hotel ballrooms. It will be called "Icons from the Age of 'They Had to Be Kidding.'" Among the probably endless examples of the absurdity of life in American urban centers at the ledge of the millennium will be a roll-them-in-the-aisles photo montage from the days of the Trendy Hotel scene.

My arrival by taxi at this "boutique hotel" marked my first foray back to Manhattan since my self-imposed exile the previous summer. I'd been summoned by my brother-in-law, Benjamin "Barracuda" Wise, as I was fond of referring to him in the privacy of my mind. He had broken into my relatively peaceful time-out with a bull's-eye shot to my emotional panic button. "I'm worried about Faith. I need to discuss some things with you in person." I drove to Boston and took the next shuttle.

My taxi had barely stopped when an elegantly black-clad boy/man shot forward and flung open the door.

Since I took him to be a fellow guest, his aggression seemed excessive, even for midtown Monday. He grabbed my bag, flashed a Chiclet grin, and welcomed me to the Baumont.

I got out, feeling prickly. I'd only been gone a matter of

months, and now even the bellboys were more polished and hip than us warriors of the old world. I transferred my irritability to Benjamin, ascribing venal and Machiavellian motives to his choice of shelter.

My inner disarray wasn't helped by the sight that greeted me in the lobby. It was hard to see in the dim greenish haze, but as my eyes adjusted I could make out bodies moving in slow motion, by New York standards, as if they were so evolved and beyond the need to keep up they could afford the luxury of strolling.

Every single person in the lobby was dressed entirely in black. For a moment I wondered if there were in fact a dress code that Benjamin had forgotten to mention, or a new gimmick offering each guest a special outfit, singling out the truly au courant from the less enlightened hordes. Or maybe they were all vampires and by morning I too would be drifting from moderne settee to coffee bar, my black ensemble highlighting the bloodless pallor of my recent conversion to the land of the totally cool.

I registered and was led into the tense silence of the dark, crowded elevator like some attendee at a cyberspace funeral.

We stopped and I stepped out into more darkness, almost colliding with an enormous unmounted mirror that was leaning against the floor. I realized, rather quickly for a design heathen who grew up with nineteenth-century hand-me-downs and garage-sale knickknacks, that the mirror hadn't fallen but was supposed to be like that.

Finally we reached my door, indistinguishable from the cell-like clones around it. The room wasn't large enough for me and my guide to stand in together. He avoided my eyes, obviously familiar with such moments of discovery, the wild look in the eyes of the guest who, however fashionable, might still lose it at the thought of being shut inside a space barely big enough for two people to stand in simultaneously.

I handed the kid a five and waved him out. No need for him to regale me with the numerous special features. He seemed relieved and left without so much as an enjoy your stay, which at the moment would have seemed less ironic if said to Papillon on Devil's Island. The door closed and I felt a moment of total panic, as if I had been pushed inside an attic closet by a deranged aunt. The room was black and stifling.

I fumbled around for something resembling a lamp. A tubelike cylinder was hanging over a tiny chipped table with miniature chairs, resembling a child's playhouse. I reached inside, flicked a switch, and a greenish glow appeared. I turned toward the window, which was covered with bent discolored blinds, and tripped, stumbling onto what had to be the bed. The mattress sat on the floor, frameless and covering the entire room, leaving only enough space to walk sideways between it and a cabinet that I assumed was the closet, to reach what I could only hope was the bathroom.

Maybe the toilet and sink were in the cabinet? I walked over and opened it: a TV and some drawers. There was a God after all. The room fueled my burgeoning outrage at the accelerating insults to common sense, the racks of Emperor's New Clothes that had shoved reason and truth so far back into the hall closets of our feverish lives.

I threw down my bag and left the trick room. I wasn't even sure the claustrophobia I felt would allow me to stay there; but unless I returned in a state of total inebriation and exhaustion, sleep would be impossible. The elevator appeared, crammed with more antlike beings. The elevator was bigger than my room.

I took a long deep breath, buttoned my overcoat, and hit the street, heading for Fifth Avenue. It had rained while I was inside and the sky was that peculiar predusk afternoon gray in the winter-city mix of sun and mist that makes me feel sad and hopeful all at once. This has always seemed to me to be a particularly New York emotional hash.

I crossed Sixth Avenue and the surge began. Whenever I have been away for any extended period, I lose my street rhythm, forgetting the push, the pace required to move forward. I felt like a newly released prisoner of war or hospital patient, thrust into the middle of Olympic trials for the hundred-meter dash. I could barely keep up. Where had all these extra people come from? Had some breeding experiment hatched a whole new generation of businesspersons in the past six months?

I raced along, too consumed with the effort to fit in and stay afloat in the churning sea of midtown minnows to decide what to do with the two hours I had to spare.

I paused before the bright post-holiday windows of Saks, brimming with vignettes of frozen party life. Alabaster people molds clad in clothes no one ever wears, preparing for scintilating social moments no one ever has. BUY ME and you too can live in a glass window in a pricey designer gown with cheerful fake tots, an ascot-adorned hunk, and a permanent grin. In I went, perambulating the ground floor cosmetics section aimlessly, as if I'd wandered into never-neverland. A midlife male who mostly bought his clothes mail order and never dated the same woman long enough for couple's shopping excursions, I had no memory of the last time I'd been in such a store. Creams, scents, lipsticks, and lotions, bloated aisles and counter streets glistening with serpentine mega-gallons of glamorous girl stuff.

It occurred to me as I moved around, inhaling the sweet alien fragrances, pleasantly lulled by the hum of commerce and Muzak, that what they were selling, what really everyone who sells anything is selling, is fear or fantasy. Buy me and you will stay young, be beautiful, attract Prince Charming, hold on to King Arthur; resist me and you will lose.

Women of all ages, styles, finances, shapes, and sizes were being cheerfully manipulated by the salespersons, who all seemed to be the same, almost a separate species, maybe grown like bacteria in laboratories and genetically coded with personality characteristics that fell somewhere between Baywatch Barbie and Rasputin.

"You are soooo—dehydrated!" one of them hissed at an attractive woman, who visibly blanched. I half expected the security guards to rush forward and cart the poor parched victim away.

I retreated, dashing across the street and up the steps into Saint Patrick's. As lapsed a Catholic as I was, I still preferred sacred oil to Estée Lauder.

I had been away a long time.

Certain rituals bring comfort. Genuflecting for one, lighting candles for my long-dead mother for another. I performed both rites and sat down in one of the center-back pews usually occupied (however sparsely) by tourists and timid non-Catholics, unsure of what might be expected of them.

I knelt reflexively and closed my eyes, resting my forehead on my threaded fingers. Flashes of memory flooded me, snapshots of my childhood, a family collage of communions, baptisms, funerals, and confessionals. "Hail, Mary, full of grace.... Forgive me, Father, for I have sinned." Granny O's amber rosary, comforting, hypnotizing, bought by my mother in Rome at Saint Peter's itself.

How I had envied my grandmother her faith. Faith. My Faith. I prayed for her to be okay. I prayed to a God I was barely on a first-name basis with anymore that whatever my brother-in-law had to tell me the next morning would not be too bad.

I let the pictures flow. Faith sobbing at the loss of her favorite doll, Granny O sitting beside her bed. "Say the Saint Anthony prayer, darlin'." Six-year-old Faith, gulping tears, believing completely: "Dear Saint Anthony, look around, something's lost that must be found." Her doll was found. Everything prayed for was always found; Saint Anthony almost convinced me, until we lost our mother. Night after night in the dark, I'd hear my sister whispering into her pillow, "Dear Saint Anthony, look around," but our mother never came back and we both stopped believing.

We pretended for Granny O; let her trot us up to Saint Augustus on Sunday mornings; took communion, the body and blood of poor old Jesus pinned up all alone on the wall, those spiky twigs pushing into his head—as frightening for a kid as any Stephen King movie, I am here to tell you.

The church and the fifth ward were my grandmother's life, and it became our lives too, or a big part of them, the other part involving Trinity Church and Bailey's Beach Club and the Newport branch of the New York Yacht Club, the dark side of our moon as we tromped back and forth in our gravity boots on those spaced-out Sundays before we were shuttled back to earth by the Duckworths.

What I had never allowed myself until that moment, bowed down in the late-afternoon stillness, after the tourist rush and before the five-thirty mass, almost alone in the great fake Gothic church, was to drop my defenses and accept the comfort. I knelt in the quiet, warm house of God, smells of candle wax and furniture polish triggering memory.

In my rush to flee the hotel and the teeming secular bazaar of Saks, I had stumbled back to the foundation of my childhood, an unseen hand gently pushing me up the stairs and toward the solace of the bended knee, the closed eye, the power of silence that I was, in some way, already preparing to lean on. My unconscious knew something that I was still spared. *Something's lost that must be found.*

I stood up and left quickly, daunted by what I had done. It almost felt like something to be ashamed of, as if I might be caught leaving and find my face splashed over the tabloids, LAPSED CYNIC SEEN LEAVING SAINT PATRICK S. FRIENDS STUNNED BY ABERRANT BEHAVIOR. "I never would have believed it! Not Jonny!" I might as well have emerged from a Klan meeting or a voodoo sacrifice.

What did it mean? Was this a step forward or would I entirely lose my urban persona now that I was untethered from my old life, friends, and career? Would I turn into one of those loopy island exile types, spouting religious mystical liturgy, becoming a vegan and hanging out in New Age bookstores in Provincetown dressed in Russian army uniforms and flip-flops? For the first time since I'd left New York for the Cape I felt shaken by my choice.

I still had an hour and a half left until I met with my agent (who also happened to be Benjamin's brother Andy), so I decided to try and see my sister and my niece.

I grabbed a cab and headed up Fifth Avenue, wishing I had time to walk and think these unsettling thoughts through.

I knew I was breaking Benjamin's unspoken rule, not to see Faith until after he gave me his view of her condition. He was always thrusting himself into the center, creating one of those triangulations her analysts were so opposed to. Maybe if I saw her first, I would be a better advocate when I met with him.

The truth was he intimidated me. I hated like holy hell to admit it, but that cocky self-made rich man's righteousness really pushed my buttons: the unsaid always being that he, coming from the Bronx and nothing, had conquered the world, and I, coming from Yankee royalty and privilege, had basically bubkes to show for it.

My main achievements, several journalism awards and a true crime best-seller that had become a movie, meant nothing to a guy like Benjamin Wise. All he really respected in anyone was the power of money and the kind of particular idiot savant smarts that knows how to make it and take it away from turkeys like me. So, screw Benjamin. I got out at the corner of Fifth and 65th and walked up the block to their building.

The regular doorman was off and I waded through the scrutiny and the calling up and the final approval and made my way past the Chinese urns filled with fake flowers and tripped as always on the threadbare Persian covering the blocks of black and white diamond-patterned marble, glancing at myself in the dusty beveled mirrors, and turned past the second-tier impressionist prints.

This was the preferred lobby look of the truly "in" New York co-op. Anything too clean or blatantly costly was considered bad form and unnecessary. Why waste the lucre on the lobby, which was basically only inhabited by Puerto Rican janitors and Irish doormen, Chinese food deliverers, dry cleaning dropper-offers, and pimply teenagers from Gristedes?

The elevator had been converted to automatic, and Samuel, the old black operator, was long gone, replaced by a panel of buttons. Samuel always remembered my name and let my niece ride up and down with him for hours on lonely-child-of-rich-busy-parents afternoons, when by some miracle or other she was freed of all play dates, ballet and gymnastics classes, piano lessons, and the dread weight-management sessions.

The elevator was paneled with wood and carpeted. It smelled like the club car on the Metroliner and always made me feel melancholy. There was something arid and gloomy about it, the passive carrier of prestigious bodies, up and down on their endless journeys to see and be seen.

It was as if, in those private moments inside its polished walls, they relaxed just a bit and let a piece of their true selves loose: fragments of longing, rage, frustration, loss. A sigh, a fart, a tear, a secret laugh. An alligator-shod foot stomped in anger, a silicon tit re-jigged inside a Chanel suit. Moments of unguarded truth, all the energy absorbed and housed. The force of it settled over me, a kind of emotional poltergeist, as I whizzed up or down. I asked Faith once if she ever felt like that in there, and she said that she felt like that everywhere.

The doors opened, and my niece was waiting for me.

"Uncle Jonny!" she said, as if it were a wonderful thing; somebody on earth really glad to see me.

We called her Pebble, despite the fact that Faith and I hated those seven-dwarf nicknames our father's line was so fond of. I can't even remember how Penelope became Pebble, but Pebble she had been since infancy.

She had my gray-blue deep-set eyes and my grandmother's sharp upturned nose with light brown freckles running almost masklike over the bridge and across her wide high-boned cheeks. It was a strong beautiful face, topped by a Shirley Temple mop of squash-colored curls.

She had that same sunny gap-toothed Shirley spunk too, the hyper cheer of the sensitive, which gave her a kind of ultra-high pitch, as if at any moment the good ship *Lollipop* could morph into the *Titanic*. Smiling through tears is an image that comes to mind, though you rarely saw them.

I've read this is often the case with chubby children and it codifies if they turn into plump adults: as if by being very jolly, she would be saved from ridicule.

To me her sunniness for all occasions was palpably transparent, her vulnerability clear. I'm sure Dr. Hofbrau would have a field day with this, but I often felt as if Pebble were mine and Faith's, and Benjamin was just the 'parent' who provided the goodies that let us raise her in luxury.

So, okay, a little incestuous fantasy between friends. But also the barren yearnings of a middle-aged loner. At forty-eight, I loved and was loved by three people on the face of the earth. My ninety-year-old grandmother, my nine-year-old niece, and my depression-dogged sister.

It must be that God protects us from more than we can bear, more loss of hope than is absorbable, by only giving second sight to raving lunatics and Nancy Reagan's astrologer and a stray Navajo medicine man and Nostradamus, because if, stepping out of that haunted elevator on that early winter afternoon two years ago, I had seen the future and known what was to come to the three women on earth who held my heart... well, I'd rather measure Hale-Bopp's sodium tail with a ruler than go there.

So, Pebble was chubby. She was still young enough and pretty enough to pass under the "baby fat" label, everywhere but near her father and the mercilessly brutal world of other children. At home, with me, her mother, and Tilly, their Filipino housekeeper, she was safe.

She jumped up, throwing her soft arms around my waist, startling me with the sheer force of her affection.

I could feel the mash in my chest. No one had hugged me in a very long time.

"Uncle Jonny! This is so cool! No one said anything! Momma didn't say you were coming! I'm like major psyched! My life is so basic, I never have surprises!"

She let go and I felt the loss of her sticky heat, an absence now in my life.

"Your mother didn't know. I'm kind of a mystery guest. I don't even have any corny presents."

She took my hand, her small moist fingers straining to hold on, and pulled me through the doorway.

"No biggie. You're the best present, anyway."

Tilly came bustling out of the kitchen, wiping her hands on the spotless white towel she kept permanently attached to her apron. No matter what Tilly was wearing, she also wore her towel and her apron. She was a tiny fifty-something woman with bifocals and permed gray hair, who looked like the schoolteacher she had been in Manila.

Tilly and her husband, Ely, had left seven children behind, the grown ones caring for the still growing, to come to work in America. And work they did, but Tilly was never anything less than jovial. Singing in the kitchen, whistling while she scrubbed the tubs, Tilly made me grateful as hell to have been born in America, even though she seemed a lot more satisfied than any American I knew.

Faith and Benjamin's apartment always reminded me of the old *Topper* and *Thin Man* movies. It had a circular marble entry with a winding spiral staircase, perfect for dramatic exits and entrances. I could envision Billie Burke and Carole Lombard slinking down, dabbing celluloid tears with silk hankies, reeling from one faux domestic crisis to the next, while bewildered and slightly simple spouses playfully patronized them.

It was Benjamin's theory that real estate in New York was what instantly separated the players from the aspirers. Theirs was most assuredly a major player's spot. Faith had not been allowed to touch it, Benjamin's fear of Granny O's Irish-heirloom sensibility overriding his regard for my sister's sense of style.

One of those pseudo-macho interior types, sort of 007 with a swatch book, had done the entire place right down to the pot holders in Tilly's kitchen.

Faith hated it, Pebble hated it, and I would rather have lived on a bench in Central Park. Behind Benjamin's back, Faith and Pebble called it "Dynasteria," having decided it combined the staginess of the *Dynasty* mansion set with the sterile coldness of a hospital cafeteria. Everything was chosen to impress, rendering everything unimpressive.

All the right labels were represented: Staffordshire, Limoges, Lalique, Chippendale. There was just one too many of everything. One too many tasseled sofas, one too many porcelain pooches, English hunting prints, celadon flower pots, Queen Anne chairs. It looked like the final day at the Park Avenue Armory antiques fair and made me yearn for one of those small rooms in a seaside hotel on some lesser-known Greek isle with whitewashed walls, blue tiled floors, and a single wooden bed draped with sun-bleached sheets.

Two rooms had been spared, mainly because Benjamin figured no one important would ever see them: Pebble's bedroom and the small sitting room where Faith lived her true life.

Pebble and I mainly hung out in her room, which she had decorated herself to look like a combination of a downtown artist's loft and a Sharper Image showroom, humanized by her collection of strange homely stuffed animals. Pebble was drawn to all the creatures no one else wanted: the skinny teddy bear, the black Barbie, the green frowning ape. Pebble dragged me toward the stairs, Tilly trailing behind.

"Uncle Jonny, I have tons of new stuff to show you! I've been experimenting with putting my animals onto my own Web site. I'm like totally inventing it, like a play with my own characters and graphics. I'm calling it Pebble's Puddle, and I'm trying to start my own chat room. I got this idea in a dream...."

Tilly headed her off. "Pebble, let me get your uncle something for drink. Let him calm himself, have some snack."

Pebble stopped and I could see the dark under the light. "Oh, Uncle Jonny I'm such a dork! I didn't even think. We've got some of those great oatmeal cookies and all kinds of special teas Momma's into now. I'm so sorry."

"Thanks, Tilly, but I had a late lunch."

She nodded, her coffee-bean eyes magnified by her bifocals. Pebble and I resumed our climb up the thirties tinseltown stairs.

"So, where was I? Oh, I remember. I had this dream and I was like all alone in outer space, just kind of floating around, and I was really lonely and I was thinking, Okay, you can deal with this, it's your dream, so if you wanted to talk to anyone in the entire solar system, who would you choose? and I thought I'd choose kids just like me."

Pebble opened the door to her room and pushed me inside. Several posters had been added to the wall, all featuring black-leather-clad rock groups I'd never heard of.

"Ah, but there is no one like you, Pebs. You're special."

She sighed and flopped down on her futon. "Maybe to my only uncle, but you know that doesn't really count at school. What I meant by that was, you know, other porkies. So's I'm not always the only one, like at Dalton."

Not being a parent, I had no experience with how to foster distrust by softening the truth. I tried to talk to Pebble the way I would talk to anybody worthy of my respect.

"You're the only kid with a weight problem?"

Pebble shrugged her shoulders. "There's a boy a grade above me, but he's so totally disgusto I don't count him.

"The point is, I got this idea to create a chat room on the Internet for chunkos. I thought we could hang out and tell each other all the mean things other kids say to us and all the dopey things our parents do and the stupid doctors and the dorky diets and how awful it is to be hungry all the time and watch all the normal kids pigging out and if you so much as eat one tiny french fry, everyone is rolling their eyes and acting like you've just swallowed a refrigerator or something, and how mad it makes you. I think it could be very helpful, instead of all of us floating around in the universe thinking we're the only one."

A lump was pushing so hard against my throat I was afraid my voice would come out sounding like Kermit or one of Pebble's other prized specimens. "I think it's a fine idea, possibly even brilliant, and I'd be honored to help you with the text part. You're far beyond me on the technology."

"I knew you'd get it. Momma likes it too, but promise you won't tell my dad. He'd freak."

"The thought hadn't entered my mind." We sat facing each other: me above her in her one grown-up size chair, she below me, cross-legged on her bed.

"Are you here because Daddy wants to talk to you about Momma?"

"Yep."

She sighed, and her eyes clouded again. "I don't think it's anything bad; he thinks it is. It's something she wants to do, but it's not, you know, like one of her schemes. I like it a lot, mainly 'cause it would get me out of Dalton. Is that, like, too selfish?"

"No, unless it involves the destruction of others for the end to be achieved."

Pebble giggled and threw a mottled brown bunny at me. "Uncle Jonny, you're so funny. Don't make me tell you, okay? Then even under torture he couldn't make me admit it."

"Is that how your father usually extracts information from you?"

"Nope. He doesn't have to. He just gives me that 'God has sent this child here to test me' look and I lose it."

I checked my watch, ruminating on how much more I wanted to scoop up my niece and hit the movies than rush over to the Regency to meet Andy Wise, "the Anteater" (my private name for him), who would have made a fine addition in stuffed animal form to Pebble's menagerie.

"Gotta go, Pebs. I have an appoinment with your other uncle. You *do* have another one, you know."

Pebble jumped up and padded across her bed, throwing herself against my waist. "Nope. He doesn't count. He never even *looks* at me, and he wears Polo, and he's mean to Sari, and he talks with a fake voice."

The mention of Andy's wife, Sari, made me feel better. "Is he really mean to Sari?" I extricated myself from Pebble's hug and moved toward the door.

"Not like domestic violence or anything, just kind of like she's not a real person." She skipped in front of me, racing down the stairs just as Tilly headed up.

"Mr. Duck. I am so sorry. My sister is calling me. Her husband Fumar, he is oby gynie for swine, and their pig is making babies. It is a very important pig in my family. Do you want some drink now?"

"Next time, Tilly."

Pebble slid across the stone floor in her stocking feet and opened the door. I leaned over and kissed her on each cheek, each eyelid, the tip of her nose, and her forehead. I had kissed her good-bye like that since the first time I held her. "So long, princess. Keep those cards and letters coming. Tell your mother I'd like to have lunch with her tomorrow before I go back. I'll call her in the morning."

"I will. She'll be psyched." She looked up at me, her shiny face solemn. "Uncle Jonny?"

"Yes?"

"I love you huge."

The lobby lounge at the Regency Hotel on Park Avenue is one of those elegant power-breakfast and drink spots, with a laid-back atmosphere that could almost convince the wheeler-dealers their meetings were really not about something as frigid and unrelenting as business. I say almost, because in the eyes darting about, sliding over each new arrival, the tactile alertness of the vigorously serious player was still present.

The walk over had felt good and had given me time to prepare myself for Andy. Andy had no sense of irony and therefore almost no humor. He took all his spins and spiels with sodden earnestness. People whose egos are so thin they can't bear any scrutiny, let alone irreverence or teasing, are perversely interest-ing. But to actually have someone like that as part of your life is something else.

I let Andy represent me when my book took off because he was, in a sense, family and therefore safer to trust than a stranger. And also because of his wife, Sari the sensational, Faith's closest (maybe only real) friend. The logic was, if he's married to her, there's got to be more to him. If there was, I still hadn't found it. But by now, he was a fixture, like a frayed lampshade in the parlor that has been there so long you keep forgetting to replace it with a spiffier one.

Not that there had been any real need. I was a year overdue on my second book idea, journalists being notoriously unreliable as long-form writers even when hightly motivated, which I wasn't.

But Andy occasionally called, sniffing around with that long aardvarkian schnozzola of his for another "deal," having little to lose beyond a couple of martinis a year.

I chose a table in the center and settled in. Andy was never first; it was a little power-play trick he had picked up in LA along with his bottle tan, buzz cut hair, bizarre diets, and spiritual philosophies. I ordered a drink and waited, trying not to over-think his reason for inviting me. *A healed mind doesn't plan* was one of Faith's self-help maxims.

I didn't have time anyway; he appeared, pausing at the the entry, checking the room, a big tall man in a big suit, big brief-case, big shoes. Everything about Andy always seemed slightly out of scale. Watching him scan the room, surveying the terri-tory like a retriever put out on the new porch, brought it into focus for me, too.

When he began his promenade, sauntering in his tall man's postured ease, I half expected him to break into some Gene Kellyesque soft-shoe routine, tapping his way around the tables. He glided over to Raquel Welch, seated in a see-without-being-seen seat and they air-kissed, she wearing some kind of Mafia pants and suspenders, flaunting a chest most women her age would have long ago wrapped up. Around the room he went, shaking a hand, patting a back, walking the walk, and talking the talk, which was his job as well as his avocation. Andy loved to schmooze.

I was his last stop, and for a moment I thought he might just give me one of those slightly unfocused, not-quite-eye-contact hellos saved for those less than stellar dudes he didn't want to be pinned down by, squeeze my shoulder, and keep moving. One could hope. However, he settled into the empty chair, looking annoyed that I had taken the power seat for myself, which forced him to face sideways into the room and miss the entrances.

"Doesn't Raquel look fabulous?" (Andy always assumed I knew these people.)

"Fabulous." (Andy was not much for greeting protocol.)

"Haven't seen her since Ascot." (Andy spent a lot of time abroad on business, which always seemed to be conducted at fancy country houses or lounging by pools in exotic Middle Eastern countries or on remote tropical islands, mainly without his wife.)

"Raquel Welch goes to Ascot?"

A moment of doubt furrowed his sun-tanned brow. "I think it was Ascot. Maybe it was Cannes."

"Raquel Welch goes to Cannes?"

A sharp look, could I be ironic?

"I'm kidding, Andy."

He motioned for the waitress. "Still have the old edge, Jonny."

A smiling young thing with ample hips and black lipstick approached carrying a tray with my martini and his "usual," which appeared to be red wine.

"Thanks so much, Lois," he said, giving the girl a wink. Andy never went anywhere he wasn't known, not even to a coffee shop for a burger. It had to be one where he knew the owner, and the waiter gave him his order without asking what he'd have.

The girl wiggled away. He watched her. I watched him.

"Look at that sway. That's a woman who's been ridden hard and put away wet, and she is giving me a chubbie."

He seemed to have forgotten I was sitting there. "Really? She reminds me of those Catholic schoolgirls in Newport."

"I like that look. It's so wantonly innocent, so un-LA with all that processed flesh. LA girls look synthetic and identical. They're pumped up and emaciated at the same time. Imperfection makes women vulnerable. They're so much sexier when they're off their stride."

"Are we still on women, or have we moved back to Ascot?"

He sipped his drink, ignoring what I thought was a very good line.

"Jonny, you've been in my head this week. I was at this

Holotropic breathing workshop at the LA airport Hyatt, working through some postnatal biography issues, and I saw you ..."

"Well, I'm surprised, because I'm much more into *pre*-natal biography issues, though it is kind of hard to fill those journals."

"This work doesn't go back that far. It's very complex, but in a nutshell it uses deep-breathing techniques to mobilize the healing of the psyche. It releases stored negativity. Really incredible!"

He had me now. "You attended a *breathing* workshop at LAX? Wouldn't that qualify as oxymoronic?"

He smiled his preaching-to-the-heathen smile. "It's brilliant marketing, because CEOs can fly in, do the two days, and jet out without having to deal with the city at all, and you can get there from anywhere."

"So what you're saying is executive types zip into a city where a deep breath in the best of circumstances is all but impossible, even miles from the fume-polluted airport, go to a second-class hotel, and pay a fair amount of bucks to sit in a banquet room and breathe for two days?"

"It's very powerful for focusing energy toward goals and moving toward wholeness."

"Ass or just general wholeness?"

"Don't be so judgmental. I did major business. I've been pursuing a brilliant New Age guru with a fantastic book idea, and she was there. She's involved in the Birthing of the Universal Human event."

"I thought God did that a long, long time ago."

"No, no. This is the universal human that's housed within each of us and holds collective intuition, so you can break limiting patterns and find the essence of your being."

"Aha, and where do they hold this, the Astrodome?"

"Oregon. You should try it. Ten days of developing your innate ability to reach desired mental states through cellular reproduction. They try to break the spiritual sound barrier; that's in their brochure."

"No shit? So did you?"

"Well, I think I would have. There was an enormous energy charge moving through the place, but I was helping my client put together this proposal, so I missed some of the most transforming sessions."

"I see. How disappointing after all that to miss the actual birth. Do you even know the sex? Were all the toes and fingers and everything okay? I wonder what Emily Post would recommend as the appropriate baby gift for the universal human. Maybe something, you know, cute and kind of basic, like one of those neat little hats from Baby Gap."

Andy motioned Lois for more drinks, which by this point we both needed. "Don't be such a cynic. Some of this new thinking is really powerful. It opens all kinds of new life and career paths, which you seem to be in need of. It's sure helped me with some issues."

He took off his glasses and wiped his eyes, and for a moment I had a ray of hope. Maybe he would open up, and I could let my guard down, and we could be buddies, and—

"Well, enough about my inner journeying." He put his glasses on again, and the moment vanished. "As I was saying, I saw you during my breathing meditation and I trust those flashes, so on a whim I called Gary Zane, the producer who loved your first book, and just lightly pitched the new one, told him you'd gone up to the Cape to work and gave him a very brief summary, and he flipped."

Lois arrived and I drained my glass and waited politely for the new drink, thinking of my hotel room and my need to return completely blotted. I think my feelings were hurt.

"He *flipped* is too general. It doesn't give me an accurate visual. His lid? Over? Out? Is this flipping good or not so?"

"Of course it's good! Try and be serious for once. He said he could sell it to Disney in a Siamese second."

"Now, once again, I don't mean to be picky, but is a Siamese second shorter or longer than, for example, a Yugoslav second? I just don't want to get my hopes up, only to have them dashed."

"It's show biz, Jonny. They mean it when they say it. But I need to tell him where you are on the new book. There's an art to this. Timing is everything. If we have Hollywood first, it can bring up the book advance."

I popped an olive into my mouth, pondering an appropriate response. I hated to let him see me earnest or eager or any other of the inner-child emotions that usually released the latent sadism shared by the Anteater and his brother the Barracuda. Maybe in fact the universal human had fish or lower mammal qualities. Or maybe it had been stillborn.

"Well, Andy, your karmic flash may be in the cosmic pan. I haven't even finished the outline. I'm not on the Cape staring at lighthouses, though that was my plan. I've taken over the editing of an entire local paper for a sick friend. I've hardly had time to open a can of Campbell's clam chowdah."

Andy frowned slightly. "I had a different vision, and I trust my vision."

"Look, I certainly don't want to trigger some crisis of metaphysical doubt or anything; maybe it's happening in a parallel universe and all of a sudden my alter ego will beam down and hand me the manuscript. However, I have to admit this bit of encouragement has perked me up. I may go back to Provincetown and buckle down, free my poor blocked psyche, and just do it."

Andy grinned, causing his nose to descend toward the dimple on his chin. "I knew it. My intuition was necessary to communicate with your blocked energy. You needed this push."

"Okay, so I'm pushed. I'll take some time and go through my notes and give you a call. Where are you going to be next week?"

Andy checked his huge gold watch, suddenly realizing he had spent several minutes too long on a minor client. "I'll have Naomi send you my winter itinerary. I'll be on the island for the weekend, and then I think I'm due at Lord and Lady Fitzgibbon's cottage in Bermuda for several days, but I'm always connected."

I watched him signal for the check, amazed that he would now conclude without a single family member being mentioned, even off-handedly. I finished my drink.

"Is Sari going with you?"

Lois trotted over and produced a check, which he signed to his house account, no plastic necessary. "No, no, she's finishing a screenplay. Work, work, work, poor dear."

I couldn't remember when I'd ever heard Andy refer to his lively and luscious wife as "poor dear." Something was afoot.

"Well, give her my best. I'm going to see your brother in the morning." I decided to leave Pebble and Faith out of range.

"Yes," he said, with a slightly sinister tone. "I know."

There is an almost euphoric rush that comes with having unplanned time alone in New York, kind of like the adult version of all the presents under the tree being for you. Where do you start? You can go anywhere and do anything.

It was a clear chilly night, still early enough for the streets to hold life. The brisk air felt great, enhancing the martini rush and the high that follows a tricky social encounter. Lately, I had begun to look at interactions with other people in espresso metaphors. They should be taken like strong coffee, in short intense doses, and not too many in any one day. Pebble and Andy had been my two cups, and that was enough.

CHAPTER THREE

When I opened my eyes the next morning, the blimpish blow-up of the Mona Lisa that served as my headboard was leering down at me.

I crawled across the mattress and into the bathroom, eager to depart my roomette. I shaved, showered, and threw my bag together so quickly I was almost out the door before I saw my message light blinking. I punched into my sister's tinkling, raspy voice.

"Jonny, it's me. You rat! Sneaking in on us like that. I'll forgive you if you meet me at noon at the place. I love you, 'bye."

My day now had a form and something to look forward to. I had an hour before Benjamin was due, time to find a coffee shop and scan the papers for a column I was doing in the *Provincetonian* made up of tidbits of absurdity culled from various news sources.

New Mexico: "A man on a weekend fishing trip with his sons decided they were possessed and beheaded his fourteen-year-old while the younger brother and witnesses watched in horror. As authorities chased the man, he threw his son's head out the car window."

For a fee a New Jersey private investigator will administer the 'fidelity test' for any woman who thinks her man is cheating. The 'test' is to hire a luscious model, wire her with high-tech recording equipment, and send her into the suspect's favorite haunt to seduce him. So far thirty such tests have been given. Not one man has passed.

According to research psychologists who evaluated dozens of studies of violent behavior among children, *high* self-esteem is more often associated with violence than low self-esteem. The scientists concluded, "The societal pursuit of high self-esteem for everyone may literally end up doing considerable harm."

I had gotten so engrossed in my read-and-rip that after two cups of coffee I arrived back at the hotel ten minutes late for my meeting with Benjamin (but don't discount a tad of well-placed passive aggression.)

Benjamin was never late. He was seated in a banquette against the wall talking on the phone. I hadn't seen him in some time and I'd forgotten the Mephistophelean power of his presence. I saw him glance at his watch as I approached, while using the same hand motion both to greet me and to stop me from verbally greeting him.

I nodded and sat down, suitably contrite for my tardiness.

One of the waiter/models strutted by. I pantomimed what I hoped was a description of a cup of coffee and settled back to observe my host.

Benjamin was one of those men who suffer withdrawal symptoms when disconnected from his cell phone. He took it everywhere. I wouldn't have been the least surprised at some future date to find that he'd had one surgically implanted. For now, he put it on restaurant tables and walked with it on the beach, like a pet.

I'd once bumped into him at a Kienholz retrospective at the Whitney, which was filled with scenes of successful workaholics like Benjamin with transistor eyes and telephone chests, among other exaggerations of the toll of the Post-Industrial Age on the human spirit. He was strolling around whispering into his phone while caricatures of people like himself mocked him across three floors of interactive art. He was not the only one.

Benjamin looked nothing like Andy. He had a large round head, wide high-boned cheeks (the only physical trait he shared with Pebble), and moonstone-shaped black eyes that glinted in seemingly pupilless clarity against pure white corneas.

His thick dark hair was worn slicked back, a hold over from the Gordon Gekko "greed is good" days. He sometimes wore little round glasses, which gave him a disconcertingly cherubic look, further accented by a cleft-chin dimple, shared with his brother.

He was smaller than Andy, but broad, well developed from obsessive daily sessions at one of those power high-rise gyms with position names: VERTICAL, HORIZONTAL, LATERAL, maybe even PRONE. He had been a swimmer and came close to making the Olympic team, and he walked with that slightly pigeon-toed walk all swimmers seem to have, as if their cracks were sore or they'd forgotten to pee in the pool.

Benjamin was always impeccably dressed but, despite Faith's efforts, the look was a little too slick for our New England taste.

The Bronx had been erased but his voice had a different affectation from Andy's, who sounded more pseudo-Brit, or the sort of cadence seen in poor little rich boys who've been shipped off to Swiss boarding schools and raised among strangers. Benjamin's was more Brahmin yachtsman, which was the world he coveted as reflected in his choice of wife and lifestyle.

His movements were spare and graceful, almost delicate, as if he was were constantly preparing for an important triple gainer off the big board. Even I could see he was attractive to women; he radiated magnetism: animal and kinetic and just so slightly unsavory. Intimidating, as I said before.

Benjamin did have a sense of irony, if not humor, though I sometimes suspected he'd developed it as a way of having a leg up on his brother, with whom he was inexorably competitive.

Faith and Sari refused to take any more joint vacations after the brothers' rivalry disintegrated into a fracas during an arm-wrestling contest at some Caribbean resort that resulted in a broken wrist for Andy and a black eye for Benjamin (who, being the less seriously injured, immediately declared himself the winner.)

My coffee arrived and I drank, knowing in advance this third cup (like too many people in one day) was a mistake I would pay for later, but at least it gave me something to do, rather than sit with that dazed-goofus look of the phone-conversation eavesdropper.

"Andre, my friend, my comrade in arms, I look to you first. You know that, right? I trust you to bring me the best, the freshest plums from the ripest trees. My group has the assets waiting; they're burning up for a deal. They want vacation travel—that's where they're weakest, and I think this industry is still embryonic in potential. Andre, do it, baby. Make me happy."

He clicked off, sharing his brother's antipathy for polite pre- and après-ambles and stopping me from grabbing the phone and warning poor Andre. Ruthless is just one of the adjectives I'd heard used to describe Benjamin's business dealings.

Now I had entered his field of light, his lunar face and moon-calf eyes beaming through me. He had a way of seducing, of turning all his attention on the object of his momentary desire as if there truly were no one else on earth he would rather be talking to. This charisma, combined with his business genius, was probably the key to his success as a mega dealmaker. With women, it was devastating. I had even seen withered dowagers glaze over in a romantic version of the dry heaves after mere moments at the receiving end of his charm.

Benjamin half rose and extended his tan manicured hand, his huge glowing eyes never leaving mine.

"Jonny, good to see you. It's been awhile, can't even remember when."

"Newport, last Saint Patrick's Day."

His smile tightened. Benjamin hated anyone to best him on anything. I tightened too, realizing I might have unleashed the lunar forces.

"Oh, yes, of course. Your grandmother's house. The uncooked corned beef."

I'd asked for it, I guess. But to have him use the moment of my proud old grandmother's greatest humiliation, and all the sorrow it caused those of us who loved her, made me want to punch his moon-man head in. I didn't. I did the next best thing. I was silent, which he also hated.

He sat back and crossed his muscular legs, revealing expensive silk socks and dark green alligator loafers. He kept smiling. I had this fantasy that, if he stopped, the light would leave the room like a penumbra and he would cease to exist.

I held my silence, but it cost me. I could feel the tension of too much coffee and not as much detachment as I needed to pull off this power play.

"Let me ask your opinion, Jonny, vis-à-vis my conversation with Andre." He'd blinked first. "I know you've traveled extensively. Don't you agree the travel industry is limitless in potential? Aren't we all in our own way restless and longing for escape and also seeking new kinds of stimuli? Look at these maniacs bounding up Everest with their laptops and satellite phones. Why? Because it's not another package tour to Paris or Colorado rafting trip, or whatever was in last year. It's about the creation of memories for the ego. 'I was here, I had a life, I saw the world from the highest mountain on earth.'

"Don't you find in your own search for meaning that travel has given you an entire world of memory and experience that highlights your existence? Don't you think everyone is looking for those highs?"

His charm was working. I relaxed. "Well, leaving your comfort zone tests you, shakes up the unconscious, even if you're just toting the kids to Great Adventure. That's partly why people crave it. But it takes a resilient inner structure. A whole lot of people rarely leave the town they grew up in, or they go on vacations and hate them, because it's too lonely and stressful. New York isn't America, Benjamin, so if there's no deal out there maybe that's why. Maybe the balance has been reached."

"That's my point, Jonny! There's a market for all those people too. Designed recreational experiences close to home. Low cost, little emotional risk. I'm convinced it's a huge oil reserve that's just beginning to be tapped."

"Well, you know best. Frankly, I'm traveled out. I could wander the Cape Cod dunes and stare at the Atlantic Ocean for a very long time; maybe that's because I've done the other. It's not where I'd put my money, which may be why I don't have any."

Benjamin leaned forward, crossing his polished hands over his powerful knees. "I see. So where *would* you put your money?"

"I guess I'd have to go along with Andy on this one. I'd put my money in the self-doubt industry, because it's endless; it will never reach terminal velocity unless mankind ends. The products are much less expensive, too: books, CDs, videos, seminars, workshops, retreats—you only need a tent, some folding chairs, and a charismatic sociopath with a new spin on Jung or the Old Testament."

I wasn't sure I liked what was happening to his smile, but I waited, holding on to my own self-doubt with both hands.

"You mean like Deepak Chopra and all that?"

"Exactly. I was stuck on an Amtrak train one day with nothing left to read and someone had left an audiotape. I popped it into my Walkman, and I must admit *The Seven Spiritual Laws of Success* is the most mesmerizing hour or so of horseshit available without a degree in agriculture. The guy has a voice that makes you feel like someone's spooning warm honey into your head. He's saying something about getting rich and famous and having all your dreams come true by doing nothing. Well, not quite nothing. You've got to meditate two hours a day and spend serious time hanging out in the natural world in order to reach the 'pure potentiality of the universe.' Then you have to follow the law of less energy expended, an idea that includes some quotes from Kafka about sitting in a room and waiting for the universe to writhe in ecstasy at your feet, which it has no choice but to do if you follow all seven laws faithfully. This could be a little unsettling. I mean, would the thought of anyone, let alone the entire universe, writhing in ecstasy at your feet really appear on your wish list?

"Anyway, 'the less you try the more you get' is the deal. 'A bird doesn't try to fly, it flies. A flower doesn't try to bloom, it blooms.' Stuff like that. I don't know how this fits into the real world. He's so murky, it sounds more like the Seven Spiritual Laws of the Bag Lady, but it sure is an attractive message. He's sold countless millions of books. Ask Andy about it. He's hustling several wannabes with their own shticks. Right now, anything that has 'the universe' in the concept is very hot."

Benjamin shifted. He hated it when I saw Andy alone. "Andy and I have done battle over this guy. I told him if it's so infallible, why doesn't it help the fifty million or so starving Indians who really believe it. It works if you're Donna Karan but not if you're some poor untouchable living in a sack on the streets of Calcutta? Andy is the last person I'd ask about anything." Benjamin recrossed his legs. "I haven't been tracking any of the softer investment opportunities. I'm out of that loop. I heard Tony Robbins once, and that was enough."

"You mean, Gumby for grown-ups? 'Yumbo' rah-rah-cocka. At least Chopra is mellow. Imagine the two of them onstage together, the rum and Coke of the mind-fuck industry."

He leaned forward, I had triggered something. "Did he tell you about Sari?"

"Just that she was working on a new screenplay. Is something wrong?"

Benjamin laughed. "I wish you could see your preppy Irish mug, Jonny. Andy didn't tell you Sari left him?"

So many emotions were surging through me, I felt like a blind man on a roller coaster, swept into space and unable to discern up or down, pleasure or anxiety.

"No. He never mentioned a thing. When?"

"Actually, I think it was New Year's Eve, but she didn't tell anyone until last week. Faith told me because Andy has been out of touch. Last time we talked he accused me of being judgmental and I said, 'Everyone is judgmental, for chrissakes. Who's more judgmental than God! What the hell was the chosen people? Talk about elitist judgments!' And he hung up on me, although he denied it—said he was in a tunnel and the signal got lost.

"He always says that when he wants to get off; either that or he spends more time in tunnels than a Con Ed repairman. I'm shocked. He seemed fine."

Benjamin looked disappointed. "I'm surprised to hear that. I thought it would have thrown him. He hasn't gained weight again?"

"His body wasn't high on my attention list, but not that I noticed. Is Sari okay?"

"I don't know. I haven't seen her. But actually, she's very much a part of what's going on with Faith and why I wanted to talk to you. Obviously, what's happening is coming out of this separation. I would say Sari's not thinking so clearly and, now that it affects my wife, I'm concerned."

I was as ready as I was going to be. I pushed my cup away. "What exactly is going on that we couldn't talk about on the telephone?"

He sat back, leaving creases on the pant leg where his fingers had been. "What's the matter, Jonny, you don't want to see your brother-in-law every so often? Or is it just that Duckworth side of you, all those Yankee cheapskates who'd squeeze a penny till Lincoln threw up? Relax. I paid your hotel bill."

Mixed emotions again, running me around. "You know me better than that, Benjamin. That's one gene I probably could have used. I can pay my own fucking hotel bill. In fact, if I'd been given a choice and hadn't been so worried Faith was going back into the hospital or worse, I would have booked something costlier than the termite mound you picked out. They should be paying me to stay here, so let's not have any grandiosity, okay? You know exactly what I meant."

He let it go instantly, as if remembering I wasn't Andy, though in many ways I was more threatening to the power he most needed, the power over my sister.

"Sorry, Jonny, just doing a little reflex chain-reacting. It's a bad habit. I could have discussed this on the phone, as it turns out, since Faith has calmed down and her new medicine seems to be working. I overreacted, but I still think it's better to talk about it in person."

"So, enough foreplay. Release me, please. What's going on?"

"Okay, let me tell it in sequence. It won't take long. It started last summer when Sari went up to the Cape, before you moved there. She was doing some research for this movie she'd been working on, and Andy joined her. I imagine this was the beginning of the end. They had a Grand Guignol of a battle that started because Andy put Sari into an auction situation that was a total disaster and killed a screenplay she'd put her heart and soul into. He's her husband, but she wasn't important enough as a client for the son of a bitch to take her seriously."

He chuckled. "In the heat of it, when she found out he'd totally shafted her, she said to him, 'Ya know, Andy? I just figured something out. Being an asshole isn't just a phase you're going through.' Sari and her wild Italian mouth. Anyway, she stormed out and started driving back from Provincetown and she was pretty upset, so she pulled off the main highway near Truro by the state park with those Lawrence of Arabia dunes. She was driving down this side road past a strip of motels and cottages, and she saw an abandoned inn with a FOR SALE sign. Can you see where this is going? The short version is she bonded with the fucking place, which is a wreck as far as I'm concerned, not that anyone's listening to me. She found out all the details. It's owned by a couple of dykes who can't keep it together and have a better gig managing some fancy motel close by. So the next thing I know, I come home from Switzerland and there's Faith and Sari and Pebble, and even Tilly, all glassy-eyed with fairy-tale fantasy. Faith wants to buy it with Sari, renovate it, and spend the season there running it. When I balked, she had a backslide into the old black dog. I went and talked to her doctors because I was worried this was another one of her desperate schemes. I'm the only skeptic, but I'm concerned about this for numerous reasons. The main ones are pretty obvious."

He sighed, and for a moment I saw the man under the hotshot mask. Whatever his games, he loved her, which made it even harder for me to come to terms with the opacity of their bond.

Her side was simpler. She loved him violently, passionately, and completely. Her total surrender to his authority, his will, and his ego was one of the most difficult facts of my life. Granted, I had different problems, having never been brave enough to risk making more than a short-term superficial or sexual commit-ment to anyone, but the reckless abandonment of her own separateness distressed me. I was more pleased to see his love for her than I wanted to be.

"The main reasons for my concern have nothing to do with the money involved. I could fund the entire investment out of petty cash. They're both savvy, talented, tasteful women, and their spreadsheets and sketches for the renovation are thorough and quite sophisticated, so believe me it's not any of that.

"To tell you the truth, in a selfish way this actually comes at a very good time for me. I've got deals under way all over the fucking planet. I'm hardly going to be here for most of this year and next. It would give her something of her own to focus on and take some of the pressure and guilt off me. So, I want you to understand I'm not trying to be self-serving here. Also, for Pebble, she hates Dalton, so this might be a good thing for her. Pebble's been up to interview at a school Faith found. She liked it, and she'd spend more time outdoors, get more regular exercise, so it might even help with her weight."

He sighed again. "My main concern is that something might happen between Sari and Faith. You know how seriously she takes relationships. If the Korean manicurist forgets to send her a thank-you note, she cries.

"I know what partnerships can do to really centered, tough people. I don't think she could take it if they had a breach. It's hard enough with Sari on the verge of being her ex-sister-in-law. It's just lucky that Andy really doesn't give a shit about their relationship, or that would be trouble enough. I've stayed away from talking to Sari, because it would undermine Faith—and Sari would probably tell me to shove it high anyway. But coming from you, Faith might listen. The owners are hungry to make a deal and there is other interest, but the broker has given us an extension. They want an offer by next week. I've got to be in Kuala Lumpur, so I'm trying to resolve this quickly. Besides, if they intend to open by Memorial Day, they're already way behind.

"The truth is, Jonny, I don't know if this is the devil or the deep blue sea. I know you're going to see her today, so pay attention. Her doctors think this is a very positive thing, and I haven't seen her happier since I first met her, and I must say one of the pluses for me and for them is the coincidence of your being up there. Of course, having Sari, Faith, and Pebble plop down in the middle of your midlife crisis, or whatever the fuck took you there, might be the opposite of what you need, but it *is* reassuring to us."

He smiled. "So that's about it. Better by far than Payne Whitney, but I do have serious concerns about the future. She could be free-falling with no backup chute."

If someone had put a gun to my head and forced me to make up a story about what I'd thought Benjamin wanted to discuss, I couldn't have invented this one.

He checked his watch. "Jesus, I got carried away. I've got a meeting downtown in twenty minutes."

I took this to be my cue. "Well, I'd agree with your concerns, but I do think, with the people we love, we've got to have trust. Faith's needed something to believe in for a long time. You do tend to consume all the available energy. There's not much she can contribute unless she's going to abandon Pebble and bop around the planet waiting in hotel lobbies and airline VIP clubs for you, and we both know what a disaster those attempts have been in the past."

"Yes, we do indeed." His globe eyes lowered, covering his pain. "The worst thing would be to treat her like a child or a cripple."

"You know, Benjamin, life does provide these sidebars every so often and they've got to be read, no matter what they mean. I'd love to have Faith and Pebble nearby, and I'll give them all the support I can."

He nodded and pulled a sheet of paper out of his jacket pocket. "Here are the owners' names and the location. Will you check it out locally? I know how Cape Codders are about outsiders pushing into their communities. It's going to be hard enough for two fancy New York women to fit in without my hounds sniffing around. The place is a dump, but the location is great and they can do it in stages."

We both stood up. "I'll be back there tonight. Give me a couple of days."

He extended his hand again. Gentlemen, if nothing else, was what we were. "You meeting her now?"

"Yes. I'll check out and go straight to LaGuardia after lunch."

He started to move toward the stairs. "Sorry about your room. I thought the place would amuse you."

"Benjamin?" He turned, and I looked directly into his eyes. "I'll tell you how she seems and I'll check this place out, but I won't be your quisling."

"Oh, I know, Jonny boy. I always know the bottom line." He descended swiftly. I could see his chauffeur waiting in the doorway.

I'd stood my ground, but I felt the same way I always felt after encounters with Benjamin. As if I'd lost something, I wasn't sure what, but something really important.

CHAPTER FOUR

When Henry Clay Frick, then president of the Carnegie Steel Corporation, wanted a place to live and display his art collection, he bought the site at the northwest corner of Fifth Avenue and 70th Street, that had been the home of the old Lenox Library. In 1914, with the help of the architect Thomas Hastings, old man Frick built a beautiful beaux-arts house, one of the last grand mansions on Fifth Avenue.

Faith and I began meeting there when we were college kids, and it became our place—partly, I think, because it reminded us of the Newport mansions and partly because the rooms were so tranquil, the steel and frosted-glass domed courtyard so calming, that it combined the comfort of church with the glamour of our hometown. We met there even when it was out of our way.

I knew she'd be waiting on a marble bench in the enclosed garden, where the sound of water trickling from the bronze frog mouths into the fountain delighted her, but I couldn't resist taking a quick rediscovery walk through the rooms.

I circled the Fragonard salon, pausing before the Progress of Love panels, Madame du Barry's fantasy and a perfect blend of irony and eros befitting the mistress of a French king. I crossed into the massive green velvet and carved mahogany great room, scanning Rembrandts, Titians, Turners, and Bellinis, and paused between two Gainsborough beauties with attitude flanking the elaborately etched archways leading to my sister.

She was sitting on our favorite bench reading something. Her head was bowed and her fine blond hair, held with one of those Hillary headbands, fell forward, the light catching it, highlighting the strands near her face. Orchids and ficus and ginger plants and dwarf palms surrounded her; she fit right in, a visiting delicate bloom among the perennials.

Faith always wore variations on the same clothes, and she was wearing one of her Catholic girl's school–inspired ensembles: white sweater, navy wool blazer, camel slacks, and plain black loafers. I stood and watched her for a moment, reverently, I guess, like the Piero della Francescas in the icon room.

She seemed to be smiling at what she was reading, and that made me happy. There was a stillness in her posture, an unawareness of herself, a state of momentary grace that so rarely comes to any of us. I hated to intrude on it, hesitating the way a parent would before waking a child from a nap, wanting her to have every single second of peace possible on earth.

She finished the page and raised her head, her myopic gray-lime eyes slightly straining. She saw me and smiled, and I smiled, and we both waved and I started toward her, still taking her in as if seeing her for the first time.

Faith Hope Duckworth Wise, my only sister and closest friend. On that winter day in January she was forty-five years old, with the kind of deceptively simple-but-complex good looks that could render her ravishingly beautiful or placidly plain by a slight alteration of light or expression. She had an outdoors, breezy look, good white teeth, clean, slightly ruddy skin that showed the effects of too many summers of sun and wind, and a small wide upturned nose. But what gave her face its arresting character was the slight oriental uptilt of her eyes and lips. There was something doll-like and provocative about her expression, as if she were preoccupied or amused by some secret thought. It misled people. It made her seem almost cocky, which was very far from the truth.

She was taller than average, and we shared the same slender frame, the Duckworth legacy that helped us overcome our Irish mugs with that side of our family. It didn't help us in the fifth ward, with all the solid hard-working peasant stock built much like Granny O, bodies designed for planting potatoes and dropping children.

Faith carried herself well, but she never seemed as tall as she was, because of her small bones and gentle presence. It was as if, by not embracing her height, she hid from her own potential power, a power she could only claim by allowing far-too-frightening feelings to surface. No one had ever managed to get her to talk about them, but everyone knew, the doctors and we who loved her, that she hid things, in the deep, spidery basement of her consciousness, secrets she protected us from by denying them to herself.

What she did to survive was care for others. She buried her needs and pushed her truths way down in the corner of that cold creepy cellar, secreted behind the rusty furnace and the abandoned boxes of discarded household objects, chipped and damaged pieces of her psyche. She had unscrewed the one dirty bulb dangling over the webs and dust, swaying back and forth, searching for something worthy of its dim but prescient light.

I sat down and put my arms around her, smelling her fresh citrus smell. We held one another for a long time. We were back together. We were safe.

She kissed my cheek, and I could feel the flutter of her soft lashes. She took my hand and threaded her long slender fingers, unadorned except for one major square-cut diamond, which

Benjamin had insisted she wear. "It's enough that you keep on buying those quasi-convent outfits," he said. "There has to be something to show I take good care of you. The way you look reflects on your husband, so wear it for me."

He bought every piece of jewelry and expensive item of clothing, her purses, even her shoes. She wore them and enjoyed having nice things; it just never occurred to her to covet them or buy them for herself.

When she bought things, it was usually for other people. She had Granny O's do-gooder heart and truly believed, because she had been granted financial good fortune through her marriage, that she must give back. Faith never left her apartment without pockets full of dollar bills for the street beggars. She gave to every one of them, even the ones she knew were scamming.

"If they have to lie to live, that's sad enough," she'd say, perfectly content to play the patsy. She was the ultimate sucker for any hard luck story except her own. But there was also a compulsiveness about her altruism, as if by not giving continuously, by saving more of her energy for herself, she would be punished or struck down or shut out of the world of others for the sin of selfishness.

The result of this over-giving in her relationships with other women had been endless heartbreak. She chose out of her wound and got just the friends such a choice provides. She was used, manipulated, and taken for granted. She was hurt. She was incapable of understanding that other people were not like her.

She truly believed that inside all the women friends she had tried so desperately to please was her own thoughtfulness and compassion. She never saw envy, simply couldn't imagine that anyone would covet her beauty, her magazine-perfect apartment, her rich and powerful husband, and the elegance she brought to everything she did, whether arranging a bunch of flowers or whipping up a soufflé for twenty of Benjamin's investors.

She was kind and unaffected, attentive and funny. She was a

nice woman, which made it tougher for her competitors to deal with, because gossiping about her or being cruel made them feel not so great about themselves.

The payoff was that eventually they dropped her—or Benjamin, having enough of her unhappiness, convinced her to drop them. After years of social turmoil she had given up, settling down to a lonelier but far more grounded life.

She replaced ladies' lunches with yoga and meditation and volunteer work at a suicide hot line and the running of her family's daily life. She rarely talked about her loneliness, but one day when we were eating lunch at some upscale midtown spot, one of a group of women she knew was celebrating a birthday and she started to cry. "What is it?" I'd asked, and she paused as if not quite sure she was strong enough to tell even me something that rendered her so vulnerable. Something that caused her shame.

When she spoke, her voice was raspy and slightly hoarse, as if she'd just finished choking on something. "Oh, it's nothing, Jonny. I'm just feeling sorry for myself. I always wanted to be invited to the party, but I never was. I've never known how to have friends. I can never make them see me, for some reason. They like me all right, and they'll come if I set something up, but I never matter to them. I'm not on anyone's birthday party list, I still don't know why. Something's wrong with me. I don't fit anywhere."

Hearing her say that about herself I felt the way I had as a kid, her big brother, her protector. Fortunately, I didn't have my old baseball bat in hand, or else the urge to bash that table of vain pampered women who had hurt my sister might well have overtaken my sense of consequences.

I took her hand and held it between my own. "Faithie, there's nothing wrong with you! It's who you choose; you know that. Anyone worthy of you would be honored to have you as a friend. When you stop needing it so much, you'll have it. They'll be groveling at your feet. Besides, look at that group of Vulgari dames. That's not you, sis."

She wiped her tears. "Oh, I know, Jonny. I didn't really mean *those* women, but it's hard, you know, because they're essentially my peers. With women who have serious careers or a lot less affluence, it's so out of balance. It doesn't bother me, but it makes it difficult for them. All the girls I went to school with in Newport just dismiss me now. All they can see is that I'm wealthy, they don't see *me* at all."

"Look, I know I'm a guy, and men handle this slumber-party shit differently; we don't expect other men to be our soul mates. We're all pretty wary and defended, so we set better boundaries and we don't expect so much. But, gender aside, you and I are both solitary souls; we always have been. There's a great quote from May Sarton: 'Loneliness is most felt with other people … alone we can afford to be whatever we are and to feel whatever we feel absolutely.' If you can accept that, it makes you stronger."

"Oh, Jonny, you always make me feel better. You're my medicine of choice."

"Don't give them the power to cause you such pain. Remember what Granny used to tell you when we were going through all that lunacy after Mother died? 'You're a Stradivarius. You shouldn't be handled by every front-porch fiddler that strolls by.' "

"I do give everyone the power. They all cause me pain. But you're always there to kiss it and make it better, so really I'm one lucky Duckworth!"

I've thought back on that lunch many times since her death; it was one of several signposts I missed. No one ever saw quite how fragile she was, how much she needed to be valued by the people she cared about.

Sometimes I feel rage at her self-absorption, fury that it wasn't enough that she mattered to me and Pebble, but then again I hadn't gone through all the staggering betrayals and karate chops to self-worth that she was still to face. Somebody once said about suicides that it's not that they want to die, it's only that they want the pain to stop. At that lunch, and later in the courtyard of the Frick, I still didn't know how deep her hurt went or how, with each new injury—each new scab ripped off before healing had taken place—the pain widened, spread from the original wound to fill her entire being, infecting every part of her till it broke her heart.

No one saw her as needing anything. They saw her as *having* everything. It was the trap of the poor little rich girl; her outward good fortune diminished her humanity, making her feelings less real, less valid than the feelings of the less overtly blessed. One of God's better jokes, the isolation that comes with having it all, whatever that means, anyway. Tell it to the engineer on the Number Six train. Tell him this human being lying in his path needed nothing. Tell *him* she had it all.

But that day at the Frick, her wonderful face was still full of anticipation, the optimism of trust in life and in her fellowman. She stroked my hand so tenderly, the way I remembered our mother stroking it. "I should be mad at you, bro. You didn't tell me you were coming."

"It all happened pretty fast. I thought something was wrong."

She laughed. "Oh, ye of little Faith, as they say. I bet Benjamin scared you, stacking the decks in his favor, poor dear. He just can't help it. He means well, but he treats me as if I were Humpty-Dumpty I'm far more resilient than that."

I looked into her slanty teasing eyes, trying to see if I believed her. "Well, you're right. He did play up the red alert part, so I was afraid you were in trouble. But I have to say, even though God knows I hate to give him an inch, he seems unusually balanced about all this, and he *is* trying to see the venture from your point of view." I paused, realizing my feelings were hurt too. "Why didn't you tell me about it? You were obviously up on the Cape, and you never called me or said a word."

She sighed, squeezing my hand harder. "I'm sorry. I always tell you everything, but this time Sari made me promise. There were too many uncertainties, and you know how superstitious she is. Besides, then you would have known about her and Andy, and she wasn't ready for the finality of that yet. Forgive me?" She raised my hand and put her face against it, kissing my knuckles.

"No, I'll never forgive you."

I withdrew my hand, afraid I might actually cry, and looked at her, searching for some sort of gut feeling, a fog light searching the bay; a cautious captain, edging slowly forward into the mist, seeking a sign of safe passage.

"So, okay, I'm here. I've heard Benjamin's version. How about yours?"

She let my hand go and crossed her arms around her waist, a ritual of self-comfort she had performed since she was a tiny child. She would curl up in a corner and hug herself, holding her wound tight, protecting it from further harm.

"I don't want to sound all sappy, Jonny, but I really feel like God sent this. It's just the sweetest place, and I see exactly how to make it wonderful. It's going to be up to me to supervise the renovations, the hirings, and all the details, because Sari is writing. I mean, she'll be there and she'll handle a lot of the administrative stuff, but she *is* a writer first, and at the moment she has prior commitments. I don't mind that one bit, because it means I can do something I control.

"She doesn't care at all about the decorating or the garden. She wants to cook—you know how she's always wanted to have a little trattoria. She sees this as a way not to be so dependent on Hollywood, to put some balance into her life. She's bossy and she loves to run things, and I don't. I love the behind-the-scenes parts, planning and designing and seeing something beautiful come out of this poor old wreck of a place. It's just sitting there, pleading for someone to care, to save it. I know we can make it work, and we'll learn so much. I just know I can do this."

I nodded, feeling uncomfortable with the idea that she felt she had to audition for this part. Benjamin controlled everything in their lives, all their assets. There was something wrong about her having to convince us.

"Faith, I'm on your side. It's enough for me that you want to do it this much; I know you hate living in New York full-time. Benjamin said he's going to be gone most of the year anyway. The whole thing sounds good. Now, tell me about Pebble."

Her face was buoyant with excitement. I could not remember ever seeing her this joyful. It had none of the reckless urgency of her manic schemes, though there had been few of those. Most of the time she just cut right to depression without even getting the momentary charge of a euphoric phase. It was like drinking without getting high, but still waking up with one helluva hangover.

"Pebble's the very best part! She loved it, almost as much as Newport! There's a great little school, and they were so nice to her. It gives her a chance to just be a kid without all that pressure and competition."

"She's got our genes. No one on either side of our family ever liked school, pressure, or competing."

"But Benjamin adores all three. He's determined to send her off to fat camp this summer (heaven forbid his daughter isn't number one, outside and in). But I think if we put her to work, scraping paint and scrubbing and digging in the garden, it might do as much good and break her out of that feeling of helplessness about her weight.

"You should see these brochures he keeps giving us. *Cheer up chubbies! Lose weight, gain self-esteem.* She's so sick of it all. I don't think this is running away, I think it may allow her to find her own path. She asked if she could have a puppy. If Benjamin's not there much and we have a yard, she could!

"Oh, Jonny, I feel great about this! My head is so full of ideas, I can barely sleep. And the best part, the part that really makes me know it's the right thing? You're nearby! Can you imagine? It's just perfect."

I was doing fine until she used that word. *Perfect* is not one of my big words. In fact I basically hate it. It always seems to be a harbinger of disaster, mostly because nothing and no one is or can be. But I didn't have the heart to snuff even one candle on her joy cake. I didn't say what I should have said. I didn't say, "Nothing's perfect, sis." Not that it would have changed anything, but I would have felt better. I would have at least provided the fog horn, sending a faint mournful warning into the barmy treachery.

CHAPTER FIVE

O n the way to LaGuardia I had a strong impulse to see my grandmother and get some feedback on Faith's plan. The weather was on the verge of turning into real winter and I knew the propeller flight to Rhode Island would be choppy, but I was consumed with a strange urgency. I even sprang for a taxi rather than waiting for the Newport shuttle.

There is a blissful sensation that overtakes me each time I cross the bridges that now link Aquidneck Island to the mainland. When the Pell Bridge was completed in 1969, connecting the slender finger atoll of Jamestown to Newport, it changed the insular, gruff feistiness of Aquidneck subtly but permanently. Some think the change was for the better and others, old-timers mainly, think otherwise, but the bridges themselves are magical.

The Jamestown Bridge is first, and I've always thought of it as preparation for the main event waiting just a few miles away. It's a teasing bridge, foreplay really, beckoning the traveler, sailboats bobbing below in the royal-blue waters of Newport Harbor in summer and the churning froth from tankers on the empty sea in winter.

The Pell Bridge soars before you, a monolith, high enough to accommodate navy vessels and freighters from faroff lands, the four-hundred-foot spans arching high, curving into the sky like giant silver harps. When the day is clear and the clouds feather like angel wings, it looks like the road to heaven, sweeping you up, then releasing you at the southern side of the bay by the old Point section of town.

The route then carries you past the cemeteries on Farewell Street and deposits tourist and local alike on America's Cup Avenue, where the ghost of the Cup still hovers around the yachting museum, sucking up linguini and littlenecks with the old salts at Salas or wandering the lawns of Harbour Court, the sprawling estate on the curve of land between Newport and Narragansett bays where the New York Yacht Clubbers converge to regale fellow yachtsmen with tales tall and sometimes even true. Stories from the good old days, when J-class sailing yachts still competed and the Cup was where it damn well belonged.

If you follow America's Cup Avenue to the Memorial Drive intersection and stay right, it becomes lower Thames Street. Thames is a street of dreams and demons that has reinvented itself over the past three hundred years or so from wild and sordid avenue of iniquity filled with brothels and seamen's dives to the now gentrified site of trendy galleries and quaint Victorian B and Bs with more seafood eateries and coffee bars than even a town full of day-trippers in August can fill up.

I've always known that Newport specifically and Rhode Island generally was America's best-kept secret. Most of us who love it breathe a sigh of relief when each summer season passes without the "in" crowd—the movers and shakers from the Hamptons and the Vineyard— figuring out that right across the way is this basically untouched paradise of fabulous bays, beaches, coastline and exquisite American architecture without the prices and the mayhem. Fine by us.

Not that Newport isn't social; it invented the word. The remnants of the robber-baron grandeur, the struggling heirs of Vanderbilt and Auchincloss, Cushing and Brown, still reside in the faux châteaus and Victorian "cottages" on Bellevue Avenue and Ocean Drive, hosting catered lawn parties under pink-and-white circus tents, promenading for their kind like peacocks in some glorified colonial barnyard. But their numbers have dwindled, most of the mansions are owned by the Preservation Society and the parties they house are rent-outs ... You too can be Daisy Buchanan for a day!... Have your wedding at Rosecliff! Hold that deb party at Hammersmith Farm, where Jackie danced the night away and JFK twirled her about on their marriage day.

These days, the limos lined up for such occasions have New Jersey plates and the brides have frizzy hair and acne pits and the grooms sport oily sideburns and powder-blue rental tuxedos, but that's only up close. From a distance there's still the glow of glamour. Members of the Old Guard continue to hold formal dinner parties most every evening, attended by women of a certain age in cocktail attire, platinum-blond hairdos coiled into lacquered helmets, oversize tinted glasses worn day and night to shield glazed, surgically tightened eyes, blood-red lips frozen in grim powder-creased smiles, veinous diamond-laden hands weighted on their satin laps.

The men who attend these widowed or many-times-divorced women are what you'd expect: gigolos with fancy titles from evaporated Eastern European countries, men who dye their hair and wear vaguely official gold medallions on ribbons around the necks of their dinner jackets.

There are also the bachelors, manicured popinjays of the other persuasion, human cigarette lighters and shawl holders whose personal lives are so utterly devoid of purpose they would accompany Medea to a family barbecue if the food was decent and the champagne French.

You can always tell when the season begins in Newport by the arrival of these folks. Luxury cars suddenly appear—Bentleys, Daimlers, even an occasional Bugatti—driven by ancient chauffeurs who often double as escorts for the truly decaying dames, those out of money and cachet, hanging on to the gossamer goblins of the past by the loosening threads in their sequined ball gowns.

These are the last of their kind, the gold-leaf scrapings from the Gilded Age, before income tax and inflation, minimum wage, and the crash of '29, when the WASPs ruled the country and Newport was the place to flaunt your bloodline as well as your backhand.

This group, however fabled, is really only a small part of the place and far from the true sensibility of our tiniest state, a land mass that would fit comfortably into the city of Los Angeles. Newport is mainly a community of craftsmen and fishermen, of Portuguese, Italian, Irish, and Yankee immigrants, who have carved stone, whittled wood, lobstered, and farmed since the 1600s.

Roger Williams, the founder of Rhode Island, was a Cambridge educated Englishman exiled from Boston for his radical belief in individual conscience. He had emigrated from England in search of freedom of expression, only to be routed by the Bostonians and cast out into the treacherous lands of the Narragansett Indians.

He called his philosophy of religious tolerance "soul liberty," and he fervently believed there could be no peace on earth without tolerance for every man's opinions. Williams founded the colony of Rhode Island on that belief, and religious refugees began to arrive from all over the world, and Anabaptists, Quakers, and Jews as well as the Narragansetts, whose tribal rites he protected from zealous conversionists.

To understand Rhode Island, it is essential to understand this: Newport has the oldest surviving Jewish synagogue in North America and a Quaker meeting house that is the country's finest medieval structure. It has a town cemetery that is non-denominational, the colonial churches sharing a common burying ground with a section called God's Acre that houses the largest gathering of pre-Revolutionary tombstones of black Americans in existence.

Tolerance. It isn't a word that is used much anymore. It's a word that always makes me feel proud and patriotic and choked up simultaneously, sucking at the sardonic pieces of my armor like a straw in a cabinet (Newport word for milkshake).

In the summer, between the weekenders, the college kids lurching around Bannister's Wharf and upper and lower Thames in a continual bullish haze of Sam Adams and too much sun, and the dowagers and their dynasties whizzing about in Mercedes-Benzes and Rollses, on their way to lunch at Bailey's Beach Club or tennis matches at the Casino, the real Newporters seem lost, slightly dowdy and out of place and a tad churlish and defensive, like the original settlers with British soldiers marching about, spoiling everything.

Tolerance, I would whisper to Faith and myself and Granny O's cohorts, the locals who grumble and grunt their way from Memorial to Labor Day. Tolerance. Without the summer folk, Newport would shrivel up like the skin on the hands of the ladies who lunch at LaForge.

In fall, winter, and early spring, however, Newport works very much like the seventeenth-century town it was. It is a living museum of colonial architecture, all the buildings still occupied, historic registry plates in place, people working and living much the same as before the Revolution, when the port bustled and the streets were alive with the stuff of commerce: pewterers and silversmiths, cabinetmakers and chandlers. Now there are T-shirt shops and pizza parlors, but there are also the others.

The lobstermen at the Aquidneck Lobster Company still unload their catch onto the dock before the eight o'clock whistle that wakes up the town each morning, and the harbormaster still sits in his lean-to and watches the bay, and the lighthouses are kept, and johnny cakes sizzle in diners all over town.

Tolerance. The word echoed in my head as I zoomed over my bridges and cruised through town, past the gentrified wharves, Long, Bannister, and Bowen, and down lower Thames, past the restaurants and galleries and into the fifth ward, where the houses need paint and old ladies, stooped and worn from long lives of bending work, sweeping and scrubbing and shoveling snow, sit in their windows waiting for spring, while their ruddy Irish grandsons toss salt onto their small icy porches. Home.

My grandmother's house has been owned by Irishwomen for over a hundred years. It was bought by her sister, the first of the O'Brien clan to emigrate, with money left when her husband, a fisherman, was swept overboard in a storm. She had no children, so when my grandmother arrived, widowed herself on the hard passage from Dublin to New York, heartsick and pregnant with my mother, it was to her sister in Newport that she came.

My mother was born in that house, and when my great-aunt died many years later it was left to my grandmother, on condition it never be sold but remain in "O'Brien hands until the Lord decides otherwise."

One of the many interesting quirks in my grandmother's character was that she relished change in everything but the O'Brien house. She loved the seasons, cherishing every single minute of each one, tending her garden with fervor and joy, as each time of growth and renewal, rest and rebirth, came and went. She loved new ideas, new people, and new advances in science and technology.

She was an inveterate brain picker: Pebble's (who was the only one keeping up, anyway), Faith's, mine, or Benjamin's. When

Benjamin came, she spent days reading *The Wall Street Journal, Barron's,* and *Fortune* so she could grill him on what he was doing.

With her house, however, this spirit of adventure ran aground. Nothing new had entered the sagging oak hallway since World War II. The only exception was the huge Sony television we brought for her eightieth birthday. I then spent an entire weekend holding her hand, until she was able to decide to move a couch three feet in order to plug the damn thing in.

All our pleas to repaint, remodel the kitchen, and replace the old refrigerator with a Sub-Zero fell on conveniently deaf ears. Every family picture, crucifix, antimacassar, and figurine was exactly as I remembered it from my earliest childhood.

When her parlor couches finally gave out, the upholsterer was told in no uncertain terms to fix them up and recover them in exactly the same material; when they were returned in a color that seemed to her a shade lighter, she sent them back.

Nothing changed inside or outside the O'Brien house on lower Thames, no matter what was going on around it, and for me and my sister there had always been comfort in that. Regardless of how we complained and tried to make her fix it up, it gave us the solace that it obviously also gave her. And it was immaculate. Her life's work besides raising us was to keep the little legacy she had been left spotless and ready for the day it passed onward.

Granny O's garden was as much a part of this plan as the house. Her garden had won awards and been featured in *Newport This Week*, and the neighbors brought out-of-town visitors to view it in the late spring and summer.

It was just a small town garden, a little plot really, with one weeping beech and one flowering cherry tree, but how it bloomed. Her daffodils were always the first, harbingers of spring popping up like lemon lollipops.

Around the fifth ward she would go, slower each year but still taking her little foil-tipped bouquets to neighbors, the counter-men at Sig's Deli, the proprietors of the liquor store, the regulars at the Irish Social Club.

"Spring's ready," she'd announce, plopping her posies down and moving on.

Her tulips drew raves, and then came the bearded iris and the peonies, the clay pots of impatiens, and the French hydrangea bushes by her front steps.

"Rich people's plants," her nosy neighbor Mrs. Callahan would sniff, so jealous she could barely keep from hacking the luscious greenery to pieces and blaming the college boys.

My grandmother had even built a small fish pond in the back by her brick wisteria-covered wall, where two very large golden carp kept company, shielded by moss and lily pods. There were six Sheer Bliss rosebushes, geraniums, red poppies, and purple foxgloves, and shocking-pink azaleas. There was an old metal French garden table and chairs that my mother had brought from the Duckworths' basement, which further enraged Mrs. Calla-han. "Putting on airs," she sniffed, to anyone who wandered by.

Faith always said Granny O's garden was a mirror image of her heart, and she was right.

By the time the cab pulled up in front of my grandmother's house, it had started to snow. I could see Mrs. Callahan's dyed red head poking out between the curtains in her parlor. Across the street, Mr. Finnegan, who was more than one hundred years old and bore a striking resemblance to Edvard Munch's painting *The Scream*, sat where he always sat in the winter, on a rocker in his dining room window, watching the action through his banged up binoculars. Not that there was much to watch on a snowy night in January at the nongentrified end of Thames Street. By morning everyone in the ward would know that I had come a-calling and by taxi.

My grandmother opened the door before I'd paid the driver,

thanks, no doubt, to Mrs. Callahan. She looked smaller and weaker than the last time I'd seen her and she was leaning more heavily on her cane, but her eyes were still sparkling blue and her pure-white hair was braided up high on her head. She still stood straight, and her clothes, all of which she made herself, were well fitted and pressed.

Proud is how my grandmother looked. Not hubristically, just matter-of-factly, the kind of pride that comes from knowing the content of your character and telling the truth. There was no nonsense about her inside or out, no self-pity, and little introspection.

Even at ninety, she didn't dwell much on the past. She was one of those tough but big-hearted country colleens used to hard luck and making do, believing completely in the will of God, good and evil, right and wrong, and beginnings, middles, and ends. "Get on with it," she would announce, tapping her cane on the worn but shining wooden floor of her kitchen, when Faith or I would wander off into hyperbole or psychodrama, ascribing motives to the behavior of others or taking too long to tell a tale.

This was a brisk woman who had been denied the luxury of self-absorption. Her only love had died in her arms of pneumonia in the rat-infested bowels of a rusting freighter carrying Europe's castoffs to freedom.

There'd never been another man, and if Dr. Hofbrau or one of her colleagues were to speculate, they might attribute some of her caustic vigor to repressed sexuality, but as her grandson, I'd never found this idea of interest.

She neither gave nor received compliments, believing that flattery was too easily used to manipulate or mislead and that if people were to amount to anything, they'd damn well better figure out for themselves who they were and what was good and not so good about them, or they would spend their lives at the mercy of others. She was completely right, of course, though this approach probably worked better for me than for Faith. We both always knew she loved us.

She hated gossip, vanity, and phoniness and she loved children, Jesus Christ, a good straight shot of Irish whiskey, and Willie Nelson, and no one who valued her goodwill ever got between her and a *Beverly Hills 90210* re-run. Go figure.

"Jon, come inside. Callahan's going to call the newspapers in a minute."

I grabbed my bag and raced up the steps, snow falling on my hair. My grandmother always called me Jon. If she was angry at me, she called me Jonny. If she was furious, she called me "Mr. Duckworth," but that hadn't happened since I was nineteen and she caught me in the back seat of her Chevrolet with one of the less bowlegged Salve Regina sophomores, half naked and reeking of gin. (The sophomore, actually; I was fully clothed and comparatively sober.)

She stood aside to let me pass, pausing for a moment to glare at Mr. Finnegan, Mrs. Callahan, and the numerous other residents who had joined them at their windows to see the return of the famous grandson.

For the fifth ward, having a movie made and a book published and appearing on *Charlie Rose* and *Larry King* qualified as fame. Faith qualified because she was rich and had been photographed by *Town and Country* at some Newport benefit or another. Our arrivals were always big news in the neighborhood.

When I leaned down to kiss her, I could see the worry behind the steely blue gaze, and I was immediately sorry for not calling first.

"Nothing's wrong, Granny O," I whispered, holding her close, feeling the sparrowlike quiver of her brittle bones, smelling her smells: flour, mothballs, and vanilla, with a touch of Ivory soap underneath. "I was in New York to see Faith and Benjamin and I missed you, so I came on a whim."

Whims were not big in my grandmother's frame of reference. Her days were as orderly as the rows of daylilies by her side porch. I let her go, seeing the relief and what looked like a fullness in her eyes. My grandmother, like myself, was not much for public display of emotion.

She leaned a bit harder on her cane. "Courage is just fear that's said its prayers," she said, telling me paragraphs about how frightened she had been to see me appear out of nowhere on a bleak winter night. Never having been a parent, I tended to forget such anxieties, which obviously no parent ever outgrows.

"Granny, I'm sorry I scared you. How about letting me sweep you up and carry you over to Christy's for some chowdah and a nip or two?"

She smiled, revealing her original and still usable white teeth. "Irish charm isn't a virtue, Jon boy. It's the real curse of the working class." She turned and made her way slowly toward her kitchen.

"Is that a yes or a no?"

She kept moving, but I could feel her smiling in spite of herself. "You're too late, boyo. I've had an offer from another visitor. I'm becoming so popular I may have to change my phone number."

Before I could inquire further, we reached the kitchen, me trailing behind, slowing to her pace, contrite and slightly confused, filled with all the feelings of coming home. A place so familiar and so strange, every step triggering memories: the cherrywood banister we slid down; the crucifix clock in the chipped case, the hands of Christ telling the time; the sampler my mother crocheted and framed in silver—NO REGRETS, it said, though God only knows she must have had some—the brass umbrella stand I broke my toe on, chasing our old cat across the hall.

Memories of feelings, of scents, of poems found and lost. "My life now smells of roses and the sea," Faith wrote somewhere.

Shadows of fear dancing in firelight on the front-room walls. My mother's body lying in her casket, open to the air, the pity, and the stares, Faith and I speechless with terror at the sight. What behooves them? Corpses in the parlor, as out of place, as glaring in their presence, as a nude in church. Mourners murmuring platitudes, patting our heads, waiting for the food and booze to appear. Sipping and chewing with the pale powdered body of our mother lying footsteps away.

I remember the rage, the urge to rush forward and slam the lid, shout them all out of the house. To cover her, wrap her up and lead her away from the eyes prying her lifelessness for secrets to hiss about over cheese puffs and slices of corned beef. The sin of sins: a Roman Catholic suicide.

Somebody was standing at the sink, holding a steaming colander filled with dripping noodles. Aromas of garlic and basil and onions wafted toward me, tickling my senses. Rusty ringlets, springing forth from a small oval head. Chaos hair. Sari's hair.

Sari turned and I felt a small shift in my stomach, a flutter of nerves or excitement. She smiled and I remembered how much I liked to look at her. She was captivating, not just because she was beautiful but because her face was so electrically alive and filled with storms of expression, changeable as New England weather.

She was small and voluptuously built with clear olive skin, yellow-brown almond-shaped eyes, and a wide full mouth. Her nose was long, slender and high-bridged, and hooked slightly downward when she laughed, which was often, and her hair was a frenzy, a Marx Brothers wig of unorganized waves and ripples, falling all around her face in a wild confetti of disorder. She was fun to look at. It always amazed me that Andy was so indifferent to her.

She gave the colander a final whack and came toward me. "Well, well, look what the snow blew in!"

She threw her arms around me and hugged hard, and that sensation rolled around in my stomach and I hugged her back, feeling the softness of her ample breasts and the warm flesh of her back.

Granny O set a bottle of wine down on the counter next to us. "Enough of that, the pasta's going to turn to laundry starch," she said.

Sari let me go and returned to her noodles, her gingery smell lingering in my sinuses. "Granny O, I respect and revere you, but never tell a Sicilian how to make spaghetti! Right, Jonny?"

I was busy opening the Chianti and trying to recover that balance inside my lower intestine. "She's right, Granny. You should try her Sicilian littlenecks sometime. You'd forget all about that junk Mrs. Alessio brings you."

I poured three glasses and passed them around. My grandmother was still standing. She would never be the first one to sit, so I carried the wine and my glass over to the kitchen table and sat down. "Since I know I can't help, I'm going to watch. It's been a long day."

Granny O was right behind me. "When I was your age, I'd just be hitting my stride about this time," she said, traces of Ireland rounding her vowels. She eased herself slowly into her favorite chair at the head of the long oak table. Battered and scarred, it bore memories of uncounted kitchen disasters: spilled burgundy, cigarette scars, forty-year-old water rings.

We settled in, Granny and I catching up, Sari whistling away as she prepared her earthy magic. No one seemed unsettled at the extraordinary coincidence: that Sari, stopping on her way up to the Cape, and I, following some inner guidance straight out of one of Andy's New Age "experiments," should both appear. Synchronicity, he'd call it.

I couldn't remember another occasion in the eight or so years that I had known Sari when the three of us had been alone together, sharing a meal. But it seemed as familiar and comfortable as if we'd been doing it daily, and I could tell, knowing my grandmother as well as I did, that she was enjoying the whole thing immensely.

She'd once told me after a sip too many of her Irish malt that I should find a girl like Sari, even if she wasn't Irish. "Someone with heated blood in her veins and something more than the Atlantic Ocean in her head, not like all those icy stick figures you're so fond of."

Sari set the pasta platter down before us. "Martha Stewart, move over."

My grandmother put down her fork. "I don't like that woman. I watched a Christmas special with her doing these crazy things, taking piles of broken toothpicks and sticking them into mounds of cranberries, pinning them on a Styrofoam tree, making it seem like nothing at all, when she has all these helpers working for her, doing the tasks. What sort of fool would come up with such silly ideas, with all the things to be done with your precious time on earth?

"Painting her own porch, indeed! Sitting there in her fancy clothes, scraping paint all calm and cool. On my poorest day, I could still find some neighbor boy to scrape my porch!

"These fancy women with their busy lives, sitting out in the hot sun scraping paint when they could be in Acapulco, or wherever the hell they go. There, she gets me so riled, I cursed!"

Sari leaned over and kissed her cheek. Neither of us had ever seen my grandmother so emotional over somebody outside the family.

"She does the kind of stuff you'd do if you had a sponge mop for a brain and a guaranteed lifespan of ten thousand years. I should call my second cousin Gino in Palermo and arrange a little terminal glue-gunning, get this woman out of our faces."

I laughed, but Granny shot her a stern fellow-Catholic look.

"Sari, remember your catechism." She paused, resisting the smile playing at the sides of her mouth. "I'll pay for this at confession, but I do rather like that idea. Maybe your cousin could just paste her hands together, keep her from stringing kumquats and bay leaves all over the place. Oh, Father Murphy is going to make me pay for this!"

Sari raised her glass. "Father Murphy probably never even heard of Martha Stewart. Don't tell him! You're ninety years old, and if you miss one confession the Lord in his infinite mercy will forgive you. Besides, I'll bet He doesn't like her either! God likes a little serendipity, you know. He's never been much for perfectionists. Look at Noah's Ark. If that wasn't a raggedy-ass make-it-up-as-you-go-along gig. Not to mention the Garden of Eden. Martha would've had a stroke, serpents crawling all over her best fruit trees! What about Passover? Unleavened bread? A total table disaster. And the Last Supper wouldn't even get photographed as a before shot in Martha's mag. God's on our side.

"Now, I want to make a toast to you, Granny O. Faith and I are going to need all your wisdom to make our inn wonderful. We need your recipes and every gardening tip you've got, and Martha can just go prune the poison ivy."

She turned to me. "Jonny, Faith told me she'd talked to you about our plans, so here's to new adventures and to Granny O for inspiring us all."

As much as my grandmother hated any fuss or flattery, I could see she was moved. She shook her head and waved her arthritically thickened hands, but she was touched. She had never allowed a party in her honor, which served her needs, martyrlike though they may have been, but denied those of us who loved her a way of paying tribute. Sari, an outsider though almost like a second granddaughter, had more leeway. And of course, in the endless Catholic competition of the ward, Sari's being Italian further loosened Granny's rigorous standards. Italians couldn't be held to quite the same measure as the Irish.

Late that night, with Sari asleep in Faith's room and me staring at the ceiling in my old room, watching the menacing shadows from the streetlights dance the way I'd done as a kid, I realized that, as much as I'd enjoyed Sari's company, I felt cheated out of a private talk with my grandmother.

I got up, grabbing an old plaid robe that had probably been hanging on the coat rack by the door since I went off to college, and stepped out into the hall, hoping she was still awake.

My grandmother, even when she was still young, saw sleep as the enemy, a necessity to be endured as briefly as possible, a thief that stole precious time away from more important things. The light was on under her door, so I tapped.

"Enter," she said, as if she'd been waiting for me. She was sitting up in the only American bed she had ever slept in, her long white braid hanging down over her shoulder, her glasses, rosary, and book resting on her lap.

I came in and sat down beside her on the old rag quilt she had patched together before my mother died, feeling the slight bony bulge of her leg, barely visible under the covers, and I said what I always said when I was given the rare privilege of sitting late at night on my grandmother's bed.

"Tell me the story."

She nodded and took my hand in her swollen fingers, still warm and soft despite the ravages of age and arthritis. "When it was my time to give birth to your mother, your Aunt Katherine put me up here in my bed and the midwife was called and the pains started.

"The labor continued for almost three days, but the baby refused to be born and the priest came and gave me last rites, and then, in the middle of the third night when we were all halfdead from exhaustion and fear, your mother pushed her way forth. Even after all that struggle, she was as beautiful as the first rose of summer. But she didn't respond. The midwife said her chances were slim and we should go to the hospital, but I refused. I asked them all to leave and I held her to my heart and I prayed.

"Somewhere near dawn, I felt her little heart stop beating and an anguish worse than any I had ever known gripped me and I shut my eyes tighter, begging God, who had already taken her father, for her life. And all of a sudden, my room was washed with a golden light, so strong it burned my face like the sun, and when I opened my eyes the angel of your grandfather was standing right there, and he reached forward and put his hand against your mother's wee back and he smiled at us with all the love of the world and then he was gone. The light was still shining, an afterglow, and your mother took a gulp of air and started to bawl, and when I got up that morning and looked in the mirror my hair had turned pure white. I was only twenty years old, but it was as white as a communion robe."

The thing about this story was that everyone she had ever told it to, even Benjamin and Andy, believed her. Maybe it was having the ultimate wise old granny telling the ultimate bedtime story, but I found it enormously comforting. Long before angels were fashionable and so over-merchandised they showed up on everything from personal checks to key rings, making me loathe the very sight of the pudgy pink munchkins, the image of my grandfather watching over us calmed me down.

When she was through I felt like I was four years old and had just finished a great big glass of warm milk and cookies, and I think she probably felt the same. We sat for a while, listening to the creaky old pendulum clock ticking away in the downstairs hall. Sari was going to drive me up to the Cape in the morning. I always thought, when I left my grandmother, that it could be the last time.

She spoke first, as if reading my anxiety. "I'm really fine, Jon. Spindly, half deaf, and slow as syrup in a snowstorm, but the doctor says my heart is fine and all the other parts are still under warranty. I could make a hundred if I don't slip on the stoop. That'd give old Finnegan something to fret about. So take that 'Oh, dear, the old gal's gonna croak any minute' look off your face.

"Being ninety is much more frightening to you young people than it is to me. The way I see it, I'm playing with God's deck now. The doc even told me I can have a little bigger nightly nip than I allow myself. So worry about your sister, if you're going to worry."

"Should I?"

"Well, I didn't want to say anything in front of Sari, seeing her so happy and all. Divorce is a mortal sin, but I'm no fool; half the Catholics on the planet do it and a whole pack of other sacrileges, so if she's got to, at least we won't have to pretend that silly man is other than what he is.

"I know how much this means to her and double that to Faith, but Jon, I must tell you the truth. I got a chill, right down into what bones I've got left, when she told me. Something doesn't feel right. It's not about Faith being all starry-eyed or anything, like she sometimes is when she doesn't want to know the turd on the table isn't a biscuit. This is different. I don't know why, I just have one of my feelings. Don't try and stop her, that would be worse, but keep your eyes open."

My grandmother's instincts put the entire psychic movement to shame. Her words alarmed me. I wanted to believe that this venture was going to bring my sister happiness. I went back to my boy-bed, but not to sleep.

Of all the wonderful things that my little state has to offer, drivers are not on the list. I have never quite decided whether the problem is one of heredity or environment, or simply a dearth of properly trained instructors, but the fact is the worst drivers on the entire planet come from Rhode Island.

Boston, which most Northeasterners think has the patent on bad drivers, has gotten a bum rap. Boston drivers are mean, surly, and aggressive, but Rhode Island drivers are mean, surly, aggressive, *and* totally incompetent. Things like looking left and right before entering oncoming traffic or checking the rearview mirror before exiting a driveway or parking space never occur to them.

I felt safe with Sari at first, because she was from Middletown, Connecticut, but it soon became clear she had learned to drive at her Uncle Freddie's house in Warren. She was even scarier than Faith or Granny O. (The happiest day of my life was when even the state of Rhode Island decided my grandmother's career behind the wheel had come to an end.)

Sari possessed an inability to absorb the concept of *other drivers on the road*, which extended into the hazardous area of changing lanes (which she did without a single glance in the rearview mirror). I had a moment of sympathy for Andy. If she drove like this in Los Angeles, divorce would be a reasonable option.

I, who had been taught to drive by one of the Duckworths, a former commodore of the Ida Lewis Yacht Club and a New Yorker, had escaped the state disability.

"Sari, here's the deal. Either I drive or you drop me off at the bus station in Fall River, because I'll never make it to the Cape this way."

"Ah, come on, Jonny, where's your spirit of adventure? You can track Jimmy the Chin all over Little Italy for five years, but my driving is too scary? A little break here."

"I'll take the mob over a Rhode Island lady driver going through a personal crisis any time. Pull over!"

Much to my surprise she did, almost sideswiping a semi filled with two-by-fours and an Isuzu Trooper filled with small children. But she did pull over, which I liked immensely. I had been prepared for a hell of a lot more feminist fencing and flexing.

I got out and walked around to the driver's side, ignoring the furious fuck-you pantomimings from our fellow road warriors, and slid into her seat, smelling that gingery smell and feeling the warmth where her fine round ass had so recently perched. Then I pulled her Saab convertible back into traffic, relaxing for the first time.

She watched me, chuckling the way women do when it's all they can manage to keep humoring us lugs. "Happy now?"

I nodded. "Roadkill isn't one of my fantasy deaths."

"You're just lucky that I'm still pausing before the meno."

"You don't sound much like a woman on the verge of marital meltdown. You're much too cheerful and calm."

"That's today. Yesterday I was hysterically insane. Last week I ate an entire Balducci's chocolate cake and was asked to leave Tower Records on lower Broadway for insulting a clerk (you know how out there I had to be for them to even notice a tone of voice), and two restaurants for sobbing and upsetting the other diners, and an Indian taxi driver put me out in the middle of Second Avenue for hyperventilating into an empty coffee container. He thought I was possessed by the Goddess Shiva."

"Well, I'm glad I got you on a good day, then, since violent hysterical women are not one of the things I do best."

"You don't know until you've tried one."

We were silent, letting that thought rest between us, like an odd new aroma that on first sniff was neither pleasant nor unpleasant.

"Hasn't Faith sent you off to one of her shrinks?" I asked finally, having decided the scent was too fresh to evaluate.

"Oh, puh-leez. After seven years with Andy, I never want to hear the word again! Naw, actually I'm very encouraged by how I'm handling this, because as emotional as I've been, behaving badly in public and all, I'm feeling the stuff. I'm telling the truth for a change. It's denying the sucker that hurts; that's what fucking kills you."

That something turned over in my stomach again. "Do you want to talk about it? I'm a pretty good listener."

She smiled and her nose tipped down, giving her face a soft, slightly goofy look.

"You sure? I can really get going on this, not having a therapist or a masochistic girlfriend in sight."

"I'm sure. *Imus* is over, and I know your taste in music. Besides, venting about agents, even about to be ex-extended relatives, is always healthy."

"Well then, Chuck, you've come to the right bumper car. Shall I start with the Jewish Buddhist from Malibu he's been screwing or the seven years of noisy despair?"

"Your car, your story, your choice."

"I think I'll start with the Buddhist, since it was the last straw and also a very good scene in a movie that I may or may not write someday. Okay, so Andy had been spending a lot of time in LA chasing all of those helium heads around, and I'd been in New York, even though I should have been in LA, or so Andy was always telling me. I'd been pouring everything into a screenplay about—well, it was about a marriage and what happens to this couple when their baby dies—which, you know, is what happened to us and so it was really tough but also very powerful, and since we never—and I mean never—talked about it, it was also a way for me to grieve.

"So I finally went out to join him and there's this woman staying at the house he'd rented for us in Malibu, which looked like the public space on a Carnival Cruise ship. I kept expecting Kathy Lee to pirouette into the living room singing 'Come Fly with Me' or something.

"According to Andy, she had this really high-concept book about healing the tadpole within, you know the drill, and of course he's helping her with the proposal—she's between karmic cash-flow peaks, so he's moved her into the house, and it takes me about a microminute for my warning light to go on, but being a nice Italian girl and all I don't act on this. I wait."

Sari pushed her seat back, kicked off her boots, and stretched her legs on top of the dashboard. She was incapable of sitting anywhere for very long without taking her shoes off and putting her feet up—cars, movies, houses, and restaurants included.

"So Andy's put together a dinner in her honor, if you will, and invited some 'people,' because he thinks he can turn her into the next Marianne Williamson or whoever, and I'm cooking it no less, and she wanders into the kitchen—one of those blondes with the boob job and the nose job and the lipo scars on the insides of her knees.

"I mean, you'd think the man would have more class after living with me all these years! Anyway, she's looking in my pots! Well, you know how I am when I'm cooking. So I politely—or I thought it was politely—ask her to leave my pots alone, and she sits herself down and lights a cigarette, pours herself a large scotch and soda, and takes a big hunk of prosciutto off my chopping block. Then she tells me she's a Buddhist, and she's been chanting for twenty-three years (I failed to mention that she's no spring lambette), and since she's been chanting she's gotten ninety-eight percent of everything she wants.

"Well, what do you say to a piece of insanity like that? I say, 'Oh, yeah, I understand. You owe all your good fortune to chanting and transcendental *medication*,' which I happened to think was very witty, but she just kept on stuffing my twenty-dollar-a-pound ham into her collagened purple lips and there's this edge, kind of competitive, sort of snide, in her attitude."

She moved her fuzzy-socked feet closer to my side, impairing my sight line, and I ever so gently pushed them back, attractive though they were.

"Now, I say *snide* because she was very tall, and when you're very tall and nasty, people see you as being sophisticated and nonchalant. But if you're small like me and snide, they just think you're a bitch. That's the way it is and I accept it. It takes me a little longer with very tall, devious women to sort it out, but my guard was definitely up, and so I waited, and she ignores my remark and goes on about how when she lived in the West Village she could never get a parking place, so one day she chanted for a parking place and she never had trouble finding a spot again. Then she tells me she was recently in Paris and it was raining and she chanted for good weather and the rain stopped and the sun came out.

"So I said, 'Oh, then you're, like, God?' and she just smiled and stuffed some more pig into her face and said I could scoff (her word), but all of life was cause and effect and it was totally under her control and she hadn't been unhappy or depressed since she developed her own form of Buddhism (and here she looked really snide, as I recall), and she said, 'I absolutely never feel any guilt.' "

The fuzzy feet slid back but she removed them before I could, robbing me of the pleasure.

"Well, by now I am trying to keep myself from taking the cleaver that I have been using to debone the veal and ever so gently inserting it into the top of her blond bimbo skull. 'No guilt,' my Aunt Rosa's ravioli! I have also pretty much decided I don't really want to finish cooking this dinner in honor of the Buddhist from Brentwood, so I slam down the cleaver and pour myself a nice big glass of chardonnay, which I find to be a very good confrontation beverage, and I ask, in my small Good Bitch way, 'Excuse me for my naïveté, but I thought Buddhists were vegetarians and abstained totally from alcohol and tobacco?' and she smiles and takes a deep fuck-you drag and says, 'There are all kinds of Buddhists.'

"There's this long silent moment—the two of us kind of suspended in time—and I don't for the life of me know quite why I did it like this—in fact, I don't think I had any idea I was going to say it until the words flew out of my big mouth—but I said, 'So while you were chanting for parking spaces and sunshine, was my husband on the mantra list?' And she took her time, licking the grease off her fake fingernails, and she said, 'I didn't even have to chant for that.'

"So I untied my apron, went upstairs, careful not to bump into Kathy Lee in the middle of her commercial, and picked up my suitcase, which—call it premonition—I hadn't unpacked yet, and I left. I guess I was ready for the information. It was really a relief, because it made leaving the bum so much easier. It's always great to get to be the one who looks good, righteous indignation and all that.

"I just went to the airport and waited for the red-eye and came home. He went a little crazy, I will give him that, and he came after me and we had a little last attempt, but then he totally betrayed me on my screenplay, just blew it off—never even read it, said it would be too painful, but that was a lie. He never wanted the baby anyway. So it never sold, and New Year's Eve I told him to move out. If I was a chanter, maybe everything would have come out better."

I looked over at her and saw the tears streaming down her lovely face, and I knew what had been happening in my stomach—what really happened every time I was with this woman and had never admitted to myself.

I was falling in love. Maybe I had always been half in love with her, but now I was careening downward, the poor shmuck in the front car of the Space Mountain ride, free-falling down into darkness, without any idea of where I was going or when the next loop would appear.

I pulled one of my father's old hankies out of my pocket and handed it to her, and she smiled at me. "No Kleenex?" she said. "I don't think I can blow my nose into silk, it's way too Marie Antoinette," and she didn't. She sniffed it all back in and wiped her eyes, and we continued on, but the journey had changed. Everything had changed.

CHAPTER SIX

*B*each towns in the off season tend to be morose, gloomy places, the locals wandering around, not quite remembering why they were so anxious for all the summer people to leave. There is the lingering sense of loss that those who remain always feel: the left behind, the used. Restaurants shuttered, stores closed, houses dark, and still the same faces, most of which were not all that cheery and attractive in the summer sunshine, let alone in howling, damp desolation that never brings out the best in anyone.

I thought I'd come to terms with my loneliness and could handle the isolation. We were used to one another and knew how to accept our ups and downs, lusts and longings. But I had never poked one toe in the tide pool of my neediness. I would rather have admitted to sins against nature than to needing anyone other than my own sorry self. Loving was okay, needing was not. Yeah, sure. Tell it to that gift horse galloping by with the feisty Italian *dama* in the saddle.

I have always felt pretty much the same way about gift horses as the Trojans did, so maybe it was because it was winter and the aching reclusiveness I wore like an old pair of favorite slippers was more intense, or maybe it was because Sari Sardella Wise had blindsided me, or maybe it was just because I was tired of manning my emotional barricades, but I let the damn Greek gelding trot right onto my borrowed bed.

I had not left New York and moved up to Provincetown to find myself, lose myself, or write a novel about a middle-aged man trying to do A or B. I was not a drunk, a disgruntled Vietnam vet, a dropout, or a hermit. I was just sick of the absurdity and mayhem of my life and I needed a break. I wanted to smell the sea every day and adjust to the new century. I hadn't had any big plans or expectations in a very long time, which all the gurus seem to think is good but which I think isn't something anybody chooses, goals and expectations being part of the human deal, but comes more from a sort of low-grade apathy and lack of direction and ambition.

Whatever. I had responded to a call from an old friend from the *Times* who was battling AIDS and needed help running the local paper. The job was temporary, which was fine, and he had given me the use of a very nice cottage on Commercial Street, close to the levee that forms a breakwater bridge to my favorite Cape atoll for long Moses-like walks, marching rock to rock for a mile into the sea.

I liked Provincetown because it broke through all the rigid snobbery and stiffness of New England. It was genially outrageous. Since HIV, the town had undergone a bizarre but extremely relevant cultural switch. The male homosexuals were weakening, their postured narcissism decimated by the Virus; the power had shifted to the women. Gay women were coming into their own. Bronzed butch goddesses and fem beauties, hairy heavy-legged schoolteachers from out of town, gorgeous Manhattan models tantalizing the tourists—all flavors of the ladies of

Lesbos had risen up and staked their claim. Amazonian roller bladers in black leather shorts, tattoos, and buzz cuts defining their rage whizzed past emaciated, hobbling men, leaning on one another like skeletal baseball-capped bookends. The women were getting bigger and the men were shriveling.

A week in Provincetown totally skewed your worldview. What I admired was its fierce honesty; it was a place where everyone was in your face and no one was. DON'T FUCK WITH ME was the unspoken town motto, and being real was the unspoken town goal. My favorite T-shirt read, HE WHO DIES WITH THE MOST TOYS ... STILL DIES. It might as well have been the town proverb.

Being straight gave me privacy and it, too, was accepted for what it was. The other thing about Provincetown, which reminded me a bit of Newport, was the tolerance. Gays and straights, families with children and transvestites, all got by together, catering to the day-trippers and taking pride in this lovely little piece of real estate, the site of the first step onto land by the original settlers.

The idea of church bake sales and town potluck suppers occurring side by side with drag shows featuring pumped-up Puerto Rican dykes with navel rings and boa constrictors wrapped around their waists is—well, kinda what America is all about. A nice bit of Founding Fathers irony.

I had intended to go to Truro alone the next morning to see the inn without being influenced by Sari's enthusiasm, but by the time we reached my little cottage in Provincetown I was so confused by the tsunami of emotions unleashed by the presence of my sister-in-law once removed, or whatever the hell she was, that I agreed to join her and the realtor handling the deal for a tour and a drink.

We were early. The back door was open, and I let Sari drag me inside the musty, mildewed wreck of someone's dream. I've always been a hotel kind of guy. I love them. I love the fancy expensive ones and the funky tacky ones off the interstates with little coffeemakers and minuscule bars of Dial soap. There is just something about the interruption of daily life, whether for pleasure or business, that intrigues me.

I try to see hotel rooms through the eyes of the maids, witnesses to every folly, foible, and peccadillo possible in human nature. I attempt to please hotel maids by being tidy and considerate, as if there were some invisible cosmic guest-approval rating and someday I would be singled out for my thoughtfulness. I always tip them, even if it's just one night at a Holiday Inn. So a deserted old salt box on a hill, at the end of the motel strip across from the National Seashore Park that runs for miles down the Atlantic side at the tip of the Cape, was my kind of spot.

There was a large weathered Cape Cod house, fine-boned though seriously neglected, with a sweeping bay-view dining room and deck. The main building contained a wing of rooms, and outside was a cluster of individual cottages, miniature versions of the main house with decks facing the bay beach.

I tried my best to be detached and objective, not swayed by the joy in Sari's face, but I failed. It was like *Home Improvement* meets *This Old House* soft-porn, a setup for every maudlin hope-over-experience fantasy any two slightly bruised and battered grown-ups ever had.

I followed Sari like a kid, letting her paint the picture. Where the little wine bar would be, how she would create an open kitchen with a wood-burning pizza oven, what Faith had planned for decor (white with comfy chairs and couches slipcovered in sea colors). On and on we went, she my Merlin, waving her magic wand at the reality, erasing the dank deserted rooms with their rust-stained toilets and rotting floors.

Pieces of the past haunted the place like friendly ghosts. A broken pail, a torn sweatshirt that said, GROW YOUR OWN DOPE ... PLANT A MAN, draped over a shadeless plastic lamp, an old kayak leaning against a sagging porch. Memories of families in the summer, clam bakes and hot dogs roasting on the grease-crusted hibachi left to decay in the sand.

Summers at the shore, full of faith and hope, my sister struggling for the same. This had been a place relatives went seeking pleasure. They had taken what they could and gone on, draining it eventually of energy. Someone had once swept the sandy steps and picked up the damp towels and scrubbed the sea stains from the decks. People had cared about it.

Sari came up beside me, her eyes sparkling. We were both in this fantasy now, like two Stephen King characters, the writer-lovers from *The Tommyknockers*, euphoric with delusion and the stamina of desire, not seeing the menacing seductive evil inside the dazzling lights.

"We have a name," Sari said, smiling—too close for my new discomfort. "We're going to call it the Inn at the End, because it is. It's so simple. Not another Sandpiper or Sea Breeze or any of those."

We were standing in the last cottage, and though there was no bed there was a partially inflated raft on the floor, which must have spurred my completely out of character and impromptu decision to kiss her.

Just pulling her toward me was enough to give me the most agonizingly sweet erection that I had had in memory. She felt it and I heard her catch her breath, and for a moment we both stopped breathing or moving, frantically scanning for negative risk factors: two novice bungee jumpers testing the cord connection before stepping off the platform.

She sighed and my head filled with the ginger smell and she kissed me back, pulling me and my poor throbbing cock tighter against her. "God," she said, "I've thought about this."

That was all the encouragement I needed. I was as ravenous as a starving man drooling before a luscious buffet with his hands manacled, then suddenly set free.

There was nothing tender about it. It was winter; it was freezing;

there were layers of clothes and a raft. I managed to free her heavy pink-nippled breasts from her sweaters and bra, sucking her until she gasped, coming in spasms, her tongue pushing into my mouth, moaning into me.

I opened my pants and she knelt down on the raft, wobbling forward, grabbing onto my legs for balance, and took me into her sexy full lipped mouth and that was that. I saw cartoon balloons. Pow! Kazam! I dropped down on my knees beside her and held her against me and we caught our breath. Bungee survivors at the end of the drop: exalted and unnerved, foolish and relieved, and grateful to have survived together.

Voices. The click of high heels. Before we could assimilate our actions, reality reappeared. Sari refastened her bra and jumped up. "Shit! It's the broker!" Sari's jumping up tilted the raft and I fell forward. My hands were occupied, replacing my prick in its proper place, and I banged my chin on the boards. Sari raced around to help me as I thrashed around, half on and half off the rubber tormentor, my chin bleeding from its encounter with the rough wooden floor.

"Oh, my God, Jonny, you're wounded. Blood! There's blood! Let me help you."

"I'm okay, I'm fine, never mind me, head off the damn broker, I'll clean up." I stumbled to my feet, looking, I'm sure, not much less disoriented than I felt and grateful now that Sari had declined the offer of my father's handkerchief. Sari hesitated, not wanting to leave me in such a sorry state.

"Go. Go."

I did my best to restore myself to the realm of normalcy and went to find them.

I heard the broker's voice before I saw her, but I knew instantly who it was: Rita Riley, bulimic, anorexic, shopaholic, workaholic, talkaholic, and, as she put it, my O.F. (occasional fuck). Of all the gin joints. Rita had once been married to the Linen King of Las Vegas, and had a bulimic eighteen-year-old daughter named

Emily, who obsessed her and snapped me out of any self-pity about not having children.

"We throw up together, it's our bond," Rita said, to anyone who'd still listen.

She was attractive in what my grandmother called my "icy stick-figure-type" way, but the ravages of her illness and compulsions had taken a toll, exacerbated by numerous plastic surgeries. We had formed a pleasant enough get-lemons-make-lemonade kind of relationship, at the end of the season in a mostly homosexual town.

Rita, clad in high-heel red patent-leather boots and some sort of endangered fur cape and matching hat, was standing with two unlikely women, scrutinizing us beneath her sunglasses.

"Well, what a truly teensy world it is. I was just regaling your sister-in-law with the story of how we met. Remember, Ducks? Last August, the crowning of the Mardi Gras queen at the Upper Deck? Just you, me, and five hundred drag queens who all looked more like Joey Buttafuoco than Miss America."

"How could I forget? The bartender with the Dolly Parton wig won. You could see his five-o'clock shadow halfway across the dance floor. How are you, Rita?"

"Pretty lousy. What the hell happened? You dancing in the dark again?"

Sari, Rita, and the two as yet unidentified females (though one was borderline, genderistically speaking) all turned and stared at me. I was still holding the bloody handkerchief under my chin, which hid part of my face from their laser gazes.

Being quite out of practice in the dating game and unused to such focused female energy, I could feel hot red blotches pushing outward onto my cheeks and neck. "I—uh, tripped over, a raft in one of the cottages."

"Well, the owners are here and the place isn't covered for indoor floating accidents, so don't sue." Rita lit a cigarette, losing interest once she had figured things out.

"Are you okay?" Sari said, in one of those mothering gentle tones that kind women use on grown men who are feeling like small boys.

"Compared to falling down a septic tank, I'm dandy. Compared to sitting in a small cafe in Orvieto listening to Puccini, I've been better."

She smiled and turned back to the three sets of eyes watching us.

"Jonny, I'd like you to meet the owners, Debbie and Inga."

I looked at Sari. I had never seen her behaving so politely. Her demeanor was more like a teenager with someone else's parents than her usual self. Could it be she really believed what Rita had told her in brokerese parlance, that there was "other interest" in this quaint pile of matchsticks?

Inga, who looked like exactly what she was, a butch German aerobics instructor from Munich, put out a large sunburned hand. She was wearing a barbed-wire bracelet, which disinclined me rather overtly from the impulse to shake it, but sensing Sari's anxiousness I did, suffering only a minor scratch on my wrist, rather than a severed artery.

Inga was about my height, nearing six feet, with broad shoulders enhanced by a Celtics jacket with a button pinned on the pocket that said I'M OUT OF ESTROGEN AND I'VE GOT A GUN, which I accepted as sacred truth. Her head was nearly shaved, she had numerous piercings of the nose and ears, and one gold ring coming out of the side of her lower lip. "It is an honor. I read your columns in ze paper. I very much enjoy your viewpoints."

Sari grinned, her nose doing that goofy thing. A fan was always a plus when facing what might be a complex real estate negotiation. "Why, thank you. It's nice to know somebody's reading it."

At this point Debbie wiggled forward, holding on to a small white poodle with a large rhinestone collar. Debbie looked like a David Hockney painting of a Miami housewife. She was wearing a fluffy pink jumpsuit with matching boots, the sort of outfit that mothers with sentimental instincts and no taste buy for two-year-olds, who have no choice.

"I was your fan first, Mr. Duck. I started Inga and all our friends reading you. I remember the first column, when you ran all of these cuckoo items, one after another. Oh, Lordy, they were fun-nee! The man in Ohio who couldn't afford a sex change and cut off his own weenie and *tenticles* and put them in a pot in his fridge! That was a hoot! 'Member, Ing?"

Mercifully, Rita, who had the attention span of a fruit fly, had had enough. "Yes, he's quite the social commentator. But my ass is freezing off, so let's get going to some nice warm bar. Since you've—uh, had the tour, Ducky, we might as well talk in a more comfy locale."

Inga moved toward me, her army boots kicking dust onto my already filthy pant leg. "I haf a better thought. Let's go to our place. Mr. Duck can clean his wound. We haf quite a nice assortment of beverages, and it's not far."

I was so relieved to get out of there and avoid an appearance at our local watering hole, bleeding, disheveled, and with my pickup pom pom squad, I would have agreed to almost anything.

I slid behind the wheel of Sari's car before she could protest and followed Inga's Trooper to the motel they managed.

Sari watched me out of the sides of her Sicilian cat eyes. "So, what's with you and Rita? When I told her who was with me, she looked a little green around the gills, but maybe that's just from all the vomiting and stuff."

"Rita and I are pals of convenience and have rolled around together a few times. She's really not a bad lady, just disenchanted with her lot, but she does keep fighting to stay present and I admire that. Mainly, we're buddies."

"I get it. She's an 'um' relationship. Like 'This is my—um, friend, Rita."

I laughed, falling faster. "Not even an 'um,' really."

She chewed on her lip, thinking it over. "Okay, I'm jealous. It's too soon and I'm freaked that I would be, but I am." She paused and then burst into gales of gleeful laughter.

This confused me. I had gotten out of the rhythm of guy-gal exchange and had forgotten how unpredictable female reactions were.

"Why is that funny?"

Tears were pouring down her cheeks and she kept laughing. "I'm sorry. I just had an image of the three of them bursting into that cottage and finding us in the midst. God, my reputation would be over before it began!"

I was blushing again. "Just promise if you ever write about it you'll make me sixteen and Chinese. Falling off a raft and almost breaking my jaw because my hands were trying to stuff my cock back into my pants was not exactly what I had envisioned for our first moments of romance."

We both laughed then, gales of mirth, causing me to swerve and drawing the attention of our platoon leader in the jeep. The three sets of eyes turned back, seeing us guffawing in ecstasy. There really is nothing, not even wild passion, that does as much for the solace of the soul as a long deep laugh. By the time we had pulled ourselves together we were at the motel.

One thing Benjamin had taught me was always to know your goal before entering any discussion, whether business or personal. "If you don't know what you want, you're dead," he said, and he was right. But I was too sore from the new aerobics being done by my heart muscle to think much further than the next minute. We got out and followed the gang into the manager's unit.

It was clear the decorating had been done by Debbie. It was sort of Debbie Does Dallas with a stop at Disney World. The carpet was powder-pink shag and all the tables were plaster-of-Paris knockoffs of Louis XIV. Cheap gold-painted cherubs held gold-flecked glass tabletops in their hands or on their heads. The couches were turquoise and covered with plastic, and the walls were covered with oil paintings on velvet of cats and clowns and cowboys. The floors were lined with enormous stuffed creatures: a snarling German shepherd, a black swan, a gray-haired gorilla. There were also ornately framed photos of Inga exercising and Debbie clad in cowgirl gear, dancing what appeared to be the Texas Two-Step with various weaselly-looking men.

Debbie wiggled over, flashing a gummy smile and revealing large yellow teeth, smeared with burgundy lipstick. "So you've found my wall of memories. You are looking at Miss Two-Step. I toured all over Texas and Oklahoma. I wasn't much for conversation, but boy could I dance!"

Inga came over and handed me a glass with some sort of whipped liquid in it. "House drink. Mud pie. You vill like zis."

Since her tone did not leave room for an argument I took it, longing for the clear stillness of cold vodka.

Inga handed Debbie one of the concoctions, slipping her well-muscled arm around her pink furry shoulder. "She is correct. How she danced! I was visiting my uncle at the university in Norman, Oklahoma. He is a professor of German literature, and we went to this place and she was dancing with some little man with no chin and I fell in love."

Debbie sighed and gave Inga a kiss, leaving burgundy marks on her cheek. Rita and Sari, who had been talking about termite inspections and plumbing problems in the corner, joined us. We all looked at Debbie's dance photos.

I had now exhausted my conversational repertoire and, feeling slightly buzzed and also nauseated by whatever the hell I was drinking, I excused myself and headed for the bathroom to clean up.

Give me ten minutes in someone's bathroom and I can tell you more than their kinfolk about their fears, vanities, and personal struggles. I'm not proud of my snooping, but then again, I am a reporter and there are worse vices. While I waited for the water to heat up, I discovered that Inga took Prozac and Debbie took antianxiety and blood-pressure medications. Someone got a lot of headaches, someone had fairly frequent bouts of flatulence, diarrhea, and/or heartburn. Someone had unwanted facial hair and not enough head hair.

I knew their tans were from a bottle and somebody's teeth were from a jar. Their eyesight was not glassless naturally and somebody's toenails had fungus. Warts were another problem. Inga (I assumed) needed heavy-duty deodorant, and Debbie (I assumed) was addicted to nail polish and antiaging preparations.

One (or both) read daily inspirational messages and stories about angels while on the toilet. One had recurring yeast infections and Debbie had recently been treated for bronchitis. One had just stopped smoking and Inga was recovering from rather extensive and painful bikini-line electrolysis. Both had trouble sleeping and somebody was battling irregularity.

Of course there was the possibility that one of them was wonderfully robust and the other a wreck, but that was unlikely. I had learned a lot. I considered myself to be the Conan Doyle of medicine cabinet sleuthing, having started as a way of learning more about women I was interested in, as an odds balancer. For example, finding prescriptions for Thorazine, Antabuse, or sexually transmitted diseases was a clear warning.

Was this paranoia or just sane caution? Now, suddenly, I had Sari's mythical medicine cabinet to worry about.

I picked up a powder-blue washrag with yellow bunny rabbits leaping across the top and soaked it in hot water, creating my fantasy of Sari's bathroom. Strong on hygiene products. Toothpaste and soap. That gingery perfume. A clean hairbrush. Some aspirin. (I knew she was human, after all.) A few basic cosmetics, without fruit acids or whatever the hell the new youth promise was, and some bath oils (showing that she was self-nurturing and liked a little sensual pampering). I could dream couldn't I?

I rinsed my face, seeing the beginnings of a bruise and a scab, and took a cotton puff from a fish-shaped glass bowl and wet it with peroxide. It stung and I winced, feeling suddenly lost and frightened. What was the matter with me? Was I so calcified in the crustaceanization of my bachelor shell that I had just reduced the first woman to open my heart into a collection of hygiene articles? It was Debbie and Inga's products that showed me their humanity. In their over-the-counter battles with their demons, I had seen who they were under the casual grotesqueness of their packaging.

I turned the water off, and the voices coming from the other room pulled me from my angst. Maybe because I'd been raised by women, with few men ever appearing in any real way, I always found their conversation as comforting as it was foreign.

They were all unnervingly bondable. Put the most unlikely assemblage of females together (like the ones loudly conversing outside the flimsy bathroom door), and they were capable of immediately finding connections, talking without hesitation about things men wouldn't tell their closest friend or the guy they fought next to in a war.

Most men found this girl thing enviable and terrifying. The problem with it, as I had told Faith over and over, was that it created a false truth. Women seemed to be capable of trading bundles of intimacies without really being intimate. It didn't mean they were your friends or that they were trustworthy; it was a web of illusion and like all webs and, all illusions, it was easy to get stuck or misled.

"I'm not having a bad-hair day, I'm having a bad-hair life," Rita was saying, while the others clucked approvingly. "I lived with this man for thirteen years, had his child, put up with all his shit—gambling and snorting and hanging out with the worst mob scumbags in Vegas—so you can imagine. Nothing I did was good enough. He totally controlled me by putting me down. And it was Las Vegas! The most beautiful women on the planet everywhere you turned! Holy hell. He treated me like a second-prize porker at the county fair. It was only a matter of time before he'd make me open my mouth and check my gums for slop rot.

"So, okay, I shopped. I shopped and I binged and I threw up, and when I was thirty-five he brought home this sheet from someplace called the Liposuction Institute of the Desert. Well, that struck me funny. I mean, deserts are so dry and lipids are so moist. I don't know, I started to laugh and Joe just stared at me. "Don't laugh, read it and weep and then fix it."

"I can still remember every single fucking word it said. At the top was a headline, EFFECTS OF TIME, GRAVITY, HEREDITY AND SUN EXPOSURE, and below was a time line.

"Age 35: First signs of aging appear, fine wrinkling, dull skin color, baby fat under chin, blotchy pigmentation."

"Age 45: Upper eyelids begin to droop over lowers. Jowls thicken and start to sag. Lipstick begins to run along vertical folds. Double chin forms. Sun spots begin to grow and darken. Moles get larger."

"Age 55: Heavy eyes with many lines. Skin folds deepen. Jowls sagging. Turkey neck and double chin."

Sari sighed. "Jesus, you memorized it."

"Yeah, and I never read it again. But it was seared into my brain like the ten commandments on the tablets. This guy had me like one of those brainwash jobs, Patty Hearst, like that, and it was the same as my father had done to my mother. Beat them down, tell them they're shit (which obviously they sort of believe to begin with, or they'd have chosen better), make them so dependent they no longer think they can take care of themselves, and then slip the warning under the door. You can be replaced at any moment, and then you're dead."

Inga jumped in. "But zat is such victim bullshit! You hat choices. You vanted some macho ass wit big bucks and then you don't like za price. I hate zat game. For your mutter, I understand.

It vas a different time for vomen, but not for you. You ver just lazy."

Sari's voice. "Hey, that's a little rough. Excuse me, Inga, but you really have a different point of view, more the macho ass part of the story. I know how easy it is for even really grounded women with self-confidence and their own careers to get lost in a relationship. I did it too! I'm really pretty good at figuring people out and I've always trusted my instincts, and *I* married the biggest jerkazoid this side of a *National Geo* discovery and I stayed for seven years!

"Almost every woman I've ever met has some sort of victim script, even if it's really tiny and hidden away. Why do you think there's a whole damn cable channel like Lifetime that pumps out programs about women fighting back after being victimized? I get asked to write this crap all the time. Damsel in distress. Abused by father, mother, evil embryo, boss, secretary, best friend, or all of the above."

Debby cleared her throat nervously. "Ing hates those movies."

"The point is"—Sari was not going to fold now—"we've all got the victim kernel. I bet you do too, Inga. I mean, look at you. Don't you think there's a bit of overcompensation going on? It's like—no offense—but you're so scared of being like Rita you'd walk the streets with an Uzi around your neck if the law allowed.

"I used to be much more programmed by feminism, but it can happen to any of us and it's subtle in a close relationship—like breathing carbon monoxide: no smell, no pain, but deadly none the less."

Debbie's slightly southern girl voice. "She's right, Ing, honey."

Rita sighed. "Gee, why the hell weren't you in Vegas five years ago? Well, I inhaled big time. I bought the fear. I had breast implants and five different procedures on my face. Look at me! I hardly have any nose or eyelids left! My cheeks shift around when I laugh. My chin implant looks like I've got a walnut under my mouth, forget about the pain and time and guess what? While

I was disfiguring myself trying to keep him, he left me for an eighteen-year-old lap dancer!"

"That son of a bitch!" From the slight slur at the end of *bitch*, I figured the mud pies were continuing to be poured.

"Yeah, well, frankly it was a relief. I never would've had the guts to do it first, and since he wanted me gone he at least gave me enough to get me and my kid out of there. I didn't even try to take him to court or get a major settlement. It was pride, I guess, but also I knew how ugly he and his pals could be.

"Whatever was left of me, I didn't want my kid to find it floating in the pool or at the bottom of Hoover Dam, like two other wives I knew. Mainly, though, it was what happened to my daughter that got me up and out of town. She was already starting to binge, so for her I was finally able to leave. I came up here because I read an article and I wanted to be surrounded by water. If I never see a neon light or a desert again in my life, it will be just dandy."

Sari laughed. "You know what the biggest problem with women is? We won't admit to anyone, especially ourselves, how angry we are. I am totally convinced that if you harnessed all the accumulated chick victim rage and general frustration—just in North America—and let it fly, you'd blow another black hole in the universe."

Standing in that small overstocked bathroom, listening to women among themselves, I had learned more about Rita than in the five or so months I had known her. It seemed like a proper moment to reenter the festivities. I put a Band-Aid on my chin and opened the door.

Though no business regarding the inn was ever discussed, a lot of business had actually been done. Trust was established and jib cuts had been measured. Rita withdrew her cat claws because Sari had come to her defense. Inga respected Sari because she'd stood her ground and not been intimidated. Debbie was dewy-eyed at all the female sharing, and I, emerging from the bathroom and playing innocent, had enough information gathered so as to not stick my damp sandy wing tip into my bruised and swollen mouth and risk a new hole in the universe.

I knew the deal would proceed honorably, and it did. Benjamin took over the financial business with Rita, and Faith came up and rented a small house near mine for her and Pebble. Every out-of-work construction jock and contractor in town was enlisted, and Sari, after spending two magic and insatiable days in my bed, went back to New York to finish her script.

The present was filled with excitement and the power of possibility, and the inn project took on a life of its own. It was almost like the Enchanted Cottage. Each time we went near it, a sort of euphoric glow encased all of us, even the workers.

The locals were welcoming, not competitive. It was the kind of place the entire community had dreamed of having there, fresh and sophisticated with city-quality food. I had never seen my sister so calm, focused, and happy, and once Benjamin accepted the decision he also got caught up in the vitality.

I had Faith and Pebble near me and was really in love for the very first time, with a woman even my grandmother admired. It was as if Brigadoon had been moved to Cape Cod in the middle of one lonely winter. Everybody's life brightened up.

My friend's pneumonia went into remission, and I took some time off to go over my book proposal (though a new agent was certainly in the cards, once Andy found out about us).

Inga and Debbie recommended people to help clean, garden, and work in the kitchen. The first-round renovation goal was getting the main house and rooms ready for Memorial Day and since most of the work was indoors and cosmetic, it all went faster and smoother than expected.

A lot of it was illusion, a movie set rather than a solid structural reworking. But the effect was swift and sensational. Bones were everything, and the inn was a handsome woman with a new coat of strategically placed makeup. It was Brigadoon. Until *she* showed up.

PART TWO

Her

CHAPTER SEVEN

She was our first guest, arriving a week before the official opening. She came by cab on a hazy late-May Friday afternoon, and I can still see her, swaying slightly as she walked, the way African women sway when carrying baskets of grain on their heads.

A madonna in black linen. Glistening waist-length jet-black hair hanging straight down under her wide-brimmed straw hat. She carried one simple black bag. "Prada," Rita whispered to Sari, as she glided up the steps and into our dream.

"Good afternoon," she said, in a soft, slightly foreign voice, forcing her listeners to concentrate, to come toward it, to do all the work of hearing. "My name is Jasmine Jones. I called last week."

We had all been enlisted for this our first customer. I had taken to rising before dawn, writing until noon, and then racing to the inn for my daily fix of magic energy. I was to serve as sommelier,

Pebble was our bus girl, Rita was hostessing, and Sari and Faith were cooking.

We had hired a young Boston college girl to clean for the season and the Italian plumber's mother, Thomasina, to help out in the kitchen. Jasmine Jones was our practice run, our out-of-town preview before the Broadway opening. We were all scared to death.

None of us had ever been in anything remotely like the service business, so we were more than a tad oversolicitous in our greeting of, our inaugural paying customer, practically bowing and scraping like characters in some pharaonic morality play. Pebble ran forward with a white rose tied with a peach silk ribbon; Sari appeared from the kitchen with a slice of focaccia hot from the oven and a glass of Prosecco. I practically wrestled the one bag away from her.

The college girl, Betsy, was poised at the foot of the stairs, ready to bring extra pillows or point out anything about the workings of the place. It was somewhere between the *Wizard of Oz* Munchkin scene and Annie's arrival at Daddy Warbucks's, and not a nanosecond was wasted on *Miss Jasmine Jones, Manhattan*, as she signed the registry.

She sipped the Prosecco and nibbled the fresh bread, properly appreciative but also conveying, that she knew more about inns than all the rest of us put together. This was a woman who loved dead center stage and was accustomed to it.

"Umm, this is divine. I thought Prosecco never traveled. I only drink it in Venice, really, but this is lovely. Umm. I taste ... what? Chervil in the focaccia? Very clever.

"There's a small palazzo outside of Portofino that has the same feeling as this, all white, and draping everything with sea and air colors is so divine!

"Oh, what fabulous paintings? Who did them?"

Faith blushed and raised her hand, the new kid in class before the glamorous schoolmarm.

"So fresh! They have the feeling of some of David Salle's first beach series, but without the cynicism and heaviness. This place is more wonderful than I expected! That little piece in *Traveler* didn't do justice. I must call the publisher and have them come up and do a feature. Who is handling your PR?"

Her eyes—which almost seemed to be colorless, a pale beige with a touch of violet, fringed by thick black lashes and heavy feathered brows—scanned us all, but no one, not even Sari, who was the right answer to the question, dared speak.

It was like we'd been put under a spell.

"We all take turns," I replied, reflexively buffering Sari and taking the full force of her attention onto myself. It was what I had always imagined being struck by lightning or zapped with a laser would feel like. She turned toward me, riveting me to the spot, triggering altar-boy quivers, as if moving around or looking away while she was focusing on me would have resulted in some fiery act of divine retribution.

"And you are?" she said, in that careful Circe's voice.

I strode forward, breaking the spell, refusing to be coerced into any emotional tone not set by my own free will. There were advantages to having spent all my adult life listening to mendacity and manipulation. "Jonny Duck, and these are your hosts, my sister, Faith Duckworth Wise, and Sari Sardella. Welcome."

Something just so very slight, no bigger than a millimeter, shifted at the sides of her mauve tinted eyes and around the sweet smile on her perfectly formed mouth. It was as if inside her android being, a computer was madly collating all available data being thrown off so innocently by the humans in front of her.

Even living in New York City and having spent considerable time in other international capitals where extraordinarily beautiful women abound, I had rarely seen a woman of this magnitude of attractiveness. It was more than her physical loveliness, which at first glance seemed to be virtually flawless. It was the aura around her, as if she carried her own portable backlighting. She was alarmingly, staggeringly, ethereally exquisite. Normally attractive people, such as we all were, are not accustomed to such beings. It throws us off, unsettles our coping mechanisms.

Even if you work in the world of models and actors and are inured to people whose power comes from acts of nature and the ability to bind their allure and concentrate its essence, when one of them is taken out of context—dropped down onto a creaky porch in Cape Cod, for instance—it has an effect.

This was, after all, far from where the "beautiful people" mingle. This was no mogul's yacht in Saint-Tropez, no party at Mar-a-Lago this was a classy but still funky inn in New England where the guests would tend to be wives with potbellies and varicose veins and husbands with bald spots and ingrown toenails.

So her presence was even more compelling. If she'd floated in on Botticelli's seashell or had a third eye in the middle of her forehead, she could not have created more of a stir. We are all swayed by beauty; it is part of our human counterpose. And this woman, the possessor of such mesmerizing loveliness, knew.

At some point we all must take a good long look at our exteriors and interiors, size up the real or imaginary competition, and figure out how to get through this life accentuating the positive, as the song says, and for most of us, most of the time, we balance it out, handling our pluses and minuses pretty well.

But Jasmine Jones was something else again. Her beauty formed a wall of fantasy. It created the image that behind such purity of visage must be purity of heart. It lied, as beauty often does.

My impulse was to pick her up by her beautiful, lithe, bloodless body and toss her down the newly repaired porch steps. I was flooded with fearsome images: black widows, black dahlias, sorceresses, Phaedras, Hydras, witches, necromancers, and succubi. Gypsy women luring sailors on the streets of Naples, alien wanderers, daughters of Satan, hags of hell; flashes of the future zapped me, hurting my head.

Every single bell and whistle from the locus of my intuition had short-circuited. All the warning lights on the control panel of my psychic 747 were flashing red, and what did I do?

I looked over at the glowing, entranced faces of the women I loved and disconnected the system. A choice of champions. An utter and complete abdication of my own truth. She'll only be here two days, I told myself, alarmed at the force of my unprecedented reaction. What can possibly happen in two days?

CHAPTER EIGHT

She was, of course, the ideal guest: quiet, undemanding, impeccably mannered, appreciative, thoughtful, and complimentary without being unctuous. She was—ah, that word again, perfect.

She had read my book, seen one of Sari's films, knew the music of Pebble's favorite grunge group, and shared Faith's love of gardens. She had lived for a time in Las Vegas and knew many of Rita's old haunts, and she was a master of active listening, drawing her prey into revelations far beyond casual conversation by simply focusing those wide limpid eyes on the victim and seeming to concentrate as if every word was revelation.

I thought she was tracking us like a sniper in a tower with a telescopic lens, searching for details, defects, bits of information. She did this without a trace of obviousness. She was serene, taking long walks on the beach, reading Proust on a lounge in the sand wrapped in her own black cashmere blanket in the still-chilly May sunshine.

She was up in time for breakfast, returned in time for lunch, emerged from bath and nap just as Sari opened the aperitif bottle of Moët for the Kir Royals and set out the homemade cheese straws and nicely ripened Explorator. She ate everything with gusto, no special requests, no picky eating, no sauce on the side for our Jasmine. She played Go Fish with Pebble and hired Inga to come and conduct a private stretch class, inviting all of us to join her. As Webster's defines the word, "A being totally without flaw or defect"—perfect.

Brigadoon had now become Shangri-La. Another kind of spell had been cast. The women were not even jealous or competitive with her. She was so out of reach she was like a specimen from some master race: Wonder Woman as seen by Richard Avedon, the Lady in the Lake as seen by Helen Gurley Brown. They were transfixed by her. Hanging on her every barely audible word, racing to please her—panting pups before the haughty bitch mother, scampering over one another to get to the tasty teat.

And I roamed the edges of this passion play, pushed out of my thus far comfy spot as alpha male by this lodger. No longer were the women interested in my compliments or observations. For the first time since Sari's return from the city, she slept in her own room. ("I'm just wiped. I need a little solitude till she leaves.")

She. leaves. The two words had become very important to me. My feelings were hurt. I retreated to my house and worked on my book proposal, or rather I sat in front of my typewriter and thought about why I was reacting to a total stranger like this, a ship who would pass, sail off as she had sailed in, returning me to my rightful spot in the world of the women I loved.

Saturday evening I dressed more carefully than usual and arrived to help as host. I wasn't needed, but I came. As it turned out, Jasmine Jones had made a few calls, and several chic folk from Provincetown had made dinner reservations. The wine bar was buzzing when I entered, which for some reason made me sad, a third wheel beside Sari and Faith, who were almost beside themselves with glee. Rita arrived with her daughter, and Debbie and Inga showed up with Inga's uncle, the German professor from Oklahoma.

I shuffled my emotional deck: a howling melancholy mixed with unease. Camelot. Brigadoon. Shangri-La was now open for business. It was no longer about creating, the intense camaraderie of a dream coming true; the bonding created by imagination, sweat-of-brow accomplishments, risk, and trust. Others now were involved. It was no longer just ours to love.

I realized I wasn't ready. It wasn't supposed to happen for another damn week, but she had changed the circadian rhythm of our joy place. It was too soon. I wasn't prepared, and neither were my loved ones, but they were infected, feverish with Jasminitis.

All right, I was feeling sorry for myself: hurt, abandoned, jealous.

I should have been glad they were off to such a good start. I should have been, but I wasn't. I felt cheated. I went into the kitchen and took out the bottle of Dom Pérignon I'd bought for our official opening-night toast, popped the cork, and poured a glass for myself. Thomasina came in and I poured a glass for her. "Salute, Signore Anitra," she said, giving me a sly wink.

In Provincetown, I had bought sterling silver bracelets made of tiny alphabet cubes and had them engraved for Pebble, Faith, Sari, and Rita, each with their names and the opening date of the inn. I took the bracelets out of the drawer where I had stashed them and lined them up on the chopping block, denying myself the pleasure of giving for the quick fix of martyrdom.

I took my glass, wandered out onto the terrace, and sat down in a small wicker chair to watch the sun turn fierce and dark as it prepared to lower itself for the night. I wallowed in the loneliness that comes from not finding the eye to catch, the loneliness of being the only one who sees what you are seeing. Was that why I was afraid? What if they never came back? What if I'd lost them all? The joy of Sari had been finding someone who saw almost from inside my own head. It was a feeling of closeness I had never known, not even with Faith. A soul mate, though I had always cringed at the idea, but even she was lost to me over this guest.

No one saw what I saw. Danger, subterfuge, and something else—something worse. I swallowed, the tingling fizz of fine wine and the setting of the sun stopping my descent down a ladder of thought that could only lead me farther away from the others. Too cold, too fizzy, too fast.

"May I join you?" She was standing before me, blocking the sunset. The red glow illuminated her hair; the night breeze gently raised it off her broad creamy shoulders and pressed the black slip of a dress against her, revealing erect nipples and no visible undergarments.

I forced myself to look up directly into her incandescent, mocking eyes, testing my immunity. "Please," I said, feeling a slight reaction.

She slid into the chair across from me and placed her drink next to mine on the table. I picked up my glass, lightly clicking hers. "To our first guest," I said, cocky in my self-swindle.

We american males seem fated never to learn from the history of our own experience, continuing to believe that we can win a battle by combat, seeing through the glassy-eyed bloat of our egos, deluding ourselves that we can outsmart, outrun, outfox, or blast the resolve out of our opponents. Only in movies do the good guys really win; movie enemies are left screaming in the eviscerated agony of defeat while the heroes wipe a drop of sweat from their strong unfurrowed brows and raise the flag of victory.

In real life the only way you ever win against the bad guys— who most of the time are disguised as your friends and co-workers and not nearly as easy to pick from the crowd as a Chechnian separatist barreling toward you with an assault rifle—is to put down your gun and go home. Why is this lesson so hard for us to learn? I know it has something to do with Darwin and a lot to do with testosterone, but it still smells from herring, as my grandmother's cantor friend at Touro Synagogue would have said.

I was going to John Wayne it.

She picked up her glass and sipped, accepting her due without response, and we watched the sun sink.

"This is a beautiful place. I think they'll do very well, because it's a word-of-mouth kind of inn and there's nothing with this sophistication anywhere around here. I'm really very honored to be the first visitor."

I had already lost ground. She was so gentle. So—nice.

She smiled at me, two Ava Gardner dimples creasing the sides of her gorgeous mouth. "Coming here practically saved my life. Just a day and a half and I feel so—healed."

I laughed, I think. "Now, Miss Jones, let's not get too far afield. It's a great spot and we've put a lot of love into it, but Mecca it ain't."

A tear, one lovely raindrop of a tear, slid down her cheek. She wiped it away with the back of her hand, a gesture so purely feminine it made my throat sore.

"I deserved that, I suppose. I feel so at home with all of you, I forget that I'm a stranger and you know nothing about me. I didn't want to bring my dark cloud into your happiness. The truth is, my mother died early last week and she was all I really had left and—well, I've wandered so much in my life, I really didn't have anyone to turn to, anywhere to go. Coming here, being on the sea again and with such kindness, means a lot."

This was the moment to put my pistol back in my holster, salute the Muslim death squad, Khmer Rouge guerrillas, Kurdish hill fighters, and retreat with dignity, but I was now well behind enemy lines while still imagining myself in the no-fly zone.

"I'm sorry, that was a dumb thing to say."

"Thanks," she said, another tear caressing her face. She let it fall and took another sip of her deeply red wine. The Mona Lisa as seen by Helmut Newton.

"Actually, it's kind of ironic, because I struggled so much with my mother for so long. I guess the unresolved relationships are always the ones that really tear you up. She was very beautiful, but she married badly, and she led a completely thwarted and frustrated life." She paused and sipped her wine, and I could see the muscles in her swan neck contract when she swallowed.

"I always wanted to ask her why she never left—she could have had anyone—but I never did. I guess I was too busy being ashamed and horrified I'd end up like her. My father died when I was fifteen, and I ran off to Europe with a crazy mafioso old enough to be my grandfather. But my mother haunted my entire life. I guess I was always trying to overcompensate.

"Now it's too late. I'll never get to tell her how I felt or let her tell me. Funny, how every time we think we've figured things out, someone shakes the kaleidoscope again."

I had now been shackled and led into my new life as a POW. It was only much later that I remembered what a police psychiatrist had told me once about sociopaths. He said students were always asking him how to keep from being fooled by them, how to spot them. "You can't," he'd tell them. "That's how it works. That's what makes them so dangerous. You can't."

"I lost my mother when I was a kid" I heard myself say, "and sometimes I try to imagine what it must be like to grow older and have a mother who you keep reviewing in a way, seeing more clearly as a person as you see yourself. I can keep my mythical mother, because I never had to view her from the daylight of adulthood. Maybe I wouldn't even have liked her. She died when I was still in the adoring blind-faith stage, and that's where I've stayed. But I do understand the magnitude of mother loss, and the bad news is, it doesn't ever seem to end. It's always just there, like a birthmark or a cowlick."

At that moment I wanted to lift her into my arms, carry her off into the blazing last light of the blood-colored sun, and make ravishing, tortured love to her.

She sighed, and her breasts pushed against the silky fabric. "Even if they're still alive, you can feel that way. I never really knew if she loved me or hated me. She never told me she was sick, and she left me nothing. It's almost as if I'd imagined her. I've led a pretty self-indulgent and rootless life, really. I sent her money when I had it, but I hadn't been home to see her in two years."

"Where did you grow up?" I asked, stumbling toward the killing field.

"Oh, it doesn't really matter, does it?" she said.

Of course it mattered. She pulled a paperback from her pocket, luring me back from the observation turret.

"Do you like Anita Brookner? I suppose men don't read her, but there's a wonderful quote in here. 'It is nearly always a fatal mistake to go against one's nature, however unsatisfactory that nature proves to be. One must be authentic, if one is to be anything at all.' We do waste so much time being afraid of who we'll become and so little in embracing who we are."

"*Brief Lives,* isn't it? I like that book."

She smiled at me, revealing gleaming white teeth. "You really are as wonderful as Sari and Faith said you were."

I could almost feel Granny O jabbing a friendly bayonet point between my shoulder blades. *Watch the flowery words; flattery is the devil's weapon.* Which is probably why we all love it so much.

Before I could respond with some similar out-pouring of praise, which would most likely have gushed forth with the meretricious splash of the deluded seducee, Sari appeared, looking flushed and frantic but not oblivious enough to prevent her own danger transmitter from switching on. I knew this by the way she crossed her arms at the sight of me and Miss Jones.

"Hey, Jonny, are we vacationing? I've got a room full of thirsty types. It's gone completely crazy in there. We need you."

Jasmine rose without a moment's hesitation. "It's my fault, Sari. He was just being a good host, listening to my little tale of woe. Can I help?"

Sari looked slightly confused. "Get real. You're the *guest*! I think they've all come because of you. Word got out we had a movie star here. No. Please, I'll show you to your table."

I stood up, feeling confused and off-balance. How could I so easily be swayed, only months into the most wonderful relationship of my entire life? Jasmine Jones led the way, and I handed Sari my glass.

"Take a sip. Dom Pérignon. It was for the three of us to celebrate, but I felt sorry for myself and opened it. The bottle's in the fridge for later."

Those Sicilian ice cutter eyes looked right through me. "Confession is good for the old soul, pal," she said, and I was catapulted back into the safety of my own troops.

"I'm very proud of you both."

Pebble ran out onto the deck, her cheeks flushed with sun and excitement. "Hey, we need help! Customers keep coming in, but Thomasina is running out of pasta."

Sari held up her wrist, the silver cubes catching the starlight. "Hey, Jonny. Thanks. We love them."

I followed her in, feeling ashamed of myself, and said a little prayer to my new friend God, that this place would give them what they needed even if they weren't sure, themselves, exactly what that was.

All successful restaurants have one thing in common, no matter how simple or grand. They give off a kind of high, a pop of positive voltage. They just make you feel more alive. You feel happier being in them than being somewhere else; more with it, more connected to the energy field. This place had it. The combination of site, lighting, taste, noise level, and good vibrations— it just sparked. We were overwhelmed but filled with that adrenaline rush that comes from any success, (success being as rare as it is).

In my role as wine steward, I had found an ideal second career as a personable and remote eavesdropper, every reporter's dream. Conversations of the unguarded and overindulged were always interesting, and I absorbed as much as I could without being obvious.

Rita and her daughter, for example, were having a heated conversation over their osso bucco and polenta (which meant they would both be purging by midnight).

"You want to know why I can't just trust you?" Emily said. Because you have such a big mouth, Mom! You've told everyone I'm gay and bulimic. And I am not gay! Now people look at me like I'm this total freak-out."

Rita was scarfing her *bruschetta.* "What do you mean, you're not gay? You told me you were gay! Who says something like that if it isn't true?"

"I was just trying to hurt you, okay? I'm not gay, I'm just ambivalent. And being gay is like the new big 'in' chick scene, especially here. But I'm not. I guess I wanted to be because of Daddy being such a scumbag, but I'm not. That's not the point. It's that you *told* people! Don't you have any pride? Why do you tell everybody our shit? They know all about your plastic surgeries, everything. Why can't you be the kind of mother who just listens and offers quiet wisdom?"

"You're right, sweetheart. I guess it's nerves. I get started and I want people to like me or something, and I just blab. But I never tell stuff I think you want to keep private."

"Oh, right. Of course, like being gay and bulimic, who would want to keep *that* private!"

"But you tell people all the time! How could I know?"

"That's different. If *I* tell them, I'm choosing."

"Oh, puhleez! Give me a wee break here. Look, honey, I'm

very sorry, your signals were really mixed, but let's get something straight—being your mother is not a job I'm auditioning for, I've already got the part, okay? I'm doing the best I can." Rita swallowed a mouthful of broccoli Rabe and started to cry.

"Mom, I'm sorry I hurt your feelings. It's this getting ready to go away to college stuff, it's freaking me out. I've been thinking maybe I'm not ready. Maybe I could stay here and help out at the inn for a while and take some courses at the J.C. You're still so shaky, you need me."

Rita took a slug of the burgundy I had just poured into her glass and blew her nose. "Oh, no, you don't. You're not going to make my mistakes. You're going to college and you're going *away* to college! You are not going to be within a one-hundred-mile range of the washer and dryer. I'll cope."

This had all the makings of a movie of the week, but I moved on. A group of male antique dealers were discussing the pros and cons of full body waxing. (Painful, but worth it, was the consensus.) I saw Inga's uncle casting lecherous glances at Sari, and two newlyweds from down the beach were fondling one another's genitalia under the crisp white tablecloth and murmuring as to what they would stick where when they returned to the privacy of their wedding bed.

All in all, it was a most satisfying voyeuristic evening, and sharing this outsider's overview with me was our guest. Sitting alone at the best table, sipping her blood-red wine, eating slowly and watching: a great black cat before the mouse hole. I refilled her glass, but I kept moving.

CHAPTER NINE

S unday afternoon. A beautiful woman collapsed on asphalt, huddled
in pain. A bicycle lying beside her. "Please, I need help," she whispers bravely, tears streaming everywhere. "Please."

I, discoverer of the wounded, run, Lancelot galloping toward Larimore.
"Call nine-one-one!" I shout to Pebble from the porch. Back I trot, bringing
ice cubes and blankets, cotton swabs and Bactine for her scrapes, proffering
my silk hankie (which she takes without hesitation.) "The pain," she
moans, seeming to pass out. I, distraught, place my hand on the warm deli-
cacy of her wrist, checking for pulse, pressing the cool vellum of bare skin
under her heart, holding her goddess head, waiting for rescue.

When they lift her, she screams and we all stand, white with anxiety
and, somehow, shame. Shame that our guest, who has trusted and flattered
us and behaved so wonderfully well, should suffer on our watch. The fairy-
dust weekend ruined by this trick of fate. What had we done? Was the bike
faulty? The newly poured drive bumpy? Would she sue? Who should we call?
How bad was the fall?

We sit in the emergency waiting room, waiting. Faith's hands shake.

Pebble sneaks Snickers bars from the vending machine. Sari paces around bumming cigarettes from fellow waiters. Finally, a healer appears. No, we are not her family. No, we cannot authorize any treatment. No, we know nothing about her medical history, allergies, or preexisting conditions. She was merely our weekend guest.

What is it? Faith whispers, her eyes red from crying. Dislocated hip. Very painful, a specialist has been called. Sleeping now—heavily sedated. The shock you see, the pain.

More waiting. Exhaustion and shame. Disappointment. Everything had been so perfect. What could we do? Specialist arrives, gruff and hurried. Hip is snapped back. She must rest. Can't travel. Of course, of course. We all scamper after gurney. Trail after ambulance. Carry her upstairs to her room. Line up medications. Something for pain. Something to help her sleep. Something for inflammation. Can't walk. Oh, God! Bedpans? What to do? Calls are made. Practical nurse is found. We'll pay. Of course, of course. Bring a tray in case she wakes up.

Lying in shadow, setting sun casting grids of light through the shutters, falling symmetrically across the sheets on her bed. Our guest, Sleeping Beauty, hair billowing onto her pillows like mermaid hair. Cheeks moist, gleaming with heat and dried tears. Shadows now falling over all the golden Came-light. Brigadoon night. Sari, following me out, clutching my hand. Quiet for her, stunned into silence by this mishap. Faith and Pebble holding one another. All of us staying. Sleeping in empty guest rooms, guarding the guest. Worried. What to do? What to do?

The man who came to dinner, madcap curmudgeon Sheridan Whiteside, had been reincarnated in the shape of a dazzling raven-tressed woman and dropped from the dusty top shelf of some arcane play archive into our newly aproned laps. No white-bearded tyrant bound to a wheelchair was our guest. Within three days she was up and hobbling around, but she had become part of our lives. She had new power now. She had suffered and we were making it up to her.

This is how bloodless battles are fought. The violating of inner peace, the mining with doubt and confusion. The plastique head fuck of the sociopathic saboteur. She recovered just quickly enough not to outstay her welcome or use up our guilt and empathy quotas, and she insisted on paying for everything. What a classy broad.

And then she presented Faith with an idea. What if she took the one renovated cottage and stayed on for the season? She was still weak and in mourning and frankly she really had nowhere to go. She was just house-sitting in New York. For a reduced rate, she could even help out. She was a whiz at gardening, an excellent cook, good with her hands, and she could paint. She loved the inn, and it would give her a purpose while she put her life back together.

Sheridan Whiteside making his comeback as Venus with a straight-edge and a putty knife. Wow. Something for everybody. The Anti christ risen from the asphalt, forgiving and tossing her fairy dust into eager eyes clouded by longing.

The thing about eyes glazed with longing is they can't see very well. All the nibbling grown-up question marks about who to trust and what path to take dissolve. Anxiety is only really kept at bay by two things, absolute truth or absolute bullshit, and there is always far more of the latter available than the former for most of us questers.

Because Sari and I really did see past the sparkle but didn't want to, and Faith and Pebble didn't see at all, it breeched us, as self-deception always does, and things changed underneath. On the surface, however, the good fairy's wand was waving all over the joint.

Jasmine Jones lived up to her promises. Not only did she beguile with expertise, she pitched travel agents, critics, and fancy locals. Dinner was overbooked every night. Extra construction workers materialized, completing three more cottages before the

Fourth of July weekend; the phone rang off the hook with enthusiasts who had heard about the inn and wanted to book. And Jasmine was everywhere, beguiling, ever so gently nudging Faith and Sari into the background. They had begun to see her as the reason for their success. Then several things happened.

I'd been away from the inn for almost two weeks, having retreated to work on my book proposal, now that Jasmine was doing my job. (Andy didn't seem to see my fucking his estranged wife as any problem at all.) I went over to pick up Sari, who was about to leave for LA to meet with a producer about her new script. We were feeling the strain of the unknown thing between us and the frustration of trying to fall in love in the middle of all that was going on, and we'd planned to take a picnic lunch and find a quiet spot in the dunes.

The lobby was filled with far more stylish guests than we had ever anticipated. Emily had been hired to help Betsy, and there was a receptionist who had no idea who I was. I sat down in the parlor to wait for Sari. The door to the dining room was open and I heard three voices: Faith, Pebble, and Jasmine. I decided not to join them, eavesdropping being my information-gathering mode of choice, but also because I was feeling left out and prickly about it.

This is what I heard.

Faith: "Darling, it's not that I don't believe you. It's just that it doesn't make sense! You've been getting so much exercise and eating so well. How can you be gaining weight? When your father comes, he's going to send you to that camp in Vermont. Pebs, I'm on your side, but I'm concerned."

Pebble (crying): "*You're* concerned! It's happening to me and my own mother doesn't believe me! I'm not pigging out! I'm doing everything right, and I'm getting fatter! It's just the truth. You've got a genetic gross-out for a kid! Do you want me to starve like Rita or throw up all the time like Emily did?"

Jasmine: "Look, I know this isn't my business, but since you

asked me to help, let me try. I told you both when we started this
diet, sometimes it takes time for the changes to manifest. I've put
Pebble on the very best regimen possible and you must have
patience. If you follow it, Pebble, you will reprogram your meta-
bolic message. It's absolutely a miracle, and it will work if you
trust me and really do it. And I'll be glad to explain this to your
father or your doctor if need be. I promise it will work, and then
you'll be able to eat what you want and never be heavy again."

"See? Please, Momma. Don't tell him. I'll do better. I won't eat
one single thing Jasmine doesn't give me. I swear!"

Faith: "Baby, I do believe you. Please don't think I don't believe
you. It's just, he keeps asking and it's hard to lie to him."

Jasmine: "But you don't have to. Just tell him she's started a
very complex diet and it takes time to kick in."

"Yes, that's good and when he comes, you can explain."

"Maybe Jasmine could call him up right now. Would you?"

"Sweetheart, he's in India. Let's wait."

I tensed like a cat in a midnight alley, creeping slowly toward
juicy rodent or drunken sailor. Sari slid onto my lap, stopping my
progression into feline intuition.

"So, are we picnicking or what?" She nuzzled my neck and I
sniffed the ginger of her, realizing how much I'd missed her.

We walked for a while, trudging in deep powdered sand until
we found the ideal spot: an alcove formed by two small dunes
that spread around us like angel's wings, protecting us from sun,
wind, and the eyes of others. Sari unpacked our lunch and we
ate. I was quiet, still feeling the pull across my back, the discomfort lingering from the overheard chat; Sari filled the gaps, her
own nervousness about leaving fueling her patter.

"Here's my fantasy lunch meeting in Hollywood. I'm at a long
post-postmodern table filled with thirtysomething blond devel-
opment VPs of both sexes. They're all wearing Armani pant suits,
and they each have little laptops, cell phones, and beepers neatly

placed before them. Slightly to the side they have plates of tofu and glasses of some privately labeled water. Next to their plates they have portable blood pressure kits and finger-prick setups to test their sugar levels and cholesterol. They're all grinning, not from pleasure but as part of their isometric face-firming routine, and are simultaneously contracting and relaxing their abdomen and buttocks muscles. Small porta weights are being used on the arm that is not eating or performing medical evaluations.

"We are talking about character arcs and payoffs, and I pull out an enormous platter of mortadella and slam a jug of Chianti down on the table, tearing off my Armani jacket to reveal a black leather bustier and talking very loudly about politically unpardonable topics. Like it?"

"I think maybe you're just scared of going back to LA and revisiting the scene of the crime. You haven't been there since you left Andy."

"That's probably part of it, but the town does weird stuff to my head. I always feel like I'm six years old, new school, first day, and I've got the clothes wrong and no one will play with me."

"Pearls before swine."

She smiled and I kissed her, tasting tuna and lemonade. She lay back on the towel and sighed. "Yeah, you're right, they wouldn't get it. The last time I was out there, before the Malibu scene, we went to a dinner party near Will Rogers's old house, and I said that the most ridiculous line I'd ever heard was his 'I've never met a man I didn't like.'

"I mean, really, if in fact you liked everyone, how could you make any selections? There wouldn't be a defining principle to your judgments. So old Will making a statement like that doesn't make him a better person than the rest of us. It just makes him either a liar or an idiot."

"What happened?" I pulled her toward me and cupped one of her wondrous breasts with my sandy fingers.

"Well, let's just say lead balloons in preschool parking lots have gotten warmer receptions. You should have seen Andy's face."

"I would have swept you up, driven to Will Rogers State Park, and fucked you wildly."

I felt her swallow and tears dropped onto my cheek as I began kissing her neck, smelling her smells, now mixed with salt and sea. "Oh, Jonny, I thought we'd lost it. Something's off, really off. I thought you didn't want me, anymore."

"No, no. More than ever. I think I've figured out what's been happening. We need to talk about it. But not now, let's just do this. Jesus, Sari, I love you. I just fucking love you."

She pulled me tighter and I knew she was crying harder, which should have dampened my hard-on into something more tender, but it didn't. I felt fused to her, in need of her, from her, in a way I had never allowed in my life. I was lost in her realness. I pushed my face down into the velvety fullness between her breasts, feeling her heart pound, hearing her moan, and realizing I'd never before said to any woman what I'd just said to her.

We were gone for hours, and Sari was restless going back. She had dinner to supervise and packing to do. I decided to wait until after her trip to discuss what I'd overheard in the dining room. We drove up the guest drive to the front, my intention being to drop her off and go home. We were both still awkward about the family knowing of our attachment in so obvious a way.

Pebble and Jasmine were sitting on the porch waiting. Pebble jumped up and ran down the steps to greet us. She was holding something tightly against her chest and she was smiling. The something moved and I saw fur. A paw. Two little black eyes peeking over her sun-darkened arms.

"Uncle Jonny! Sari! Look! Look!"

Sari checked the mirror for signs of sex. "I feel as sinful as if the Holy Mother herself was coming at us with Baby Jesus in her arms. Am I blushing?"

"Yes. Am I?"

"Yes."

Pebble held the furry thing up, resting its forelegs on my open window. "Isn't she the cutest thing you've ever seen in your entire life?"

The little mutt cocked her head as if on cue, and one slightly bent white ear flopped over her face, and she licked the silver cubes on Pebble's bracelet. It was almost too cute. It was so cute it was hard to believe it was a real animal and not one from Pebble's stuffed menagerie. It had snowy-white curls all over and a snub nose. It looked like a living feather duster.

Sari and I got out, smoothing clothes and hair as we moved, avoiding eye contact.

"Here, here, hold her! She's just so cuddly! We've already taken her to the vet. Momma said I can keep her if no one comes to find her. My first puppy!"

I took the small pleasure ball and held her up, and she whimpered and stuck out her little pink tongue and licked my cheek. Irresistible. Sari took the puppy from me, cooing in Italian, holding her where she'd recently held me.

Seeing Pebble's joy, I decided to make the logical inquiries, trying to be paternal rather than act as mushy-hearted as I felt.

"Pebs, she's a gem, but where did she come from?"

"Momma and I went out to the garden to do some planting and we heard this noise, almost like a baby crying, and it kept getting louder and we were looking everywhere, and then I saw something white sticking out of one of the empty planters. I went over and I saw this tiny tail. She was inside! We called the ASPCA and the pound and everything. No one's reported her missing; it's like a total mystery! She doesn't have a collar or anything. She was all dirty and so scared. It's like a miracle. I'm going to call her Angel, because that's what it felt like. An angel flew down from heaven to answer my prayers."

Sari leaned over and gently handed the miracle with the dubious past back to Pebble. We looked at one another and I knew we were both feeling a mix of love and fear that her happiness would be wrested from her by the rightful owner. This was not the kind of pup that anybody just abandons or whose absence wouldn't be felt.

I put my arm around her and led her and her angel up the steps and sat down in the rocker, pulling her onto my lap. Jasmine sat on the wicker chaise. She was wearing a long flowing black robe over a bathing suit, and when she crossed her legs the robe opened. Her feet were bare and there was a mark that at first I thought was dirt or a mole, until I saw the outline of a heart. A small purple heart was tattooed on the outside of her left heel.

"Pebble, honey, I don't want to be the mean uncle here, but this is a very cute pup and it's pretty likely she belongs to somebody. Don't you think we should at least put an ad in the paper? It will only be harder to give her back later on."

Jasmine leaned forward and her hair, braided into one long thick plait, fell forward over her shoulder like a silken rope, a Rapunzel path to some secret place.

"I've already done that," she said, cool as cream. "It does seem for whatever strange reason that she was just put out. The vet said it was possible the mother had gone off and given birth and when she'd weaned the pup it wandered away." I've leased a car and I've driven from one end of Truro to the other asking everyone. No one has seen other pups or a dog resembling Angel. Of course you're right to be concerned."

That alley cat thing was happening between my shoulder blades again. I saw something. A slight narrowing at the corners of Jasmine's pale lavender eyes, a mime's movement.

Faith appeared in the doorway, her face radiant and flushed. "I just talked to Granny O, and she's going to come up with Benjamin and stay awhile. I never thought she'd agree. Isn't that grand."

Sari hugged her. "Granny and a puppy all in one afternoon.

This is getting too sappy. When are they coming? I don't want to miss her."

"Oh, not for a couple of weeks. He's still in Bombay, and she won't go anywhere until her peonies have finished."

Sari moved toward the door. "Let's have a quick meeting before dinner. I'm worried about leaving you in the lurch here."

"Not to worry. Jasmine and I have everything under control."

I glanced over at Jasmine, who remained sitting, as tranquil as an underground grotto. "We'll be just fine," she said, and for the first time since our drink on the deck, she looked directly into my eyes.

Theo had once entertained me during an autopsy in New York with his theory of human life. Theo believed that in the great galactic scope of things we mortals were merely thinking amoebas desperately wiggling toward the light. A bleak and certainly won't-play-in-Peoria view, but it did partly explain the human ability to fill any vacuum and rearrange even the most important relationships in jig time.

So Sari left and I resumed my role as dinner host and wine steward, freeing Jasmine to supervise in the kitchen. We soon formed a new construct and routine. Sari called daily, regaling, ranting, making us laugh, and primarily peeing on her territory. Pebble provided her with daily reports on Angel's training progress (the pup remained unclaimed and had captured the hearts of the entire inn and every arriving guest). Nothing could have been quite as effective a promotional tool as the all-time poster puppy, bow-wowing at the entrance.

With Sari gone, Faith became more assertive and decisive, with the subtle but, I was beginning to note, persistent encouragement of Jasmine. Now that I was back to semi-clear-eyed observation, I was picking up all sorts of static on my rusty inner radar.

But what quelled my doubts and enabled me to tune down the other frequency, the underbuzz of electric disturbance where the truth crackled, was my sister's emergence from the streaks of darkness that had flanked her life. I watched her grow each day from my own private perch of past and present experience. I watched her bloom.

Faith in her garden, kneeling, spade in hand, Granny's sunbonnet tipped forward, face solemn with joy. Digging, pruning, packing earth, sweat of brow, good tired, the kind well-earned, coming from honest effort, work to be proud of. On her knees, fingers caked with mud, Pebble hoeing, watering cans pouring, puppy prancing. My sister, the petless shy one, leading the way. Angel, stay. Sit. Bad dog, Baaadd dog. Good puppy. Good girl.

Moving room to room, bouquets of growing things, colors of Monet, arms full of buds, yellow and pink and peach, taller, she seemed to be, taller, striding now, not hiding, adoring puppy trailing behind. Betsy, we need more towels in Room Eight and that bed's not tucked in right. Thomasina, too much egg in the tortellini last night, let's try the dough again. Hello? This is Faith Wise, the Inn at the End.... The salmon order was short two pounds, and that is just not acceptable.

Round and round, morn to night, strutting almost, marching to and fro, mandarin smile of mouth and eyes, head high, laughing that gravelly laugh, shining bright, the crushed-heart look gone, gone that silent blinking cry for help, freed of it, lime eyes lit with fancy, a good fairy's augury, lighting her path. Mantra humming under her breath, round and round, "Pom pom, pom pom," murmuring, twinkling with her secrets, healing something. Peace of mind, it meant, peace of mind, her own code, her own goal, always out of reach, now in sight. Pom pom possibilities flowering like the garden.

I watched, ignoring the blips, the current surges under, always under, this dream coming true, because what I saw in her was real. My sister, living the life she deserved. Pebble, I want those phlox watered and I will not ask you again.

I faxed Benjamin somewhere, "Faith is better than ever. Come soon." I felt some urgency, some desire for him to see her now, see what she had created before anything changed. Skeptic that I was, but knowing too well that such magic times always pass, often before we've thought to note them. Often, like this one, only really recovered in memory.

I see now that what happened next was inevitable. I accept the madness of my dark-side dance. We must all do at least one very long tango with the Devil sometime. I'm not going to defend or rationalize what happened. I'm merely reporting because it's part of the story.

Six solid days of proximity to Jasmine Jones had taken its toll. I returned to the inn compulsively. Showing up hours early to be helpful with chores, taking beach romps with Pebble and her pup when I should have been writing, staying on to sip after-dinner drinks when Faith had gone home.

I conned myself. I was doing it to figure her out. But you don't do battle with the Devil's army. You lock the doors and hide under the bed. You kneel before God and pray for guidance. You leave town. I was stirred, and I didn't want to be.

I had taken a shower and popped open a beer, preparing to do some work, when the chime on the front door tingled and I padded out in my robe and bare feet. I could see her through the leaded glass pane, looking somber and ruffled. I wasn't as surprised to find her there as I pretended to be, but my heart was beating too fast. Fight or flight, my alley cat blew into my already deafened ear.

"It's so late, I'm sorry, am I interrupting?" Jasmine smells floating from her hair, darkness crossing my threshold like the shadow of the angel of death passing over the Hebrew houses.

"I was just about to bite the bullet and do some work, but I'd welcome an excuse to put it off. Would you like a drink?"

"Yes, please."

I was acutely aware of my nakedness under the damp terry cloth. I felt as diffident as a teenage virgin. I resisted the urge to excuse myself and put on some pants, another strategic error. Pick up your gun and leave, Jon, the cat purred, tickling my ear.

"A beer in the bottle would be wonderful."

I left her and returned to the kitchen, opened another bottle and carried it back. She had taken off her shawl and was sitting curled on the one couch. She was wearing a long loose black dress, and I could see the line of her body underneath. I handed her the beer and moved away, choosing a large club chair as far from her as possible.

"Is something wrong? You seem upset."

She put the bottle to her pale lips and tilted her head back, and I could see her throat contract as she swallowed. She took her time, drinking deeply, providing all sorts of erotic images, which I could feel my battle-weary body responding to. She was more than a visitor in my home, she consumed the space, possessed it. She was too powerful a force for such a simple little room. I was having trouble breathing. Some exotic and voracious hot-house plant was depleting the oxygen in my rickety little greenhouse.

She lowered her head and her hair cascaded forward, framing her incredible face. Her cheeks were flushed and tears welled in her beautiful eyes. "Yes, I am upset. I never would have come here, but I just—I didn't know who to talk to about this. You've all been so wonderful to me. I was afraid Faith would ... I just didn't know what to do."

The rational voice of my feline pointed out to me that this woman never didn't know what to do. "What is it, Jasmine?" Saying her name, posing a direct question, seemed to throw her off. Her face tensed.

"Yes, of course. Forgive me. I don't mean to be obtuse." She set her beer down on the table in front of her, uncurling her bare legs and reaching over for her purse. She opened it and pulled out a paper bag, turning it upside down and emptying an assortment of candy bars of all sizes and brands onto the glass tabletop.

"Emily was cleaning and found this hidden in Pebble's room.

Faith was out so she came to me; she's very worried about her. This explains why my diet isn't working. I just didn't know how to handle it. I'm an outsider and it's not my place, but I know it means Faith will have to send her away. I just—I thought you might—"

She stopped talking and turned those eyes on me, so earnest, so caring. I could barely control my tumult of emotion. Horror at the evidence, despair and concern for Pebble, guilt and confusion because I was finding it so hard to think about anything but the suffocating presence across from me.

"You made the right choice," I said, hesitating to confide anything deeper about my sister or her family. I had no idea what Faith had divulged, probably everything, but as Emily had told her mother at that long-past opening-night dinner, that was different; that was her choice. I picked up my beer again and sipped. She did the same. We said nothing. The cat was silent, thinking I had received the information.

I remember hearing the travel clock ticking in my bedroom, that was how quiet we were. "Shall I leave these?" she said finally, the words almost like a taunt.

"Yes, please. I'll talk to Faith in the morning."

She leaned over to put the candy back into the bag and her dress fell away from her chest and I could see down into the ivory of her breasts.

She looked up at me then, still bent forward, her hair covering her shoulders like a Greek widow's mantle, and she didn't move. She just waited. The power of her confidence made this the single most sensual act I had ever seen. She was the cat now, no ragged skittish domestic shorthair, but a great big panther arched for attack.

"I know," she whispered, and she straightened, moving toward me, stirring my senses with infusions of aromas: feline, female, Jasmine, night-blooming and dizzying. She reached down and pulled her dress over her head.

When I think of her body on that morgue slab I remember her that night, the magnificence of her. I had never seen anybody like her, no real flesh-and-blood woman. She lowered herself onto my lap, opening my robe, straddling me. My erection rose, proving my weakness, my defeat. She knew, had known all along, that underneath my feigned indifference I was just like all the rest. Alley cats have no business on the same battlefield as panthers.

"Oh, God, Jonny, how I want you! I couldn't bear another day of it. I thought if you didn't fuck me tonight I would just go mad from wanting you. Please. Please!" Her tongue was licking my neck, and she lowered herself onto my prick, surrounding me with the dense wet heat of her cunt.

I sat there, as stuporous as some nursing-home geezer, but when she climbed onto me something turned.

There was a snapping to, a need to assert. I put my hands under her shoulders and lifted her off, tearing off my robe and pushing her forward, prodding her, like a stubborn farm beast, into my room, onto my bed. "Okay, okay. That's what you want, isn't it? Somebody new to try and conquer you. Somebody else to fail. This is about sex, now. This is just about fucking."

She was gasping and moaning under her breath. "Yes, it is! It is! Please, please! I never can, I never have. I can't come. Make me. Please, *please,* make me."

Jesus. What was that? The beautiful frigid seductress, begging for release? The panther *groveling* before the fur ball?

"Anything. Do *anything* you want."

I pulled her down, spread her incredible legs, and pushed my tongue deep into her pussy. She buckled and I held on; we were both blind now, or so I assumed. I would do it to her. We had ripped away all shreds of pretense. We knew what this was about. She screamed and I felt her release and I turned her over, thrusting into her ass, not caring about her discomfort, not slowing. I banged into her very being; bang is the word. I used my cock like a weapon, shooting at the enemy, firing away. I'd show her. She, screaming under me, "Oh, my God, Jonny. Thank you! Thank you! I've never ... this is my first . . . oh, God, don't stop. Never stop. Please, please!"

Please. Please. Darkness covering me. Not just the night. Ravens circling. Crows. Vultures. Blackness. Ignominy. What have I done?

When I woke up it was daylight. She was gone, her scents lingering and the hologram of her presence, like a vision behind my eyes, haunting my mind's eye, something I couldn't blink away.

On my knees, my new best friend God and I having a chat. What had I done? I forced myself up and into daily things. I showered. I shaved, avoiding eye contact with myself, letting the mirror fog. I didn't want anything to do with this tom. The worst kind of alley trash, giving the whole damn species a bad name. I had fallen. I had really fucked up.

I dressed and made my bed and placed the empty beer bottles in the recycling bin and tidied up and went out for the papers and a walk in the fresh morning air. I did it as if nothing had happened. As if I had not betrayed myself and the woman I loved and parachuted into enemy territory with no walkie-talkie or map, no clue in hell as to who exactly I was fighting and what was in their arsenal.

What did she want from me? Cold sweat dripped down my shower-fresh skin. Did I for one micro minute believe what she had said to me in the midnight madness, that I was the first man to unleash her passion? No. Not even for a tick of my travel clock. I didn't have that kind of male ego structure, anyway. That was the terrain of the Andys and Benjamins. I never fooled myself about prowess.

A woman like that. I was not on my most virile day that good, or well endowed, or whatever it is that would make someone the purveyor of such power. And certainly not last night. It had to be a game or a ploy, not that she needed one. I was gone before she turned it there. Why? What did she want with me? With us?

Was I going to blame her for what I had done? I could at least show some dignity. Jesus. At my neighborhood gourmet deli I ordered a takeout latte from Waldo, a pretty boy with blue spiked hair and eight nipple rings bulging beneath his T-shirt. I bought the papers and sat down outside on my usual bench.

My hand shook when I took the lid off my coffee, and I felt tears pushing against the backs of my eyes. Get a grip, man. I was more than frightened, I was terrified, Why? This felt darker and more dangerous than the obvious betrayal of self, or maybe I'd just never had more at stake. I'd given somebody I had absolutely no trust in the power to destroy the most wonderful thing in my life. I had delivered a gift-wrapped box of live grenades into the hands of the rebel forces, an adversary I didn't even know. What the fuck was wrong with me?

I finished my coffee, picked up the papers, and walked into town to the office. I had a column to do. I decided to work at the paper, avoiding the possibility of the panther's return.

On my desk was a message from Sari saying she was not going to be back for a few more days, and a message from Jasmine that said, simply, *Soon again?*

Behaving in an appropriately mature manner, I tore it up and threw it into my trash basket. I opened the papers and tried to concentrate, but nothing stayed in focus. I tossed them aside and turned to my computer, surfing the net for stray items of absurdity. One stood out.

It seemed that the body of a man clad completely in scuba gear, including a tank, fins, and diving mask, had been found in the smoldering ruins of a major California forest fire. The site of the fire was a wooded mountain area twenty miles from the ocean. This, needless to say, had puzzled the authorities.

The autopsy showed he had died of massive internal injuries, not smoke or burns. When he was identified, rangers went to his home, where, after recovering from the shock, his wife told them she couldn't even hazard a guess as to how he had wound up on a mountain in the middle of a forest fire when he had left early the morning before to scuba-dive off the beach near their property.

Water. Fire. Puzzle pieces began to fit. Helicopters had been dispatched to the ocean to fill huge steel buckets and air-lift them to the fire. The unfortunate diver had apparently been scooped up like a giant goldfish and dropped a thousand feet down onto the blaze, extinguishing himself and five-feet-ten-inches' worth of flame.

Given my state of mind, I let the possibly apocryphal tale absolve me momentarily. Let's say the man had a lot on his mind. Let's say as he sat at the water's edge, struggling into his gear, he'd been overcome with doubts about diving. He'd worried that he'd drunk too much the night before and wasn't sharp enough, his tank pressure gauge was rusted, he'd heard of a shark sighting just miles away. Whatever else in his life was weighing him down—money woes, marital problems—the one thing you can bet the farm that he wasn't concerned about was the possibility of being ladled up out of the Pacific Ocean like a serving of fish soup, flown through the air in a giant tureen, and dropped onto a raging fire.

So? Maybe it doesn't make any sense to worry about anything, is the point I made to myself, sitting at my desk, fending off my fears. Whatever I could conjure up as the payback for my act of lechery, it would most likely be the one thing that never crossed my mind. Worry in the end is always our feeble attempt to control life. All those amoebas searching for the sun.

Whatever Jasmine Jones wanted from me, and whatever the consequences of my actions would be, I could no more figure them out than the poor shmuck in the wet suit.

I wrote my column and finished a piece for *Boston Magazine* and started a *Traveler* article on Provincetown. I worked without stopping and I didn't make or return any calls. The inn was closed for dinner on Mondays and I wasn't expected, so I wrote until after eight before wandering over to my favorite bar and ordering an icy dry martini. I really wanted a beer, but too many recent memories were involved.

Rita came in and sat down next to me. I hadn't seen much of her since that night at Debbie and Inga's, and I realized I missed her. She was the closest thing to a buddy I had up there.

"Hey, Jono, you're a sorry sight. The broads let you out of your cage for a night?"

"Yeah, the animal rights people issued a complaint. I've missed you. I hear you've been selling swampland to widows and orphans. May I buy you a drink?"

She motioned, and Persephone, the transsexual barkeep, brought her usual. "Just a quickie. I'm meeting Emily for a bite, and then I've got a date."

"Anyone I know?"

"Don't laugh. Inga's uncle."

"The German professor from Okiehoma?"

"He's really very nice, and amazing in the old sacko. No offense to present company, but he sings 'Eidelweiss' when he's doing it. He's leaving and going back to his estate on Lake Geneva, so he's got some loot and he's crazy about me and Emily. All I know is, I've gained ten pounds and I feel almost normal. Besides, another summer like this one and they'll find me impaled on a NO VACANCY sign somewhere."

"Didn't you sell anything?"

Rita smiled. She did look better. I realized I had never actually seen her smile. To each his eidelweiss.

"Yeah, actually I did great. Two condos and three million-plus houses." Emily came in, bringing memories of candy bars. I had stuffed the entire mental and real bag away until tomorrow.

"Hi, Jonny." She seemed different too, more feminine and younger somehow. Her hair was growing in and she had taken all visible rings out of her face.

"Hi, Em. How's it going?"

"Great. We're full and there's a waiting list and two travel writers called up and want information. Faith was excited." She kept her eyes away from me.

Rita nudged her. "Don't avoid. Ask the man."

I smiled at her. "It's okay, Emily. I know. Jasmine told me last night."

She shuddered and I thought she might cry, but she steadied herself and looked up at me. "Jonny, Pebble's my friend. I understand her. I freaked when I found that bag. And then Jasmine came in while I was trying to hide it—"

"She came in? You didn't go to her?"

"Me? No way. I don't rat out my friends. I was going to talk to Pebs first, but Jasmine grabbed it right out of my hands and I didn't know what to do. Pebble adores her. Mom said to tell you, but you didn't come over today, and I guess I was hoping it would all die down. The thing is, I don't think Pebble's been bingeing. I really know that routine and she was totally into the entire Jasmine diet thing. She's been really good. She's motivated, and I've never seen her sneak stuff. Something's not right."

"Emily, don't worry about Pebble, she knows you're her friend."

Rita slid off the stool. "Hey, we gotta boogie. I'm on Emily's side. Something's funny here. As for our live-in cover girl, knew the type in Vegas. Count the silver. I tried to tell Faith, but she thinks she's the Second Coming."

I watched them leave. The gripping was back. Something was not right at all.

CHAPTER TEN

It was late when I got home—too late, I hoped, for a panther's night prowl. I could feel my pulse race as I opened the door, half expecting the great beast to leap out at me. Silence. Was I really relieved or disappointed? I took a long shower and put on my robe, triggering memories, animal panting, lust, and rage, rolling around together like the pals they were.

The bell tingled and my breathing seemed to lose its rhythm. I tightened my robe, put on pajama bottoms and slippers, a fool's flimsy armor against eros, and went to answer.

Faith. Fair head bowed, tears streaming. I opened the door and she collapsed against me, her slender body quivering. It was like cradling a wounded bird; I could feel her heart, like a little sparrow's, a fast-beating fragile thing. I led her to the sofa and she sat down in the panther's spot and shame filled me again. I brought her water and sat beside her.

"Pebble's been hiding candy in her room. Oh, Jonny, I don't

know what to do. She's never done it before, lying and sneaking like this."

I said nothing, not knowing where to go without compromising someone. She wiped her eyes and sighed, looking at me quixotically as if she were slightly amused and slightly perplexed. "You don't seem surprised."

"I saw Emily tonight." My first flexing of the truth for the evening.

She nodded. "Emily's a good kid. She must have gone to see Pebble right after she saw you, and then Pebble and Jasmine came to me. Jasmine was there when Emily found the bag."

"Did Emily tell you that?"

"Well, no. Jasmine did. She was very upset. Pebble went to Jasmine when Emily left. She just idolizes her and she was afraid of what I'd do, I guess, but Jasmine told her she had to tell me at once.

"Oh, Jonny it was awful. I've never seen Pebble so distraught. She was hysterical. She kept saying that someone had set her up. All the movies she watches!

"Who would have done such a thing? Why? It doesn't make any sense for someone to try to entrap a little girl by planting candy in her room. I think she's so desperate she'll say anything. But she never lies!

"Oh, God, I've failed her, haven't I? And Benjamin sent a fax today. He'll be back in New York tomorrow and he's going to pick up Granny O and be here by Friday. I don't want him to see Pebble like this! She's gained ten pounds! I have to send her to camp, I just have to.

"I thought being here and the diet and the puppy and all would do it, but it hasn't and I'm making it worse. If it wasn't for Jasmine, God only knows how much she'd have gained. I really don't want Benjamin to see her. He's so harsh about her weight. He's so disciplined himself he just doesn't understand. Jonny, tell me, am I wrong? What do you think?"

"It's not what I think that matters. It's what you think. You don't need me or Jasmine Jones to tell you what you know better than any of us. You know Pebble. What do you think?"

She laughed then, and her eyes and the sides of her mouth crinkled up, and my heart hurt with love for her. "Damn, you sound like my shrinks."

She picked up her water and I saw her hand tremble. "What do I think? I think my baby is in pain and camp may be what she needs. Maybe the candy is a cry for help, some sort of attention-getter because she really wants to go and be with other kids who are grappling with the same problem. The crazy thing is, Jonny, in my heart, I believe her, but I think she should go anyway and I want her to do it before Benjamin comes up."

She relaxed then; making the decision had steadied her. I tried the question out on myself and realized I agreed with her, but for different reasons—reasons that I couldn't share, either with my own sister or the woman I loved. Anything I said about Jasmine now was tainted. She had bound and gagged me, rendering me as helpless as any captured prey.

"Faith, I think you're right. I'll drive her. Just let me know where and when."

"I've already called. They can take her right away, so I thought maybe Wednesday, before she has much time to think about it."

She moved closer and I put my arms around her and we sat the way we had as children, reaching in the dark for the comfort of the other. Motherless waifs, fearful of everything. "It's going to be okay, Faith, it is. She's a fighter. She'll struggle, but she'll be fine."

We sat for a long time calming one another, but there was no real release for me. I had withheld something important from her for the first time in our lives. I hadn't been strong enough to trust her with the truth.

* * *

I dreamt that night of alley cats and jungle cats, thrashing in the sea, pulling one another under, waves rising, great foamy, slashing torrents of water pounding over them. A maelstrom, a flood of fluid, a suffocating violent womb wave deluged with fear.

Something else, within the dream but not, something pulling me up into the air. Cold air, blankets stripped, pajamas opened. Something cold and hot and terrifying and amazing. Sucking on me in my sleep. My cock hard as a sea rock, struggling toward the surface, pushing me forward out of the birth canal, seeking air, seeking land, but not wanting to go.

Ambivalence, always, every day of our fucking lives. All those endless question marks, all those possibilities: decisions, doubts, mistakes. Jesus, but it felt so good. Crashing to shore, eyes open. The panther on me, covered in black, hair tickling my thighs, sucking me off in the dawn's early light. In the rockets' red glare ... bursting in air ... Jesus. Coming into her luscious mouth, surfing my half-sleep nightmare toward shore. She sat up, my jism leaking from the corners of her mouth, licking it away with her pink panther tongue.

"Good morning, Jonny," she whispered, in that baiting, luscious tone, and she was gone. Jasmine stink, sea goddess stink, jungle queen, a two-headed beast, sea and plain, gone.

I've been raped, I thought, wildly groping for my night clothes. The ultimate wet dream, womb wet, the wild thing. Unbearable sinful pleasure and terror. Real, now, in the morning light. *Good morning, Jonny.* What had I done?

The phone rang before seven, dragging me back from my escape sleep.

Thomasina's heavy voice. "Signore Anitra, you come. Now, please."

Up and out, fear clutching me. Catholic fear, pure and deep. How many Hail Marys would it take? My mind raced as I drove, not even glancing out the window at the beauty of the day, the incandescence of the early morning light fondling the dunes and the water, the sun rising into the clouds like a giant orange. A blissful morning, warm and ripe with summer senses, a world of joyful possibility paralleling my distress. Think of the sucker in the diving suit, Jon boy; stop trying to control the information.

Up the stairs into the inn. Quiet, still enough to hear the old railroad clock Faith had found at a flea market, ticking in the kitchen. No one up or about.

I ran outside and stopped to listen. Seagull sounds and then, beneath them, anguish, snips of female despair. Faith and Pebble. I followed the sounds into the garden protected from the wind and sand by trellis and shrub. Faith's secret garden, an homage to our grandmother.

They were kneeling together, rocking back and forth like Muslim village women mourning their dead. Thomasina stood over them, her hard weathered face clenched in fury, the fury of an old woman who has seen too much of the heinous side of human nature.

Pebble was holding something, and as I came closer I saw that her arms and Faith's, which were wrapped around her, were covered in blood. She was holding something limp and white, white feather fur blotted with red.

Faith turned, seeing me, her face ruined with confusion, uncomprehended cruelty. "Jonny. It's Angel. She's been killed."

I came around and knelt beside them. Pebble held the body of the puppy as if the force of her loss could will her back to life. Blood oozed from a gaping hole where her head had been. I gulped back a fist of bile in my throat. It looked like a doll, a mutilated, stuffed thing. The head seemed to have been suctioned off its body.

I reached over and as gently as possible pried the hemorrhaging creature from Pebble's trembling arms. Thomasina picked up one of the insulated coolers we used for picnics, and I lowered the little body into the chest; she sealed it fast, marching off before Pebble could stop her.

Pebble tried to get up, but I held her and she relaxed against me, her grief filled with the innocence of new emotion, feelings never known before, pure and unrepressed.

"Who could do this? How could they hurt her? Who could hate a little puppy?"

Faith blew her nose. She had recovered enough to attempt an answer. "Maybe it was another animal, sweetheart. A wild dog might have found her, or a—maybe a raccoon."

Pebble pulled away from me, logic—the need to fight back against the outrage of her helplessness—taking shape alongside her heartbreak. "Mom, there aren't any raccoons at the beach. And how could a dog get her? She was on my bed when I fell asleep. What was she doing out here? Somebody took her, like they set me up with the candy! Somebody's out to get me! They did it to psych me out!"

Faith looked at me, her eyes pleading. I had absolutely no idea what to say, because I agreed with Pebble. Thomasina came back then, saving us from a fanning of paranoia.

"Pebble, is my fault. I come very early, and I hear the Angel scratching at your door. I think she want to go do her business. I take her out, but I go to make the coffee and I forget. So she is in the garden maybe half an hour until you come out. Plenty time for some *pazzo* dog to get her. Is no person, is just me and my stupid old brain. Is not against you, *cara*."

Pebble shook with new sobs. "No, Thomasina, it's *my* fault. She was *my* puppy. I should have heard her. I should have taken her out! She needed my help and I wasn't there! I didn't even hear you come in. It's not your fault."

"It's no one's fault, it's the will of the universe." The presence rising above us, black wide-brimmed hat and glasses shielding the face from the morning sun. We, kneeling in the grass, good

Druids fighting to keep Satan's son from his seriously overdue birth, guarding tremulously against Armageddon.

Pebble pushed away and ran to her, leaving Faith and me behind. "Jasmine, somebody ripped Angel's head off!" She fell against her in utter trust.

Jasmine stroked her back, murmuring over her. "Her spirit is free. Be glad for her."

No one spoke, not daring to interfere with the power of her words to Pebble. Faith sat beside me, tears streaming down. Thomasina watched, her face ashen. "Come now," she said. "We eat something and then we bury the doggie." She said it in the flat resigned tone of one who has buried many and survived.

I stood and pulled Faith up, feeling dizzy and debiled by the turmoil, breaking away from this ad hoc black mass or whatever Jasmine was doing. The kitchen was cool and filled with life smells, cinnamon and perked coffee and bacon, and we ate ravenously, almost happily, we the living made more aware of our vulnerability, astonished at the wonder. The earth doesn't spin out of orbit, the oceans don't cover the land, the infinity of cells and molecules within us cooperate.

I felt humbled by the sheer bafflement of existence, surrounded by dangers vast and minute: bacteria and atoms hurtling through space, plague, flood, famine; madmen of all sorts; flesh-eating viruses and malarias and cancers and bursting arteries; new dangers daily, piling on the old, challenging the delicate membrane of being, the chrysalis of creation, all swirled together by the headless remains of a child's pet.

Pebble ate nothing. She sat by the window looking out at the cooler, paying her penance and honoring her loss. We buried the puppy in the garden, and I headed for the privacy of the small cluttered office where the business of the inn was conducted. I didn't want to leave them, but I was intensely uncomfortable being there with Jasmine.

Faith had taken Pebble home for a bath and change of clothes. The sun was shining elsewhere, leaving the room dark enough to need lamplight. I moved toward the desk, not seeing her until I reached for the switch. She was in the swivel chair and she spun toward me. She had taken off her sundress and was wearing only a small bikini.

"I knew you'd come here."

I felt as if all the oxygen had suddenly been sucked out. "Jasmine, this is insane."

"Yes, it is." she smiled and her perfect teeth glowed in the dimness. She stood and moved toward me, and I backed up, hitting the wall. "Oh, God, Jonny. What you've done to me! It's like I'm really alive for the first time. I want you so much, I'm insane with it. Fuck me, Jonny. Please, please."

I grabbed her forearms and held her back. "Stop it! We can't do this! I love someone else."

She threw her head back defiantly, achingly feminine, unlike any other being I'd known. Her eyes were closed. "No, no. We must. I know you feel the force of this. It isn't possible to deny. It's the life force; it will kill us if we fight it. Fuck me, Jonny, please."

Somehow I held on, blood pounding in my head, slamming my heart against my chest, my prick pushing toward the danger. "No. I don't believe you. This is some head game you're playing."

I let go. Her enormous eyes filled with tears, riveting me with her loveliness. "You must believe me. I'd do anything for you. You're the first man I've ever felt anything with."

"I know who I am, and I'm not that special."

She moved back slowly, her eyes hurting me with the intensity and fearlessness of their contact. "This isn't about performance, you fool, it's about soul lust. Look. Look at what you've done to me."

She sat back down in the chair, spread her legs wide, and began stroking herself, never once shifting her gaze away from me, forcing me to accept her action.

"Look, Jonny, this is real!" Her breath came faster, filling the now airless space with Jasmine smells, whiffs of coffee and bacon, under odors mingling with the delicious, wanton smells of her sex.

She came, screaming out, and leapt up, jungle beast that she was, rushing me, wiping her juice on my mouth, forcing me to know it, to believe her. I was losing my way, dizzy with lust and terror, in a room where gravity no longer worked.

"Christ," I said declaratively, not quite praying or surrendering.

A knock at the door. She jumped, grabbing her dress. The abruptness of her reaction alarmed me more than the knock. She picked up her shoes and fled through the back door connecting the office to the reception room.

I was shaking all over. The wobbly old Druid, pushing the beast back into the beast mother. "Just a minute," I said, reaching for a Kleenex and wiping the devil juice from my lips. I turned on the light and sat down at the desk, reeking of her scent. I fought for air; one deep breath to return me to reality or take me away from it, I was no longer sure. Get a grip, Jon boy.

"Yes?" I said, hearing my voice shake slightly.

Thomasina opened the door and waited.

"Sorry, I was on the phone. Come in," I said. I stood up and walked around to pull out the folding chair that faced the desk. "Please, sit down."

She hesitated. "Is okay for me to speak about something?"

"Of course. Do you want some coffee?" I picked up my cup and took a gulp of the strong, bitter brew.

"No, *grazie*. I have too much. Is bad for my pressure. It shoot up again from the stress."

"Stress?" I said, trying to focus on her need.

"*Sì, la tensione*. It come when I have a trouble inside, when I see a truth, but I no say a truth."

She paused. I waited until she was ready.

"Signore, you have truth in your eyes, but I not trust nobody but my family since the war. I was just a girl when the Germans come to my village. We run in the night and hide in the mountains.

"We live three years in caves without light, afraid to move, to laugh, to cry. It was like the holy shroud had fallen over the sun and it would never be back again. And then one day we hear more tanks, but is different ... something is different ... my little cousin, he sneak out to look, and he come back, shouting! *'Americanos! Soldatos! Americanos!'*

"We crawl out and we are very weak, but we are running down the mountain. A soldier, a black man, which I have never seen before, he step in front of me and he is holding a big shiny apple. I want this apple more than I have wanted anything in my life; more than peace, I want this apple, and he is laughing, 'Don't be afraid, take it,' he say.

"But all I remember is how to be afraid, so I turn, looking for my father, but I am alone, and I decide I trust this black fellow, I reach for the apple and he salute me.

"I can still taste the liberator's fruit, so sweet! The apple and his smile, it keep my heart from turning cold. So, now, Signore, I trust you with something, because I must."

"What is it, Thomasina?" I said, moved by her stern integrity.

"Signorina Jasmine, she put somethings in Pebble's food to make her more fat, not like she say. I see her many times and I find this hidden in the larder."

She reached into her pocket, pulled out a package, and handed it across to me. It was a nutritional supplement given to bodybuilders to bulk them up.

"You saw her put this stuff in Pebble's food?"

"*Sì.* I no understand then. I think is part of the diet. But when Emily find the candy I know is something bad, so I watch more. I see where she put this and I take it. I think is why Pebble, she is more fat. And something else—very bad."

"Please, tell me."

"I no see this happen, so is wrong maybe to say, but I believe she kill the little dog. I see her near the garden before Pebble come. I think she do it. From the war, I have a nose. I smell evil."

Her watery brown eyes sparkled, and she breathed for both of us, a deep sighing breath. *"Allora,"* she said, smiling for the first time, her plastic teeth giving her old face a girlish affect. "My pressure, she is falling already."

She stood and I joined her. I took her small dry hand, which reminded me of my grandmother's, and kissed it, remembering too late what had preceded it on my lips. "Thank you for trusting me and for telling your story. *Cento Anni.*"

"En bocca lupo," she said, leaving me with a wiser wish.

I sat back down in the shadows, listening to the clock in the kitchen. Outside I heard Emily and Betsy clumping across the gravel with their cleaning supplies, whispering about the puppy; the front door opening and closing as guests arrived and departed; Faith's voice, cheerful but strained, always the perfect hostess.

A phone rang. "Inn at the End," the desk clerk chirped. What Thomasina had said about the war had happened to our dream. A shroud had dropped over us, covering the ecstasy. I sat until I knew what to do, and then I left the same way the panther had, leaving her scent behind. I went home to make a call.

CHAPTER ELEVEN

"Hey, Ducky, where ya been? I thought I musta landed on your doody list. I was at Mike's the other night and I was thinkin', Where the hell is my favorite pain in the ass? Got a lotta heavy shit goin' down lately. Coulda fed you some real smacky stuff."

"I miss you too, Daisy Mae. I've gone back to my pilgrim roots for a while. I'm on the Cape helping out a friend and trying to work on some nonviolent subject matter. How's the crime-and-grime business?"

"Summer in the city, same old, same old. I actually took a week off. Went fishin' with Theo and some of the patho boys. You ever want to understand how men and women are in no way alike, you go fishin' with 'em. What a bunch of boring bullshit. Sittin' in a leaky boat, freezin' my ass off even in July! Spendin' hundreds of dollars to catch a lousy ten-dollar fish. Boooorrr-ing. I'm actually happy to be back to real stress. So, what's shakin', Duckman?"

"I need a medium-size favor, not for me, really, but for Pebble and Faith."

"My favorite chick duo. You got it."

"I want you to check someone out for me. Her name is Jasmine Jones, but I've got a hunch it's not real. Can you run her and see if anything comes up? I know nothing about this woman except she's house-sitting in Manhattan and she's beautiful and she's moved into Faith and Pebble and Sari's lives up here at this inn they've put together, and I have reason to believe this is not a good thing."

"Jasmine Jones? Sounds like a hooker or a drag queen."

"Maybe the former, definitely not the latter."

"Oh, so you bumpin' uglies with this broad?"

"Whoa, Lieutenant, out of bounds."

"Ah, come on, Jonny. Give a horny old has-been a little perk."

"It's not part of this, okay?"

"Okay, but you owe me now. So if the name comes up phony, you got anything else?"

"Well, I may have, hold a minute."

I left my desk and walked into the kitchen and pulled out the recycling bin, grateful for the ineptitude of my cleaning lady. The two beer bottles, Jasmine's and mine, were still there.

"Daisy, I have two beer bottles, one with my prints and the other with both of ours. I'll FedEx them to you today."

"Ah, I see. Brew for two. Naughty boy. Losin' your Jonny-the-rat-with-women instinct? You usually choose the nonthreatening, non-anything types."

"Be a pal. Just run it, and if you talk to Faith, don't mention anything. She thinks this lady is a saint."

"Hey, you know me, a fucking sphinx. So, how's Pebble doin' with the poundage? Better than me, I hope."

"She's going off to one of those camps tomorrow, and we're hoping that will help."

"Hey, you sound down about it. I wish they'd had the damn

things when I was her age. I hear they can work miracles. Tell her I said so. Well, I gotta lineup to check. Send the bottles and your fax number and stuff; I'll be in touch. But I'm back at you now, no forgettin your Forgotten Woman. Friends are hard to find these days."

"Thanks, friend. I won't forget."

On Wednesday, I drove Pebble to camp. She was subdued at first. We listened to the radio and she dozed awhile, but as we crossed from New Hampshire into Vermont she started to talk, firing questions at me, trying to extract something to take with her for protection.

"Do dogs go to heaven?"

"I have no idea."

"Do you think people go to heaven?"

"Well, put it this way. If there is a heaven, and people go there, I'm sure dogs and cats and chickens and everything else does too."

"Flies and bugs and cockroaches?"

"Why not?"

"I thought you had to have a soul to go. Do you think ants and fleas have souls?"

"That may be pushing it."

"Do you think Angel has a soul?"

"Yes."

"Where do you think our souls are?"

"Big toes."

"Uncle Jonny, you're so bad!... They're not in our, you know, in our heads, are they?"

"No room. They're all too swelled up with our egos."

"What's an ego?"

"Well, basically it's the part of our brain that's more interested in ourselves than in anybody else."

"Like Uncle Andy?"

"Like almost everybody."

"Momma's not like that, and neither are you or Sari."

"I'm oversimplifying because ego is a big subject. We're only in ourselves, so we all filter through our egos, but there's good ego and not-so-good ego."

"So you don't think the soul is up there in our brains with all that ego stuff?"

"Pebs, if Angel had a soul, she didn't lose it with her head. God has a much better system than that."

"Jasmine said, 'Her soul is free now, be happy for her.'"

"Yes."

"How does she know that?"

"You're going to get me into big trouble with your great-grandmother. She doesn't *know* it, but she believes it, that's what's called faith."

"Like my mother. She believes in people. She trusts everybody. You don't."

"No, I don't."

"Do you trust me?"

"Yes."

"Momma?"

"Yep."

"Jasmine?"

"You set me up."

"No, I didn't. I'm just a kid being curious."

"I don't think so."

"You don't like her, do you?"

"Why do you think I don't like her?"

"You don't look at her when you talk to her. You only do that when you don't like somebody."

"Pebble Wise, Ace Detective."

"Momma says she's a 'godsend.' She says she's the best friend we have besides Sari and you. She says she couldn't have gotten through everything without her."

"Yes, she could have. She and Sari had already done everything before Jasmine even showed up."

"So, you don't trust her."

"No, I don't."

"Do you think she has a big ego in her brain?"

"I don't know what the hell she has up there."

"I trust her. She's my friend. She tried to help me, and she believed me about the candy."

"Can we change the subject? I'm much more interested in you."

"That's because you have a big soul and a little shriveled-up ego."

"No, it's because I have the most magnificent and entertaining niece on the planet. So how do you feel now about going to this camp?"

"Well, I'm nervous, and I'm kind of mad at Momma for doing it, but it's a lot better than being around when my father shows up. That, I was like totally freaking out about. He blames Momma if I gain weight, and then I feel bad and it's like a total nightmare, so I'm kind of relieved. I don't know. I guess I feel like a failure, but I'm kind of excited, too."

"Sounds like a very good analysis of the way most of us feel most of the time."

"Yeah, right. *You're* thin and beautiful."

"You're beautiful too, and brave, and failure is a lousy word and I don't want you ever to say it about yourself again. Okay?"

"Okay. If I think I'm brave and beautiful and not a failure, does that mean I have a big ego?"

"A healthy ego, which is different."

We were there. I was exhausted, not being used to long philosophical Ping-Pong matches with precocious nine-year-olds. The camp was set high on a hill, and as we drove up toward the main lodge, passing meadows filled with children playing soccer and tennis and splashing in the large swimming pool, I snuck a look, trying to watch her reaction.

Her lovely freckled face was solemn, almost reverent, seeing something for the first time.

I stopped, and several kids all plump as Christmas puddings came running toward the car to welcome her.

"You okay?" I asked, her silence heavy between us.

She turned, and then she smiled at me. "Jeez, they're all pudge-os! Everyone's like me! This is really great!"

I got out, swallowing hard to keep from dissolving into a puddle of sentiment, and went around to open the door for her, thanking God, from my ego or whatever, because I knew she was out of harm's way and this was going to be all right.

Benjamin at the inn. The moon man beaming down at the gathered. Toasting my sister with moon juice, wine red as Mars, glimmering in the setting sunlight. Sari beside him, just returned, flushed with success. My grandmother on the other side, sitting tall, joy twinkling across her handsome face. Joy to be here seeing what Faith has done. Joy to be anywhere, as George Burns used to say.

Faith the fragile hanging tough, glowing under the praise, warmed from the reflected light of Benjamin's radiance. Cheers to all. Empty place where Pebble belonged.

And the panther, gone to New York suddenly, some business about her mother's death. Too bad. Too, too bad. Faith had so wanted Benjamin and Granny to meet her new friend. Sari watching me, sensing something. Trudging around in zero gravity, my moon boots clunking, weighing me down with the force of my deception. Toasts all around. Faith cheery, Granny O jolly, Sari wary, Benjamin boisterous, and me the space man, separated by my portable life support system, breathing different compounds, pretending to still be one of them.

All I wanted back was my innocence. I wanted to rewind the tape and return to that night a thousand years or so ago when I opened my door to the beast. I wanted only to go back and bolt it, plug my ears, and sleep right through the tinkling of the bell.

I was shit out of luck. God does not do returns, no matter how earnest the complaint or how shoddy the merchandise. No exceptions. No refunds or exchanges. No voided receipts in the register. I was stuck with the ugly *shmatte* inside my conscience.

And being from another planet now, there was no one I could complain or explain it to. I sat with the happy group, toasting my sister and my lover's success, slipping out of my gravity boots, and floating off into infinity, the moon man watching my ascent and Sari watching too.

I waited on the deck for Benjamin, knowing he would seek me out after the reunion festivities, wanting his intergalactic gossip. He sat down, proffering a small tray with two brandy snifters and a couple of fancy contraband cigars and paraphernalia.

"Well, Jonny, it looks like I was wrong. This is really wonderful. I've never seen her in better shape."

"Yes, it's been an incredible summer for all of us."

"Andy told me about you and Sari."

"I'm surprised he remembered. It seemed to be very low on his interest list when I spoke to him."

"He must have still been boffing the Buddhist. Now he's not boffing, so he's noticing."

"You mean I need to find a new agent?"

"Not at all. Business is business. The way Andy sees it, wives are easier to replace than money-making clients. You'll know if Andy is ever going to kiss you off because you'll get a note signed *Always a friend, forever a fan.* Until then, you're still a viable product."

"This is downright heartening. I was beginning to think I was losing trust in my fellowman, but these insights are really encouraging."

He finished preparing the cigars, one of those male bonding rituals that my gay friends consider the closet version of cock-sucking.

"Cuban. The very best." He handed me one.

We sat for a while, sipping Armagnac and puffing in his moon-
light. I was still drifting toward the Milky Way, my single goal
being to not untether.

"Tell me about Pebble and the camp."

"Nothing to tell, really. She was nervous and not eager, but
when we got there, she was impressed and so was I. I think it was
a relief, and I think Faith made the right decision."

"I've been telling her that for two years."

"Well, mother instinct has its own timing."

"Ah, yes. And sibling loyalty has its own agenda."

"Are we speaking now of you and Andy or Faith and me?"

"Touché. I apologize. No quisling role for my brother-in-law. I
remember our last conversation."

"Look, there's nothing I can add to what you're seeing for
yourself. They've done a helluva job and they're a hit. It's like this
whole peninsula has been waiting for one terrific joint with some
personality, and they provided it. But the best part is what Faith
is finding in herself."

Benjamin tidied his ash; then he dipped the tip into his brandy
with his freshly manicured fingers. "What can you tell me about
this Jasmine Jones? I was concerned by the way Faith was heaping
praise. She seems too good to be true, and that always leads to
trouble. Also, Faith is giving her too much credit and power. I
don't like that pattern at all."

"Well, she's pretty damn mysterious and I agree with your
concerns, but it hasn't been the right time to broach it. I'm watching, and I'll let you know if I learn anything more about her. I'm
betting Faith will see the pattern and figure it out by herself."

I managed to focus on Benjamin. I saw Pebble's face in the
car, asking questions about trust. How much and who, our daily
plight. I took a puff, feeling slightly buzzed by nerves and smoke,
resisting the urge to confess, seeking comfort and guidance from
the moon god. I finally understood something, had an epiphany if
you will. I saw who he reminded me of, what was familiar from

my boyhood box of discarded memories: my father. I felt with Benjamin the way I had felt with my father, the desire to unload and the prickly discomfort, the edgy polite withholding, a reflexive instinct to defend myself from something I could never quite see or feel but dangerous nonetheless, more so because it was connected to such a passionate yearning that it not be true. If I was wrong, I could surrender all my needs and secrets to this planetary presence, this bigger-than-me man, this father.

"Faith's talking about making her a partner, but I was adamant about not doing it and I think Sari will back me up."

My air hose felt narrower. "Has she already talked to Sari about this? She didn't say a word to me."

"No. It all came out when we took a walk this afternoon. I think she's just thought about it, but I had the feeling this woman may have planted the idea. What does Sari think about her?"

"Actually, I don't really know. She's very charming and charismatic."

"So I've gathered. Is she as attractive as Faith says?"

"Yes, and she knows it. She uses it like wampum."

"So, are you one of the eager Injuns?"

"I'm just a loyal scout trying to keep the peace pipe lit."

I finished my brandy, snuffed out my cigar, and stood up, drained from my space walk, needing to be safely alone to guide myself back to my ship.

Benjamin laughed and looked up at me. "Oh, Jon, you are one prickly SOB. We're on the same side here. I'm trusting you with my wife and child. Can't you trust me with some simple information?"

"Really, I would. I just don't have any at the moment. How long are you staying?"

"I have to go to London tomorrow, but I don't want to. I miss Faith and I'm bone tired, but this fucking deal is like running in front of a train and I can't stop now. I wanted her to come with me, but she can't leave because this woman is away and it's too much for Sari. If they start making money, I want her to hire a proper manager. I'm very pleased about what this has done for her—and your fax was right on; she's coming into her own—but I don't want to lose her and Pebble because of it."

"You could never do that. She idolizes you. It's knowing you're out there that gives her the strength to take a risk like this."

He stopped smiling, and I saw something new in his face, something sad and unshielded that I didn't really want to see; it confused me and broke into my defenses against him.

"Yes, I know. But relationships change, brother-in-law. Needs change and people lose one another without even knowing it—" He stopped, deciding not to trust me, either. "Christ, I'm beat. I'm getting too old for this shit. Just keep an eye on this woman."

"I will."

"They're all I have."

"Me too."

The next few days, Sari was jet-lagged and busy catching up and helping Faith after being away, so it wasn't too hard to maneuver around her.

I concentrated on my grandmother, finding enormous pleasure in her pleasure. For someone who had never slept a single night of her life in a hotel, she adapted remarkably. Within forty-eight hours she had taken over the gardening and was bossing Thomasina around in the kitchen. I was spending more time there, enjoying the banter between the two tough old dames, both immigrants, both widows who had sacrificed to hold themselves and their families together, and of course they made a fuss over me, pampering the sole male and making sure I had something to put my teeth into on an hourly basis.

Thomasina and I had our own bond now, and since she was the only person who shared my fears about Jasmine, I found it far less stressful to be with her and my grandmother than the others. On Sunday I drove them to church.

The Saint Francis Catholic church in Provincetown was nothing like Saint Augustus, and my grandmother kneeling beside transsexuals and drag queens, taking communion next to a lesbian biker with a shaved head and a ring in her eyebrow, was quite a sight. On the ride home, we discussed it.

"Now, Jonny, I'm trying to have an open mind and Thomasina has been most helpful explaining these people to me, but it is a bit strange, I must admit. You know what the Bible says about whatever it is that they do to one another. I don't want to think about it, but there they are in front of the Holy Mother and the Lord himself got up like that, and the priest doesn't seem to mind at all."

"The priest is gay too."

"I don't believe it."

"Sì, is true, Signora O'Brien. Is not a regular church. Is for Catholics who are, how you say, outcasted."

"So then he's not a real priest? He certainly seemed real enough, and he looked as loving as Saint Sebastian."

"He's a real priest, Granny. It's just that the Church doesn't want him to be, so he started his own for Catholics who don't believe in certain doctrines."

"Well, mother be, this is why I stick around down here. Never a day I don't learn something new!"

"Sì, sì. Is part of this place. I take my great-aunt from Palermo, and she like it very much. She giggle like crazy lady when I tell her the nun beside her is a sex change. She say, Well, Christ looked like pretty girl, so why not? I like this church because all the people would be killed by the Nazis, for being not normal. 'Defective,' they called homo people. So when I go here, I feel like I am saying to the *fascistas*, 'Ha! We laugh in your face!'"

Granny O chuckled. "Thomasina, I like your spunk!"

"Is like, in Venezia, is a Jewish ghetto from ancient times. It is very small area like a bowl, with four bridges, and the Nazis lock everyone in, thousands of people in a space for a few hundred.

But these Jews had been locked in for centuries off and on, and because it was always so crowded and they need to have an opening to the sky to pray, they built their temples on the tops of the buildings, many, many stairs and hard for the old, but they climb and they look up into the sky and they pray until the day they took them away. People always find a way to God, even the outcasted."

My grandmother's bright blue eyes were blinking quickly, her way of filtering emotion. "Well, that is very true, Thomasina."

"Anyone want to stop for ice cream before we head home?" I felt the subject was due for a break.

They waited in the car, and I bought double chocolate-chip cones and handed them in through the windows, and their faces were as impish and happy as if I'd been performing the same ritual for two five-year-olds, which cheered me, until we were back at the inn and I flashed forward to my own old age, alone, without a grandchild to buy me treats or take my arm. A bachelor shot of self-pity. I put aside my guilt and went to find Sari, someone of my own with whom I might possibly gum ice-cream cones in the twilight years.

I found her in the dining room, helping Emily and Betsy set up for dinner. She turned and smiled when she saw me, her wild hair fanning across her shoulders and her nose doing that funny tilting thing, and I wanted to fall down on my knees before her and confess my sin and beg forgiveness and ask her to marry me, to save me from the loneliness of my old age. I had allowed myself to need someone and then, just as quickly, found a way to screw it up. Where had I read about unacknowledged needs being the ones that do us in? What about the ones we acknowledge too late?

"Can I steal you for a minute?"

"Sure, these two are far better at this than I am, anyway."

Emily laughed. "Not better, just less fussy."

"Well, that I admit. I'll go drive Jonny crazy for a while."

The sun was still high in the sky as we took off our shoes and walked down toward the water. I pulled two beach chairs together, and we sat down and she reached over and took my hand and held it so sweetly I almost forgot my secret.

"I've hardly seen you since you got back."

"I know. I'm in a kind of semicontrolled panic and Andy's coming up! There's so much to catch up with here and so much I've got to do out there.

"We have to finalize some things about the divorce, and he's going to be in Chatham, and I guess Benjamin's been tooting our horn or whatever. Mainly I think he wants to see if he can use the inn as a way of cheating me on the community property settlement. How about taking me out later and getting me piss-eyed and making wild love to me? I fear it's that or heavy pharmaceuticals."

"I'd be glad to do my part for holistic health purposes. I take it you sold your script?"

"Yeah! Well, almost. I have to make some changes, but I actually liked their notes. It's the big one, Jonny. It could change my entire career, and of course there's a little 'Fuck you, Andy' mixed in there."

"That's the best part of a dream coming true, if we're being honest; right after thanking all the little people comes flipping the bird to the thwarters."

"That's me. Miss Middle Finger herself. It's going to cause some problems with Faith. It already has."

"The inn?"

"God, Jonny, how ironic! I mean one of the reasons I wanted to do this was so I could have more control of my life and not be so dependent on a business as undependable as screenwriting, and now look! I just don't know how I can write and keep up my end here, and I can't let Faith down. Who the hell knew we'd be a hit so fast? I never imagined this. The trouble is, we're a long way from running in the black, and we can't afford to hire someone to replace me, and even if we could, it wouldn't be the same; it's not what we pledged to each other."

She stretched her legs out, wiggling her red-painted toes in the sand.

"I tried to talk to Faith about it yesterday and I could tell she was hurt, even though she didn't say much. I know she feels like I'm abandoning her, but what can I do? I promised to deliver the revisions by Labor Day and if they accept them I have a major movie deal, so why do I feel like Sammy Glick here?"

" 'Want to see God laugh? Make plans,' my grandmother always says. It'll work out."

"Yeah, well, maybe, but so far I think her first suggestion sucks. She wants to make Jasmine a partner."

"Benjamin mentioned it to me."

"And that was before I even told her about my dilemma! I am beginning to get a yellow flashing light about her highness, and it's not because I'm jealous of her friendship with Faith or her gorgeousness, though I did have to rule those two factors out before I opened my trap."

My relief at hearing that the beast had not completely fooled her too was tempered by my awareness of having lost my right to confide my own doubts, the end of that pier being far too rickety for a truth walk in the daylight. I resisted the urge to grovel at her feet, begging for mercy.

"I didn't know you felt that way,—" I stopped, feeling the aura before I saw anything. A towering darkness, smelling of night flowers, shading our intimacy.

Sari turned first, squinting up at the presence. "Jasmine, you're back," she said, flushing slightly, and instinctively I let go of her hand.

Two days later Daisy Mae called. "Hey, Duckman, when you ask a favor you don't fuck around, pal. You owe me large now.

This dame of yours has messed with my head. She's in there rollin' around with my take-out fantasy selections, and that's not okay."

"I'll make it up to you with the meal of your dreams. You found something?"

"Well, yes and no. You were right about the name. Nada plus. She's got a credit card under it, don't know how. The bills go to a PO box in Manhattan. Nothin' else to speak of. She's not payin' rent or taxes, as far as we can tell.

"She's a floater. But we got somethin' on the prints from Vegas, a juvie arrest for hooking under the name Wendy Pulski. Long ago and far away. Vegas PD had a file on her under RUNAWAYS, but they douse it when the perp turns legal, protection-of-minors jazz.

"So that's it. It's like, Get a life, babe. I'd say call girl, moll, or drug moth, somethin' like that. Can't find anything on a family, but we do have an old address in Vegas for the pimp who sprung her."

"That's it?"

"I told you, Jon boy, this was a mind gummer. We ran her through Missing Persons, DMV, and the Hall of Records. Zippo. And under the credit card just some chick charges and, oh, yeah, one weirdie. A pet store in Hyannis. She's got a heart somewhere, 'cause she bought a little white cockapoo about a month ago."

"What?"

"Am I not speaka ze English here? She bought a puppy. Why, is this part of some Provincetown kink routine? Cockapoos for cocka-twos? What's the deal?"

"You're sure about this?"

"MasterCard is. I got the printout, though I wouldn't admit it under torture just in case you're gettin' any ideas."

"No. No, I'm just surprised. Thanks, Decker. Plan on the best dinner in town when I come in."

"So? That's it? You're not gonna give me the goodies? I'm

supposed to cloud my menu planning with obsessive speculation about this chick, her puppy, and *usted*? I'm dyin for some good dish and you're holdin' out on me."

"It's a guy thing. I hate to deny you, but I just can't open the can yet. Besides, I'm just speculating. You know how we reporters are, we like to have our facts straight. First I need something solid."

"Fair enough, but since patience is not one of my numerous virtues, if you know someone in Vegas I'd lean that-a-way. I'll fax you what we got and the old address. You never know."

CHAPTER TWELVE

"**I** *know* he thought I was a real girl, I'm not like a petri growth! But I was so horny and he was so awesome, I mean, really hung, so I figure he's drunk enough and we'd done some weed and like sometimes these hi-hetero guys that don't know, they really do? I mean, my gender clinic counselor is always quoting Freud about 'the blindness of the seeing eye,' like about knowing and not knowing what's happening? Well, maybe that's not quite what she means, but anyway, so okay, I was wasted, but so was he, so I thought, Risk it, 'cause if you get lucky, whoa, woman, you are in for a great ride, so I put my hand on his sweet thing and cooed in his ear, 'I'm not quite a woman, honey, but lips are lips,' and the louse almost broke my arm!"

Sitting on a bench in the August sun sipping coffee, waiting for Rita to join me, eavesdropping on Persephone and thinking through my conversation with Daisy Mae. What did I know? I knew I had been seduced by a big black spider and had pinned my own wings to the wall like some masochistic housefly.

I knew Thomasina had seen Jasmine put body-building pow-der in Pebble's food and walk by the garden shortly before the puppy lost her head. I knew she'd bought the puppy and lied about it, and she had a sketchy and dubious past. Not a helluva lot to present to my sister, who had an almost perverse sense of loyalty.

What would Jasmine say? She'd probably deny Thomasina's account and turn the clandestine purchase of the puppy into a selfless act of kindness. Buying it couldn't lead us to conclude she'd mutilated it, and there was the obvious question (I could see the look in Faith's woeful eyes when she asked it), Why would she do any of this? What could possibly be the payoff?

Until I had some sort of supportable answer I had best keep my mouth shut. Also, if Faith confronted the beast, there I was, the ultimate sitting duckworth. All the panther had to do was roll over and reveal our secret, and I could kiss my credibility good-bye. Lips are lips, as Persephone said. The kiss of death is unisex.

I did take Daisy Mae's advice and lean toward Las Vegas by calling Rita. The former wife of the Linen King still knew her way around out there, and she was someone I more or less trusted. Wendy Pulski? Jasmine Jones was a runaway Polish girl from nowhere?

Rita plopped down beside me. She was wearing some tight shiny purple casing, running shoes, a sequined baseball cap that said WITCHY BITCH in black velvet, and huge Jackie O sunglasses. Her Walkman was clipped onto her wrist with the cords hanging around her neck. The sound was so loud, I could hear the music coming from the earphones. It was Frank Sinatra. "Is your figure less than greek, is you mouth a little weak ..." She looked surly and out of sorts.

"You look surly and out of sorts," I said, kissing her bony cheek.

"Oh, fine, I need this. First I have to get up an hour before my peak metab set point time, shlep over here to meet you on a goddam deli bench in the direct sun, which my skin doctor says I cannot do anymore or the AHA on my face is going to start sizzling like bacon on a griddle; and that crazy head case Waldo is going to spit in my coffee again. I am sure he does it, so don't start with me and as my reward, you're going to insult me?"

She leaned back and put her headset on, crossing her skinny arms across her altered breasts. "Oh, Frankie baby, take me there, darling."

I left her and went to get her coffee and bagel, eliminating her apprehension as to the possible extras that might be added to the order. I watched the preparation carefully, trying to think of the best way to ask her, now that I had offended her and intruded on her rituals, to dip back into her painful past and find out what she could about Jasmine. This meant I had to tell her something. I carried her breakfast out and sat back down beside her. She was still lost in Sinatra, humming along peacefully.

"Night and day, you are the one . . ."

I tapped her shoulder, and she sighed and took off the earphones. "He couldn't sing worth shit on the last Duets album. It made me bawl like a baby. But I'd still rather listen to him croak it out than anyone else croon, even from the grave he's hot.

"No one ever sang like him, no one ever will again. I was in Vegas in those pre–theme park years when all the great ones used to play the Strip. Now they're all dead: Benny, Sammy, Bing, Burns and Allen, Lucy, Gene Kelly, Judy Garland. . . ."

She dumped two packets of fake sugar into her coffee, stirring it with one of her long pink nails.

"Look at me! I'm tearing up! I cried for two days when *Dean Martin* died! I'm turning into one of those toxic nostalgic types."

"Sinatra chokes me up too, though I can't say Dean Martin's death had the same effect. Rita, I'm sorry I hurt your feelings. I didn't mean that surly and out of sorts was not attractive or appealing. It was just a reporter's footnote."

"I forgive you. I *am* surly and out of sorts. I just don't want it to show."

"The casual observer would never notice."

She picked up her latte, eyeing it suspiciously. "I watched the coffee being made like it was a life-saving vaccine."

Rita sipped. "So okay, I forgive you. Groveling isn't required. What's the big emergency? It couldn't wait until cocktail hour, when I'm presentable?"

"I've got to help out at the inn tonight, and I didn't want to miss connecting with you today. Look, Rita, what I'm going to ask you is very dicey, and you have every right to say no and I'll back off immediately."

"You want me to have your love child?"

"For that, I would definitely wait until cocktail time. No, what I need will hopefully only take you a couple of phone calls, maybe nine minutes, not nine months, and you will not have to send it to college. I need some information."

"From little old me? Mr. Big Brain? I am stunned." She bit into her bagel, and I could still hear Sinatra's voice from better days, crooning into her neck. "I've got you under my skin ..."

"Rita, this is strictly between us, okay? Would you call your contacts in Vegas and see what they can find out about a young woman who was known as Wendy Pulski? I know she had a juvenile arrest for prostitution and I have an old address, but nothing else. You're the only person I know with access to that kind of info out there."

She licked cream cheese off her knuckle. "I see. And am I allowed to ask why you need to know whatever it is I might find out?"

I felt the squeezing back between my shoulders. This would be the first time I had said anything about the beast to anybody who knew her, and once I did I was on a one-way highway and there was no turning back.

"Sacred trust, okay? It's Jasmine. I need to see if my doubts are real before Faith gets more deeply involved with her."

"Hey, Jonny, you think I'm just another neurotic bottle job? I already figured that much out. The minute you said Vegas, I knew. Besides, Emily's been picking up negative neutrons from her highness."

"She makes me too insecure to trust my own judgment, I can't get past insane jealousy, but I don't know what the big mystery is. Why can't you just tell Faith? Everyone treats her like she's some china doll or something. She can handle this. She's gotta know Jasmine's been to the big party. She'd be crazy to make her a partner without checking her out."

"She told you?"

"Yep. Asked me some real estate advice."

"Well, she hasn't told me. Want to know why?"

"Because you might supply what you want me to find out?"

"That's my guess. My sister takes friendship very seriously. She doesn't look at people the way most of the rest of us do. She's been sheltered and she's truly kind, so she believes others are too, and no matter how many times she gets her heart crushed, she can't see it differently. I don't want it to happen again, especially with so much at stake."

"Jonny, baby, that's not how it works. She's already into the fantasy friendship, so no matter what happens now she'll still be devastated. It's always about the old wound. It doesn't have so much to do with Jasmine now as whatever tore Faith apart long ago. You never had therapy, did you? Boy, can I *tell*."

"You're right, but I can't do much about the past."

"Not unless you're Shirley MacLaine. Did you ever see her perform with the Rat Pack? Man, they were so hip. All I wanted was to be one of them: to vamp into the Sands Hotel with Frankie and the gang in a white mink coat with everybody bowing and scraping and Old Blue Eyes whispering in my ear, 'You're a helluva broad, Rita.' Toxic nostalgia, for sure. So okay. Give me what you got. I'll make some calls."

I handed her my notes. "Did you know they blew up the Sands Hotel? They're replacing it with a six-thousand room monstrosity."

"Yeah, I cried for a week over that one. It's the end of the entertainment age, Jonny. All the propeller heads will have left is Snoop Doggy Dog and Madonna."

She stood up, tossing her trash into the barrel beside the bench and replugging her ears, returning to a less real world. "Gotta burn off the bagel. I'll call you."

"Thanks, Rita."

I watched her go, arms swinging, tight bony ass swaying. A bright straight flash in the sunshine.

And so, with only good intentions I unleashed the demon, flawed but earnest Druid wannabe that I was. The simple act of inquiry took the lid off Pandora's box, let the jungle cat out of the Prada bag, opened the gift horse and disgorged the Greek soldiers, popped Aladdin's cork, and plucked the little Dutch kid's finger from the dike.

Not that it might not all have happened anyway, but it was on my watch. I was the unofficial protector of these women. 'I was only trying to help,' as the tag line of all disastrous do-gooder efforts always begins.

I shook the stick at the serpent and the plagues began.

PART THREE
It

CHAPTER THIRTEEN

*A*ndy the Anteater at the inn, lounging on the deck, Sam
Adams in hand—the beer named for the rumpled ne'er-
do-well of our Founding Fathers, as unlike the drinker
holding it as possible—dressed for recreational success. Shiny
white suiting with short pants, Italian sockless loafers, and
panama hat. Gold neck chain with diamond infinity symbol. Tor-
toise sunglasses. Give me a Yankee break. Sari storming off,
almost knocking me down. "Where're you going?" I ask, not rel-
ishing a one-on-one with my agent so soon after lunch.

"I'm going to bronze his asshole-of-the-century award."

I approach, feeling that old infantile urge to shove it to him
that he evokes in me. He turns, smiling his Big Bird smile, the hat
and the shades and the child's clothes making him look like a Red
Grooms version of a South Beach slicko.

"Jonny, nice tan, the summer agrees with you. Sit and have a
brew while I wait for that cute little dinghy to return. It's interesting what the sun and the sea do for women; ever notice how

much more provocative and sensual they are in the summer, especially the young ones? That little waitress can row my boat any time."

"I always thought you were the oarsman, Andy."

"Well, I'm sure you remember from your Saint George's days, there's a time to stroke and a time to pull in."

Emily, as if on cue, arrived with two cold beers. She had matured over the summer. No perceptible holes remained in her face, her honey-blond hair had grown long, and her body had filled out. She looked the way Rita probably looked at her age, before the self-loathing took control. I wondered how Rita felt when she saw Emily now, if it hurt or just made her more determined to keep her kid from making her mother's mistakes.

"Thanks, Emily. I saw your mother this morning."

"I know. She's still ragging 'cause she had to get up an hour earlier. Do you need anything else?"

"Emily, is it? I need a big smile from a lovely young lassie."

Emily stiffened and looked past him to me. "Just holler if you need a refill."

Andy lowered his shades. "No smile?"

"Kiss my lassie, man." She stomped off. He seemed to have a dramatic effect on women's walking styles.

Andy's bonded grin sank slightly. "Whoa. Hot and hostile. I like a little attitude. I'd still put my canoe in the water for that one."

I sat down and picked up the beer. "Have we about finished with the sexual sea analogies, or should I trot in and find my mariner's thesaurus?"

"Jon, you're a tough nut to crack."

"Are we segueing to legume metaphors? Or maybe it's organ slang or psychological pejoratives? I like to keep up my end of the banter."

"Actually, this banter, as you call it, is true synchronicity. When you say *organ slang* and *psychological pejoratives* it aligns with why I'm in Chatham. I have a psychiatrist client who's working on a book about cultural differences impeding patient communication. For instance, if you were a Hopi Indian and you went to see an analyst in New Jersey and complained of ghost sickness, he'd probably treat you as a psychotic, when in your own culture you'd be suffering from something similar to anxiety-related depression."

"Fascinating! I didn't know there were enough Hopi Indians converging on New Jersey analysts to make a best-seller. Live and learn."

"This is cultural anthropology. Not everything I represent is commercial. The Hopis are just an example; there are many case studies."

Andy took off his hat, which had made a groove in his forehead.

"In North Africa there's a mental illness called *zar*. They believe victims are possessed by a spirit and they shout, laugh maniacally, and bang their heads, and it isn't even considered pathology. But if the sufferer were to have an episode in, say, New York, they'd commit him."

"Actually, in New York they'd probably star him in a music video."

"Very funny. It's about the difficulties of cross cultural communication. In Malaysian men there's *koro*, which is an irrational fear that the genitals will recede into the body and cause death. It can occur as an epidemic there, but if it happened in Hollywood—"

"If it happened in Hollywood it would be a mass acting out of what everybody silently wishes on everybody else anyway. Imagine an actual 'Go fuck yourself,' sort of like a human Christo event. This does have immense healing ramifications."

"It's fascinating material, not a joke."

"Well, strangely enough it reminds me of a joke, which is about miscommunication and psychology. Mickey Mouse and Minnie Mouse are getting a divorce, and Mickey's lawyer stands up in court and says, 'Your honor, Mickey wants to divorce Minnie on the grounds that she's crazy.' And Mickey gets very upset. 'I never said she was crazy. I said she was fucking Goofy!' "

"That's good. I think my author might be able to work it in as an illustration."

"There's an even bigger picture for your client, right up there with Hopis and *zar* and *koro*: cartoon character pathology. They're a veritable hotbed of rage, frustration, and seething emotion. Even if you only covered Disney, you're talking mega—how about the Little Mermaid Center for Substance Abuse?"

Andy put his hat back on. "Okay, you don't get it. How's the proposal coming?"

I put down my beer. "Sorry, Andy, I do think it's interesting—just too many smart-ass openings. The proposal's going quite well."

Before he could answer she appeared, looking so outrageously beautiful I turned my head away, expecting to see Andy with his mouth agape and his snout quivering at the sight.

But that's not what I saw; what I saw was calm. He crossed his long bare legs and smiled up at her. I was impressed. If Andy could work himself into a full head hard-on over a kid like Emily, Jasmine Jones should have been sending him into some ancient cultural frothing frenzy. But his paddle stayed in the boat. His agent instinct was providing him with the necessary cool.

"Jonny, pardon me for interrupting. Sari needs help bringing up the new cases of wine."

I was already standing, my cotillion manners clicking in. We were eye to eye and Andy was watching. "Thanks, I'll be right in. Jasmine, have you met Andy Wise, Faith's brother-in-law?"

She gave him the high-wattage full-power stare. "No, I haven't had the honor." She extended her hand, and he took it without rising from his chair. "I'm happy to meet you."

"The pleasure is mine," he said, almost sedately.

"Andy was telling me an intriguing story about the unique emotional problems of various cultures."

"Oh, you mean like *susto* in Latin America, what they call soul sickness?"

Andy perked up. "Why, yes, a perfect illustration. Have you read any articles by Gerhard Wassel? He's my client."

Jasmine moved forward and sat down in my chair, and I excused myself, leaving them to their discourse. They were really well matched: two humorless narcissists with a penchant for the New Age.

I found Sari in the storeroom, slamming cartons around. "Hey, easy there! I know he upset you, but a case of expensive broken bottles isn't going to make it better."

I took her hands and held them to my mouth, trying to provide comfort, but she was too agitated to accept it.

"That son of a bitch! He really knows how to pull my plug! Not only was he taking Polaroids of the property—for court, not sentiment—but he's asking for a full commission on my screenplay, because I hadn't formally fired him as my agent when I sold it! And this is the one he told me to forget, that no one wanted stories about relationships anymore, and I should change my name and write a thriller if I wanted to get anything produced! Steam is not only coming out of my ears, it's pouring out of my twat! God, how crude. Forget I said that. I'm off the monitor right now and we're overbooked for dinner and we've got reviewers staying the weekend. I haven't written a word."

I put my arms around her, holding tight. I could feel her heart pounding against my chest.

"It's okay, baby."

She sighed, letting the tears come. "It's just so mean and small. It's not fair."

"Ah, unlike the rest of life. How odd."

She laughed and relaxed into me. "Yeah, yeah, I know. So I

regressed to crib mode. It's hard being mature twenty-four hours a month, you know. I'm okay now. He's going back to Chatham tonight. Thank God."

"Good, so let's get on with it." I leaned down and kissed her. "I must say, however, that image of steaming pubis is lingering. Can we have a smoke-detection class at my house later tonight?"

She laughed and pushed me back. "You got it, chief. If you promise to wear one of those yellow hats and carry me to safety."

"I'll do better. I'll let you slide down my pole."

"Mr. Duckworth, I am blushing all over."

We carried the wine upstairs and she left to change. I unloaded the bottles in the bar, glancing out toward the deck. Andy and the panther were still sitting together. Maybe he would take her away with him and solve all my immediate problems. Did life ever make things that easy? The phone in the office rang, and I went to answer, trying to think of a situation I'd ever encountered where the easy way out had worked.

I gave directions to a dinner guest and was about to return to the wine arranging when something on the desk caught my eye. The mail was stacked in one of Faith's neat sorted piles. One letter was alone, next to the rest. It was addressed to Jasmine Jones, care of the inn, and it was from the hospital where we had taken her when she had her accident, the event that maneuvered her into our lives.

I picked it up and put it in my pocket and went on with the evening.

Rodentia: small gnawing mammals, bearing disease. Vermin are the dress extras of all plagues. Ours too. That night the dining room was filled with guests from urban centers and two travel magazine writers. The buzz was good, the food never better, and the room sparkled. The critics were beaming and even the weather cooperated; the glass doors were flung open, and the gentle warm breeze carried smells of herbs and roses from the garden.

And then someone screamed. Shrieked in horror.

The room froze. Glasses were suspended in air, forks and knives paused between mouth and plate. What? Who? The travel writer from Boston jumped up then and the room thawed, silverware clattering. She was still screaming. What was she saying?

"Rats! I've been bitten! Help! Help me! Rats!"

Rats? *Rats?* Chairs skidded backward, bodies banged against tables, rattling china, while pampered people in summer silks scattered, fleeing in panic. I moved toward the woman in distress, who had scrambled up onto her chair, and a fat gray rat ran over my foot. The diners fled into the night. If someone had yelled *Fire!* or *Bomb!* they wouldn't have moved faster or in a greater frenzy. Vile, filthy pests had invaded our Brigadoon. Frantic maddened rodents and frantic maddened humans were scurrying everywhere. I swooped up the hysterical travel writer and carried her out through the chaos.

Sari, her face streaked with sweat and tears, came racing across the room, followed by a herd of volunteer firemen in full gear, axes in hand, looking more terrified of the rats than of a raging inferno.

"I'm calling the Health Department!" she shouted, waving to me across the riot of rescuers, invaders, and victims. Faith and I ran back and forth trying to calm, offering reassurance, but within an hour every guest had checked out. The inn was empty. We stood in the ruins of the perfect evening, stunned into silence. There was nothing to say.

I saw my grandmother's face, her blue eyes blazing, leaning hard on her cane: my grandmother who had crossed the Atlantic with the dread creatures, packed side by side in the bowels of a rotting ship. She knew about rats.

Faith went to the hospital with the bitten hysterical woman and her husband, and the rest of us stayed while the Health Department and the exterminators and the firemen cleaned up. Endless questions we couldn't answer were asked. Sari and

Thomasina and the summer chef from New York were all in shock. "Our kitchen is immaculate. This is simply not possible!"

I watched my grandmother. There was something in her eyes I had never seen before, something more than anger. Fear, fueling her fury. She slammed her cane against a chair to get the questioner's attention.

"This is nonsense! I know about rats. I spent one solid month with the things crawling all over me! I know what agitates them and what attracts them. I can still spot a mouse dropping across a room. There have been no rats or mice in this kitchen. None! This place is as clean as a christening fountain! Someone did this. Someone did this out of pure spite!"

She leaned hard on her stick, seething with the indignation only allowed the truly righteous.

"It's the police we need here! Go catch one of the devils and test it. Whoever did this gave them something to stir them up! They hate light and noise and, unless they were drugged or provoked, they would never lay siege to a room full of people like that! I tell you, this was done on purpose!"

She was shaking. I went to her, afraid of what such turmoil might do. I saw tears spurt from her anger-bright eyes. Fear and tears, from my steel-girded grandmother. I took her arm and helped her to a chair and she let me, which unnerved me more than anything else. "Someone did this!" she said again, her voice quavering, and I thought she looked at the panther. I stood beside her, my sin between us, stunting my courage.

It was hours before we finished cleaning up, traps set, poison sprayed. Faith was still at the hospital, and Sari and I decided to drive over and bring her back. My grandmother refused to go to her room until everything was in order, but I could see the exhaustion in her face.

"Jon, I'm quite tired. Help me to bed now, will you, dear?"

She had never said anything remotely like this to me before. I took her free arm and she leaned on me and I guided her across the hall to her room. She had been with us for two weeks, calling home daily to the neighbor boy who was tending her garden but seeming in no hurry to return. I had sensed that in some way she was trying to protect us, the way she had been doing all our lives, but I didn't know why or from what. There was only the premonition she had told me about before Faith had started on this adventure.

I helped her to her room, cheered by the way she had personalized the small impersonal haven. Her rosary lay on the Bible by the bed; her statues of the Holy Mother and baby Jesus stood on the dresser, next to smiling photos of me and Faith and Pebble and her long-dead sister and husband. The special icons of her safety.

"Close the door, Jon," she said. "The walls have ears."

I did as I was told, I always had, and waited for her to tell me why, half knowing, half hoping she would confirm my own suspicions. She sat down in the rocker Faith had bought especially for her, waving away my move to help her. "I'm all right now," she said. Her window was open. I could hear waves lapping on the shore, the sound of summer laughter coming from somewhere, and a child crying in the dark.

My grandmother shook her head as if clearing her thoughts. "Jon, I've kept my mouth shut until now. I've never cast a first stone that I can remember, but I must say what I think."

"What is it?"

She looked up at me and I saw tears again. All I wanted was to kill whoever had wrinkled the starched serenity of my grandmother's devotion.

"That woman did this! That Jezebel from hell! You must find a way to make Faith see what she really is! All my life I've believed that the power of good was stronger than the power of evil and God's love was in every sorry one of us, no matter how hidden. But this woman is outside His grace, may the Lord forgive me. And my granddaughter and my great-granddaughter are not going to be her victims!"

I realized I was holding my breath, trying to dull the force of her words and lessen the impact. "I agree with you, Granny. I'm trying to find something solid to show Faith that will convince her."

She tightened her grip on her cane. "Do it quick, Jon. She is stone blind to this woman. I tried to talk to her a week ago, before all this, just from what I was seeing, the way she plants doubt in Faith about Sari and you. Very sneaky, but I heard her, watched her undermining things, playing on Faith's insecurities, and that's why I stayed. The woman has a real hold, a grip. She knows your sister's weak spots. Do something. Get her out of here."

"I'll do my best, Granny, I promise."

"Do better."

The hospital was a nightmare. The writer had already called her lawyer, she'd have to have rabies shots, and nothing, not even intravenous Valium, had been able to calm her down. Faith had absorbed all the blows, accepted all blame, and was now too over-whelmed to reclaim herself. She sobbed all the way home.

Sari put on her PR hat and tried damage control. "First, we call our own lawyer; then we call the local press and send letters to all the guests and flowers and wine and do what we can. The key is to do it fast, first thing in the morning. We can recover from this. It'll be okay, Faith. It will."

Maybe she was just too tired and pulled by her other conflicts, but she didn't convince me, which probably meant she hadn't convinced Faith either. Over and over, Faith said, "Please don't tell Benjamin. I want him to be proud of me."

We dropped her at her house and Sari came home with me. We were more worried about Faith and my grandmother than the fate of the inn. I opened a bottle of wine and turned up the air conditioning and we collapsed on the couch. She was in the panther's seat, triggering everything I was trying so hard to forget.

We drank the wine quickly, allowing the elixir to do what it had been invented to do.

"I tried to get your grandmother to go stay with Faith, but she wouldn't have it. If I stay over with you, she's all alone at the inn. I probably should go back and be close by."

"I'll drive you later."

"Yeah. Let's wait until I'm blasted and totally useless in an emergency."

"You're never useless; you've got that grit gene."

"My God, what a day! My rat and real rats appearing simultaneously!"

I refilled our glasses. "Are you hungry? We never ate."

"Starved. Want me to cook something?"

"No. You sit. I've got some bachelor vittles. I'll bring a tray."

"Great. Do you think I could take a quick shower first? I'm filthy from all that crawling around with the exterminators."

"Sure. I've got a spare robe on the hook. I may join you in a minute."

We took our glasses and I walked her to the bathroom and kissed her, sniffing in her fragrance, and went to fix some snacks. While I assembled leftovers and opened cans, I flipped on the local news in the kitchen, hearing the sound of female ablutions, comfort sounds from my childhood coming from behind the wall.

"Like a page taken from *A Tale of Two Cities*, a pack of vicious, possibly rabid rats attacked a dining room full of affluent guests at the much-acclaimed new Inn at the End in Truro earlier this evening. One woman was bitten and two other guests were treated for bruises and shock. The injured woman will undergo rabies treatment, pending lab results on one of the captured intruders.

" 'It was like a scene from the Bible or some horror movie,' was how one of the shaken diners described it. The Health Department has closed the inn pending further investigation."

I turned the t.v. off, hoping Faith hadn't heard it, and picked up my glass and the tray, carrying it into the bedroom. I stripped down to my shorts and knocked on the bathroom door. I could hear the sound of the shower, and all I wanted on earth right then was to climb in beside this precious woman I loved and hold her soft pliant body against mine and let the warm water cleanse us of the evening's horror.

She didn't respond. I opened the door carefully, not wanting to disturb her privacy. She was sitting in the tub with her legs crossed and her head lowered, and the shower was raining down on her back. I knew she must have heard me, but she didn't look up.

"Sari, are you okay?" I said, standing in the steam-filled bath in my underwear.

She leaned farther forward, the water bouncing off her shiny caramel-colored back. Her shoulders heaved. She was crying. I sat down on the toilet seat, reaching over to her.

She seemed to feel my arm coming and raised her head then, stopping me with her eyes. She held up her hand, the water still pounding down on her. She was holding something.

"You fucked her, didn't you, Jonny," she said, choking on tears and water. She reached over, opened her hand, and dropped what she was holding onto my bare leg: several very very long, very very black hairs. Panther hairs.... *And God shall wipe away all tears from their eyes,* Revelation 7:17. Lines from my childhood circled the misty, steaming shame in my white-tiled confessional.

I didn't even try to respond, I owed her at least that. I just sat there on the toilet seat in my Brooks Brothers boxers like the perfect Yankee yahoo I was and cried right along with her. Choking on the rarely used apparatus, the rusted pipes of my vulnerability.

In the predawn, long after she had gone, leaving me still speechless and blubbering in my disgrace and despair at the hurt I had caused the woman I loved and feral in my fear of the consequences, the alley cat of reason came licking my lobe, trying to help.

Jasmine had never showered in my house. The tub had been cleaned at least half a dozen times since that one night and one morning visit. The hairs must have been planted in the last couple of days.

I got up, remembering the letter I had taken from the office, and fumbled in the dark for my pants. I ripped open the envelope and carried it into the living room, where the candles were still lit and the air conditioner continued whirring, waiting for the romantic reunion they had been prepared for.

There was a bill for emergency room services and medications attached to a lab report with a lot of medical numbers and mumbo jumbo that I couldn't understand. But one thing stood out, the diagnosis.

> Fees and services for hip dislocation
> caused by Ehlers-Danlos syndrome, type III,
> hypermobility.

The room was too cold and I shuddered. I blew out the candles, switched off the AC, turned on the desk light, and thanked God for the Internet. It took a bit of time to find, but finally up it came. I scanned, scrolling through pages of medical technology.

Ehlers-Danlos syndrome, also known as India rubber man's disease. The severity of Ehlers-Danlos syndrome can range from having loose joints which may dislocate easily with few other complications, to…. The underlying features of all forms of EDS is a defect in the molecule which makes up the connective tissues (skin, ligaments, tendons)…. All forms of EDS are inherited and appear in early childhood…. The defects are in the collagen molecules…. Type III, benign hypermobility: Skin may be soft and velvety. Joint hypermobility is generalized, affecting large (elbows, knees, hips) and small (fingers, toes)…. joint dislocations are common and can often be done at will.

She did it on purpose.

I heard the chimes outside my cottage door ring. I jumped up and pulled on my pants. Sari had come back to let me apologize. The devil made me do it, darling, I would plead, throwing myself on the mercy of her court of compassion. Please, please, let me try and explain. Please!

Two officers of the law, menacing in the dark, patrol lights flashing from the street, intensifying the threat.

"Jonny Duck?"

I resisted an urge to quack in the giddiness of my misery. "Is something wrong?"

"Sir, would you get dressed, please, and come with us."

"May I ask why?" My heart was pounding so hard, I was afraid they would hear it.

"I'm sorry, sir, but we're not authorized to give any information. The detective will explain when we reach the scene."

The scene meant *crime*. I moved, somehow I dressed, and let them lead me, stunned with dread. I asked no questions, being too afraid of the answers, Catholic to my bones, wages of sin, penance left unpaid. I looked out the window, exhaling only when they had passed the turnoff to Truro. We drove until the sun came up. I opened my eyes and we were in Chatham, in front of the premiere resort. Chatham was where Andy was staying.

I followed my escorts up the stairway, past an ambulance and several officers and hotel security guards, and into one of the water-view suites. Sari was sitting on a chair smoking a cigarette, her face looking almost the same as it had in my tub, blurry with hurt.

A tall, gaunt son of New England came forward, wearing a seersucker suit, one size too small, the sign of a true pilgrim. We shook hands. "Ezra Clay. I thank you for coming, sir. Your name was with the victim's belongings, and his wife said to call you. It appears your brother-in-law's brother, Andrew Wise, committed suicide here earlier this evening. Overdose of sleeping pills."

"What?"

Sari sprang up and came over, and for that moment we were a team, unified in the outrage of the absurdity.

"This is absolutely insane! Andy would no more commit suicide than the Pope would! Andy's idea of emotional distress is ... was ... whimpering a little during *The Lion King*! He is—was, excuse me for speaking ill of the dead—shallow! Got it? As shallow as a kiddie pool. He never took a sleeping pill in his entire life. He slept like a fucking bear in winter! I don't know what happened to him, but he would never, ever, not in a zillion years, kill himself! Tell them, Jonny! This is craziness!"

"Well, ma'am, we found a note. You identified his handwriting."

"May I see it?"

The detective nodded, and a piece of paper encased in a plastic evidence bag was retrieved and handed to me. *Ataque de los nervios*, attack of nerves, uncontrollable shouting, crying, trembling, heat in chest rising to head ...

"Seems the poor fellow was under extreme stress. Maybe seeing his estranged wife triggered something. People have all sorts of hidden bogeymen. It is his handwriting."

"He was working with a client on a book about psychiatric symptoms and disorders in other cultures. This must have been from notes he was taking."

"Well, now, we've interviewed his client, Mr. Wassel. Seems he saw him for a drink. Mr. Wise seemed very tense and glum, he said. He canceled their dinner date and told him he would meet him in the bar at ten-thirty. Mr. Wassel waited until eleven-fifteen, calling his room twice. Finally, he came up here, heard the television, and when his buzzing met no response he called security. They found Mr. Wise in bed naked. He had vomited and, it seems, ejaculated shortly before death."

"No fucking way!" Sari yelled. "Andy Wise would never let anyone find him like that! If he was going to kill himself, he'd be laid out on the sofa in silk pajamas by candlelight. Somebody did this!"

Somebody did this seemed to be the theme song of the night from hell. My head was now pulsing with unwanted images. Rats and my grandmother's piercing eyes. Somebody murdered Andy? Why?

Sari's head, bowed in the tub, black hairs on my knee; puppy parts, Pebble's smile; joints, sliding at will, rubber men, mayhem.

Men like Andy didn't get murdered. They died in their sleep after a short illness at age eighty-three with their doting third wives and late-life kiddies by their sides. Andy was one of those Teflon dudes—nothing stuck; all the shit slid right off and landed on everyone else. Who in hell would *bother* killing Andy?

"Well, now, Mrs. Wise, if he was murdered—and that's for the coroner to determine—you and Mr. Duck would be the only viable suspects. However, luckily for you, the ME has set the time of death at approximately nine P.M. and we have plenty of witnesses as to your whereabouts. You'd be smart to let us write this up as suicide and let it go.

"We can all waste a whole lot of time, energy, and taxpayers' money, not to mention what the local press will do with this, and it's still going to come up suicide. We have no weapon, no motive, and no fingerprints but the victim's. We have evidence of emotional distress, the sleeping pills, and we have a note."

I walked Sari out, both of us stumbling in confusion and

numbing fatigue. We didn't speak until we got to her car. "*I'll drive you home,*" she said firmly, and I got in beside her without arguing, leaving the police cars and the ambulance, which now held Andy's bagged and tagged body. Nothing remained of all that networking and puffery and bravado, all those fancy clothes and expensive haircuts and the name-dropping and jetting about. The people Andy devoted his life to impressing would now read a paragraph about his death in *Variety* and *The New York Times* over their power breakfasts, cluck their tongues, and forget he ever existed.

We were silent all the way to my cottage, until she stopped in front. "I need you to know something. You're the only woman I have ever loved and I'm not going to lose you. I don't know what to tell you now that you could hear or accept, but I will. Whatever happened, you know I adore you. I want to marry you and live the rest of my life with you, and I promise I'll be able to convince you that one moment of weakness and poor judgment has nothing to do with my love for you."

She didn't speak or turn her head, but at least she didn't say anything final. I got out and left her alone.

CHAPTER FOURTEEN

"**T**his lounge lizard I knew in Vegas used to say that God was like an old Bourbon Street ivory tinkler, riffing away. When he hit your key—*ping!*—end of tune ... Hey, Jonny, our hero! I wish I had a video of you swooping that dame up and carrying her out like a quarterback with the last ball of the game, dodging and weaving around the rats right out the door! I'd fight next to you at a Loehmann's clearance sale anytime."

Rita was holding court in the kitchen. Debbie, Inga, Jasmine, Emily, and Faith were commiserating over coffee. My stomach did a few rollovers.

I poured a cup of coffee and sat down next to Faith. "She was all wrapped up in some kind of serape or something and she kept flapping her arms. I almost dropped her twice."

"The man is too modest. But you're right, that broad was head-to-toe Sherpa chic."

Inga rubbed her almost-bald head. "It was unbeliefable! Ze

rodents and ze death. My uncle says it is like ze Old Testament, like in ze book of Exodus—ten plagues starting wit' blood and ending wit' ze slaying of firstborn sons. Vermin vere ze third plague."

Faith tensed, and I took hold of her hand under the table.

Debbie nudged Inga. "Now, Ing, no gloom-gloom! Don't despair, Faith. The way will be shown to you."

Faith smiled, touched by the caring this unusual community of women had given her.

"Well, I hope you're right, Debbie. You've all been so wonderful, I don't know how to thank you." She looked at her watch. "Jonny, I'm going to take Granny O home on the way back to the city. I shouldn't be gone more than three days or so." She let go of my hand. "What do you think I should do about Pebble?"

"Leave her at camp. This is not the funeral she needs to start with."

She sighed. "Jasmine said the same thing."

I avoided Rita's eyes. "When are you leaving?"

"As soon as Sari finishes with the authorities and Granny O finishes packing. I still haven't reached Benjamin."

The panther rose. "Don't worry, Faith. The health inspector told me if everything checked out today, they'd grant us a waiver. We'll be back better than ever in no time!"

Faith smiled up at her. "Bless you, Jasmine."

A stirring behind me. My grandmother bustled in, her cane tapping across the floor. I rose to give her my seat, but she waved me away. She was accompanied by a small, tightly muscled woman with a thick well-oiled Elvis-style pompadour and a mustache. She was wearing some sort of repair person's uniform with a name patch that said RIKI.

My grandmother was all business and very agitated. "All right, all of you. I want you to meet my friend from church. This is Riki. She's an exterminator. We got to talking at early mass, and she offered to come have a look. I want you to hear this from her own mouth. Tell them, dear."

The first known female exterminator grinned, exposing a pair of remarkably rodentlike front incisors. "Howdy, all. Well, let me start by saying that my hobby is fancy rat breeding, which may seem kinda counterproductive for an exterminator, but one is business and one is pure pleasure. Anyways, I breed the little cuties, so's I know a thing or two about their behavior. They're smart as dogs and the friendliest, cleanest pets you could want. Now, your fancy domesticated rats are different from your wild ones. I'd bet from the droppings I found and what the boys at Acme Pest Control told me that what you had here was a Norway rat, very aggressive for a domestic. No way they just came in from the garbage or standing water. Also, your fancy rats like set paths and they don't like strange food, so they had to be going after something familiar. I was pokin' around under the tables and I found it."

Riki grinned again and her mustache wiggled. She pulled a tissue out of her back pocket and opened it, holding it out for us to examine.

Rita gasped. "Oh, my God, is that a rat turd?"

Debbie giggled nervously. I snuck a look at the panther, who remained unruffled.

"Naw, I wouldn't do that to you guys. What I have here is Purina Rat Chow. Top-of-the-line fancy rat breeder's food."

Granny banged her cane on the floor. "Tell them what that means!"

"Well, what it means, and what I'm gonna tell those health department bozos, is somebody set this up. Those guys missed it in the dark last night, but I found a whole trail of the food leading right into the dining room and planted in little mounds under some of the tables. My guess is the Norways, maybe with some roof rats mixed in, were starved, given something to speed them up, and let loose on the food path. I'm no Columbo, but it had to be something like that."

Jasmine applauded, without missing a beat. "Amazing! This should settle the whole thing. And the idea of sabotage is dramatic enough to get press attention and soothe the guests. Mrs. O'Brien has saved the day!"

My grandmother ignored her. "Jonny, will you see to this after I've gone? I'm leaving my friend Riki in your hands. Someone get this dear soul a nice cup of coffee. I've got to finish my packing."

I could tell by the straightness of my grandmother's back and the spring in her gait that doing this had helped her regain her grit. It also told me a thing or two about what she expected of me.

I was glad she was going home. She would be safe there and Pebble was safe and Faith and Sari would be safe. My hope was to have Jasmine out of there before they came back.

Rita, dragging Emily behind her, grabbed me before I could follow Faith into the office. "I know this isn't the moment, but I wanted you to stand by. I got a call from my friend out west, and he's sending me a file by FedEx. I've gotta go to the realtors' awards dinner tonight, so if it comes in Emily will bring it over to you, okay?"

"Great. I'll either be home or at the newspaper."

"No sweat, I love slave labor." Emily saluted.

Faith was sitting at the desk talking on the phone. I could tell by her tone that it was someone far away with limited English skills. I waited while she struggled to communicate urgency without specifics to this distant and indifferent lifeline. The problem, whether friend or foreigner, was always the same. Do they really hear me, and can I trust them with the information?

She hung up and sank back in her chair. She looked tired and pale and her eyes were puffy and red. Her face was too delicately balanced to handle such strain; it bent her beauty, leaving her even more transparent. She looked up at me, wariness in her eyes and body language. Her lips were pursed; her gaze held none of the affection I was used to seeing.

"You haven't talked to Benjamin?"

"No. I've faxed and called, but the time difference is impossible. He doesn't even know what the emergency is! I just couldn't put it in a message, and dealing with those desk clerks and secretaries is unbelievably frustrating. It's like they know the words but not the meaning."

"Where is he?"

"Singapore."

"I'll keep trying after you leave."

She cocked her head slightly and looked at me almost provocatively and very unlike herself.

I swallowed a mouthful of held breath. "Faithie, listen, I know this is lousy timing, but I have to talk to you about something before you leave. It's too important for me to wait any longer, and I promised Granny O."

She sighed, a short weary sigh. "Oh, please, don't tell me it's going to be Granny's Jasmine paranoia. She's already told me and it's just ridiculous."

"Faith, it's not paranoia, unless there's an epidemic. I didn't want to say anything until I had more convincing evidence, but with all that's happened, I'm going to risk telling you what I've found out. You have too much at stake here."

Her eyes narrowed and I realized she was angry at me, but I presented my case, using my sternest, most professional tone. The puppy, the powder in Pebble's food, the India rubber disease, with a lot of bad vibes and gut feelings thrown in, and then I did it again, repeating myself, working up a head of steam, doing all that we do when the connection between the object of our desperate need to convey and the information being sent has been tampered with. I felt like the Singapore desk clerk with Faith at the other end. The words were translatable, but not the meaning. Finally, I just stopped.

"I have the feeling you haven't heard a word I've said."

She sat forward and I felt the tension inside her, a stiffness and defensiveness I had only seen when she was fending off a truth about a new friend or a new passion, protecting the illusion that she hoped would bring her connection, still believing that others held that magic.

"Jonny, let me tell you something now. I know by your face that you're shocked I'm being so tough, but I've changed and my friendship with Jasmine is part of it. She's helped me see how I let all of you treat me like a child and that's why I never get stronger. Well, I'm not a child and I have to trust myself, not you or the doctors or Benjamin, and I trust my instinct about Jasmine. I know she's had a checkered past, but the rest of this is just ridiculous.

"She told me she bought the puppy. It was an act of consummate generosity. How dare you suggest she could harm it? "She did it the way she did so we wouldn't feel she was trying to ingratiate herself. She didn't try to get points for it, which is the opposite of what you're implying.

"And the bodybuilder's powder she explained to me when she first set up the diet; it has to do with certain balances in the metabolism. She showed me a report all about it from a pediatric endocrinologist. And of course, if she has this disease her hip might dislocate from a fall! For God's sake, that hardly means she did it on purpose! Why would she do any of this? We certainly haven't made it worth her while. She's worked her butt off and she doesn't know anything about how successful Benjamin is or how we live, so greed is certainly not her motive. The way I see it, she's given all of us a helluva lot more than we've given her. She's had a hard life. If she wasn't so beautiful you wouldn't even be noticing and you know it."

"That's not true, Faith. The beauty just makes it harder to see the wickedness underneath."

She stood up and turned away from me, and I felt totally disconnected from her for the first time in our lives.

"Okay, Jonny. You asked for it and I know I'm betraying Sari's trust, but I must put a stop to this before I leave you here with Jasmine. I know you slept with her. Sari came to my house last night when she left you. She was absolutely devastated, and she told me about finding the hairs. So your credibility lacks a tiny bit of selflessness.

"I saw you flirting with my own eyes. I'm not a silly dimwit, even though you all try to treat me that way. I saw the way you looked at her, the way you hung around the inn to have nightcaps after dinner, and I know she wasn't initiating it! She's in love with someone who broke her heart, and her mother's just died, so she's susceptible too. I blame *you*, not her, but it certainly explains why you'd want to get her out of here, especially before Sari found out.

"How could you have done it? The real truth is, even Sari's letting me down. I understand why, but if it wasn't for Jasmine I'd be left to keep this together all alone. She's the only one who hasn't betrayed me, and I will not hear another word!"

The room seemed to be shrinking. I felt suffocated in the hot, humid space. My sister crossed her slender arms and held tight, as if locking herself away from me. Part of me was proud of her fierceness and the force with which she'd stood up to me and defended her friend. The other part of me was shaken by the result of my blunder. Verisimilitude, prancing around like some demonic drum majorette, throwing her dime-store baton up high into the air between us.

"Why do you think I waited this long to tell you? My stupidity has nothing to do with my concerns. If you'd just keep an open mind, I'm expecting a file that may prove to you I'm right about her. I only want what's best for you. Please don't shut me out."

"I'm not, Jonny. It's just that you're always harping on me to trust myself, make my own decisions—until I do. You can't have it both ways. You have to trust me too."

Everything she said was also true. The alley puss had given up on me, leaving my ears ringing with his unheeded hissing. What if she was right and I, out of my own lust and fear and uncertainty, had completely misjudged the Panther? What if in fact, she was not a wild beast, prowling the jungle of our innocence, but the most magnificent creature ever put down before me? What if I was wrong?

CHAPTER FIFTEEN

I went home and waited in the shadows for Emily and the FedEx package, staring into the unlit fireplace. Emily never came. I fell asleep sitting there, and when I woke up I knew they had all gone: Sari and Faith and my grandmother, gone to take Andy the unmourned back to nowhere. Bury him here, bury him there, a childless, wifeless man who had lived from his ego and left little legacy behind. Someone closely resembling myself?

I stripped off my dirty clothes and performed my familiar morning rituals, and then I went back to the inn to help in whatever way I could.

It was just before nine and nothing was stirring. I let myself in, noticing that the Health Department sign had been removed, and went to the kitchen. They had worked hard yesterday, and a squeeze of guilt hit me, like a physical pain in my chest. The place was gleaming and ready to resume.

I poured coffee, remembering a short story by Sartre about a woman whose husband goes mad and she stays with him in his crazy room, hoping the sickness will fill her too and keep them together. If *I* was wrong, maybe I wouldn't have to stand alone or go away.

What if Jasmine were innocent? Could I be that disconnected from my own instincts? I carried my coffee outside onto the deck. It was one of those golden August mornings when nature has nailed it, and for a moment God is almost visible and life is simple and suckle-sweet. I sat down, the steaming jolt of the first sip and the sun cheering me. The tide was in and there was no one on the beach, just a few boats in the distance and the sound of sea birds and music floating from one of the cottages. I closed my eyes, feeling a moment of something almost like peace. When I opened them, she was there.

She came out of the sea like one of the *Odyssey* sirens, but I had only a deck chair, no mast to lash myself to, no ear wax to stop her song from penetrating my defenses.

Her hair was plastered against her head and she was wearing a simple black suit and her body was creamy beige and the sun caressed it, enhancing the perfect planes of her being.

She walked toward me, her face solemn, not revealing anything. She leaned over the lounge chair that held her things and picked up a black robe and sunglasses. She didn't speak and neither did I. I waited to be devoured or saved.

She sat down, smiling slightly, or maybe she was just adjusting to the glare. I had no idea what to say.

"Do you always wear black?" I asked, still the reporter and the well-brought-up son, who feared the social pause more than the small humiliations of idle talk. I realized I'd never asked her a direct or personal question. Why not try and see what Faith sees? *What if I am wrong?*

She shook her glistening ebony tendrils, running her graceful fingers through the tangle. "No, actually I only wear black in the summer."

"Why is that?"

"I wear seasonal-tribute clothes. Black in summer, like an old Greek village woman. Purple in the fall because it's the color of royalty, and I see fall as the imperial season. I wear white in the winter because it brightens the barrenness, and I wear gray in the spring, because I think of spring as the in-between, a transforming, rather ambivalent time."

"Pretty ornate wardrobe planning."

"Ornate?" She frowned slightly. I had disappointed her. "I think it's nicely simple and saves enormous time and silliness, because I wear basically the same clothes year after year, so I'm immune to trends and fads; also, it's quite spiritual and ritualistic and gives me a deepened awareness of the seasonal cycle of renewal and rest."

"Well, your explanation makes more sense, except for the purple. The only thing purple I've ever liked is prose."

She laughed, that soft, sultry, slightly sly laugh that melted male armor more effectively than an acetylene torch. *What if I am wrong?*

She stood up. "Well, I'd better get dressed. It's going to be a very complicated day."

"What did the Health Department say?"

She was standing very close. I could smell the scent, squeezed from the tiny white night flowers, her namesake aroma but a false name and possibly a false scent, used to elude, throw pursuers off the proper trail, redirect the hounds away from the frantic fox.

I didn't want her to leave and I didn't want her to stay.

"Everything went fine. Little Riki was enchantingly convincing, even those macho gay-bashing county workers believed her. But now we have a criminal complaint to file and of course the question is, Why would anyone do such a thing? We're not really taking local business away. We're actually classing up the neighborhood, so to speak."

I searched her face for subterfuge and she, divining this, took off her glasses, meeting my skeptical eyes with a look as clear and direct as a world-fresh tot. "Do you have any hunches?" I asked.

"Not a one." She moved slightly back. "I must go. Emily was supposed to be here an hour ago to go over the check-in schedule. It's not like her to be late."

"Do you want me to try and reach her?"

"Yes, please." She stood without glancing away, both of us balanced somewhere just off the ground, not risking a step in any direction. Her beautiful bare lips began to tremble and two large teardrops, as lovely as the rest of her, slid down her cheeks. She was braver, it seemed, than I.

"I loved you, Jonny. How could you think I would hurt any of you? All my life people have only seen the outside of me. It's not a blessing, you know. It's a terrible trap, lonely and isolating. No one ever gets beyond it. Your sister is the very first person in my entire life to really see me. Too much beauty is like too much fame or too much money. People treat you as if you're not real, as if you don't have pain and needs, as if your losses aren't serious. It's a curse, not a blessing, and you've proven it. I thought you were different, that I could trust you. You opened up my soul, my sex, everything, and then you pushed me away and tried to cut me off from the closest thing to a family I've ever really had. You've broken my heart, Jonny."

And she left, a black streak across the summer morning. I sat stupefied. Was it possible that I, who had lived my entire life trying only not to do harm, could have done this foul thing to an innocent woman. A woman who trusted me? I lowered my head into my hands and prayed for my cat to come back and lick the doubt away. Dear God, what had I done?

The morning that had seemed immune to discord was now rumbling like a quasi-dormant crater. I felt stiff, aching from muscles knotted by impending disaster. Zombie-like and bewildered, I went in to the front desk to check messages. If Emily had left one, I could avoid talking to Rita, now that I was no longer sure I wanted to see whatever we were waiting for.

Plagues, like sea storms, come in waves. I held the phone, a modern Moses waiting for the next test; muffled, choking sounds emerged, Rita's voice somewhere within, adrift in the middle of the torrent.

"There was an accident last night. Emily was driving over to bring you the file ... I'm at the hospital.... Shit, Jonny, I need help!"

The Pharaoh's army behind me, the Red Sea churning in front, and no sign of salvation from above.

Coffee down, moving into the froth, keys, car in gear, no time for any thoughts of self. Her voice, the sound of ravage. Driving too fast, wrong exit, forgetting the way. The hospital, the fucking hospital again. Park the car, out, up the stairs, asking directions, up in the elevator, so slow, too many people, sick people, frightened people, indifferent people serving the other kinds. Out, running, in and out, around corners, down hallways, there she was, crumpled up on a dingy vinyl couch, rail thin and pale, too much sun on her dark roots, no makeup, showing her tucks and pinches. Never seen her without makeup. Jesus, it must be bad. Butts all around her, wet Kleenex, she in the middle, floating beneath the debris of the terrified. All alone in the center of the barely parted sea.

I stopped and she looked up and shook her head. I sat down beside her knowing her daughter was dead.

"What happened?" I heard a voice as unlike my own as hers was on the answering machine: a detached, stripped, almost mechanical sound.

"She had the file for you, but I guess she went out first, so she was late. She must have been speeding. She wasn't wearing her seat belt and she lost control, went across the divider, and flipped. She died in surgery."

She was very calm now, her voice as flat and lifeless as any battered thing.

"I never had much, Jonny. My family didn't really love me. I was never very pretty or smart, and I couldn't seem to find a way to make myself valuable to anybody. I tried. God knows I tried. The game was, I'll give you anything you want, just don't leave me. But the more I gave, the harder I tried to make them care about me, the less they did.

"It was like I had no skin, like I'd been put together wrong and they'd forgotten to seal me up. My wounds never scabbed. Until my baby girl. Someone that wonderful and precious and special came out of me! I didn't have to pretend with my kid. Emily accepted all the stuff I hated about myself, and my love for her saved my saggy little ass. Some things are just like that. There's no way to protect yourself against losing someone you love that much, need that much, so I never even tried. She was everything good in me, everything that made this crummy struggle worth it. I pulled myself out of the mess of my life for her: to be Emily's mother and give her something better than I had. This is not going to be okay, Jonny. This is not a bearable deal for me. Some things are just not okay. They're just not."

I reached out and pulled her to me, and she let me.

Later I went to see the cops. The detective in charge was the same Yankee Doodle from the Chatham hotel room, Ezra Clay III. His huge wing-tipped feet were up on his battered-old-salt desk, and he was sucking on a corncob pipe. "Mr. Duck, misfortune certainly trails you." On the wall behind his desk were dusty, cheaply framed photos of smiling ancestors perched on piers and sailing ships.

"Or coincidence, if you believe in coincidence." I pulled out all my most impressive NY press credentials and the special letter from Daisy Mae I used in a pinch and spread them before him, covering brass paperweights, a letter opener with an American flag insignia, and a silver-rimmed picture of someone's large shaggy dog.

Detective Clay peeked at my documents over the top of his bifocals. "Hmm. Mighty impressive. How's my old friend Daisy Mae?"

"You know Lieutenant Decker?"

He flashed an almost devilish tobacco-stained grin. There was some kind of reverse snobbery regarding dental work among the Mayflower descendants. Brown, broken, and rotting teeth seemed to represent integrity.

"Oh, my, yes. She lighted up many a convention for me. Quite a dancer for a stout woman. Light on her feet and mine."

He had a dreamy Boston-cream-pie look in his eyes that told me far more than I wanted to know but certainly gave the man more depth than the other clam-boil types I'd grown up with.

"Please give her my regards."

I decided to take advantage of his mellowing. "Look, Detective Clay, I'm not here as a reporter, I'm here as a family friend. I'd like to see what your boys took out of the car. Emily was bringing a package to my house when the accident occurred."

Eyebrows raised. "Really? Well, then, she most surely got lost because she was headed in the opposite direction." His sunburned Adam's apple bobbed above his blue polka-dot bow tie like a buoy in the briny deep.

"May I see the effects?"

"Now, now, matey, you know better." He reached into a drawer by his desk and pulled out a large plastic envelope. "I can't release these to anyone right now, anyway."

"Why?"

"Because Mr. Duck, it's evidence."

"Evidence? In a traffic accident?"

"Maybe not."

"What then?" I tried to swallow, but my throat had closed.

"Not for print, you get me?"

"I told you, this is personal."

"We're going to request an autopsy. The accelerator pedal was stuck to the floor and the paramedics on the scene thought she might have been unconscious before the crash. I got a funny feeling about this one. She was going almost ninety. I checked her driving record. Not even a traffic ticket. No trouble in town, no history of substance problems, just doesn't feel right. There's a sort of dead-calm sniff about this, wind's pulling off a ways."

"Did you go through the contents?"

"Yep, and the car, every inch. I think someone thought it would blow up and we wouldn't notice the pedal."

"Was there a FedEx package or a folder of any kind?"

"Nope. Nothing. Just a young lady's purse things, cigarettes, lipstick, some CDs, an empty can of diet soda which we're testing. No folder; that I can tell you."

"Thanks."

"Don't mention it. I trust you'll return the favor if you have any information that might help."

"Yes, of course."

"You got any hunch about where the wind's blowing?"

"Yes. Too much coincidence."

"You mean, to the suicide?"

"One maybe-not car crash and one maybe-not suicide."

"I knew that's where you were headed. Looks like my first summer vacation in two years just hit a squall."

"One favor. Please don't tell the mother anything that isn't absolutely essential. This kid was her whole life."

"The autopsy?"

"What if she's sedated and unable to be told?"

"Possible."

"Well, she is. She's with friends and the doctor knocked her out. Do it, I'll answer for it."

"Okay, the quicker the better, if it's drugs."

"You've got my number. Let me know when they finish."

"Count on it, Mr. Duck."

CHAPTER SIXTEEN

"Does everyone know what happened?" Thomasina in the kitchen, face grim. "*Sì.* We know."

"Where's Jasmine?"

"She go to town for errands and to pay respects."

"How long ago did she leave?"

"Five minutes before you come."

"I'll be back."

Cottage called Sunrise where the panther perched. The door is open, a sign of hauteur. Who would dare enter the lair? Cool inside, smelling the smell of her. Neat as Narcissus. Where to look? No folder in the car. If she has it, proof. Closet with black clothes, spare and pristine as monk's robes. Some shoes, a few hats. Nothing.

On the dresser, a stack of books. Hinduism and Ecology, Lives of the Saints, A Hundred Years of Solitude, *well-worn copies. No beach*

reading, no family photos. Candle by the bed. Sandals by the armchair.
Nothing to reveal or conceal. Under the bed, under the mattress, under the
cushion on the chair, under the hemp rugs. Nothing. In the bureau drawers,
black lacy things, infused with the odor. Swimsuits, T-shirts. Black cash-
mere shawl, folded like a veteran's mourning flag. Nothing at all.

In the bathroom, where I thrive, poking in drawers and medicine
chests. A black toothbrush. Crest. A tube of sunscreen. A bottle of her scent,
squeezed from the plant. A jar of French face cream. Nothing, not even
an aspirin. My fantasy partner: not the bath of any human woman, the
bath of a pod person or an alien. A bar of mud-colored soap by the tub. No
folder, no trace of past or present. Prada bag on the hook. No hints inside.
Everything was with her, on her, traveling life so lightly, able to vanish at
any time.

Failure to find and shame for trying. More disorder within. Vein throb-
bing in my neck, and then a sound. Jungle stealth. So subtle, so sudden.

I turn, wanting to flee, to push her away and run like a jungle boy,
spearless before the prey, drop my pallet and scurry away, leaving the white
hunters to fend for themselves.

Soft, so softly she speaks. "Jonny, what are you doing?"

"I was looking for something to tell me who you are."

"Why now?"

"Emily."

"I don't understand."

Her face was damp with sea mist, so smooth, like baby skin,
like Chinese silk; no anger, only that slightly puzzled, wounded
look, curving into a smile of world wisdom gently touching the
corners of her eyes and mouth.

"All you had to do was ask me."

"Really?" She was too close now. *What if I'm wrong?*

Tears again, dropping like dew, sliding onto her goddess neck.
"I cared about Emily." She walks to her bed, kicking off her
shoes. So still, her back to me, her bare feet together, shoulders
trembling. I move toward her, magnetized by the power of her

mystery. Mindless as any lost boy, any tourist on his first hunt, his guide mangled and the bearers run off, staggering across the savanna, far away from the safety of camp. I want to kill the voices of ambivalence, snuff them and make the fear go.

She turns and I stop. She knows where I'm heading. She reaches down and lifts her short shiny black slip over her head, naked now, the shock of her body striking like a stomach punch.

"Jesus." I stand in holy reverence or devil worship or whatever it is. Jungle drums, voodoo trance, Holy Mother, all of the above. She lies down, her face opaque, her hair fanning about her on the pillows, like a dark Venus.

A line from the Magus: *Liars hate silence*. Why think that? Was it true? She seems to love it, lolls about in it without any trace of unease. She closes her eyes, raising her long ballerina arms over her head and undulating in what appears to be ecstasy.

"Oh, God, Jonny, please, please, just once more, please make love to me, just feel me, know me now. Please, I ache from wanting you. I'm so wet you can see."

She spreads her legs, lifting them slightly, and I see the juice on the inside of her thighs, dripping down onto the pure white sheet.

I climb in between, caressing her feet, the small heart tattoo on her heel. I crawl forward, licking the juice, Jasmine juice, infused with the scent, oozing from within her. She moans and I put my hands under her, holding her up, pushing my tongue into her pussy, feeling the wet heat, hearing her sounds, louder and deeper, her body moving faster—

The cat, my friend from the night alley, leaps back up where he belongs, hissing like a serpent from the other garden: *Open your eyes. Open your eyes.*

I do, seeing her face. Her eyes wide open and dead as doll's eyes, staring blankly up at the ceiling, totally removed from her words or the motions below. The truth.

Silence, only the sound of my retreat. A gull squawking on the porch. My footsteps on the plank floor, the click of the door closing, the too-fast beating of my heart.

"Detective Clay, do you have a minute?"

"Certainly, Mr. Duck. Close the door, if you will."

"I have something that may be important."

"Fire away."

"There is a woman here, her name is Jasmine Jones, and she arrived as a guest our first weekend and then stayed on. I believe she's responsible for the deaths of Emily Riley and Andrew Wise."

"And all the ships at sea. Well, now. Do you have any proof?"

"None whatsoever."

"Any indication she had ever known Mr. Wise?"

"No."

"Any connection between this woman and any of you prior to her arrival on the Cape?"

"Absolutely none, unless—"

"Unless what, Mr. Duck?"

"Unless she didn't just arrive by chance but came as part of some plan."

"Any thoughts about what the plan might be?"

"Not a one."

"Not much bait for the hook, mate."

"I'm certainly aware of that. I'd hoped the bait would be in the file I was expecting from Las Vegas, but it's disappeared and I can't ask anymore of Rita Riley. Helping me has already cost her her daughter."

"Now, now, buck up, son. You've been gaining some points here. Don't go all fish-eyed on me."

"Thank you. I appreciate the compass correction."

"I appreciate the noninformation. I'm a pretty good judge of character, like my father and his before me, all proud sailors. I think you have a solid keep. Is there anything else at all that might help us? We don't get a lot of cunningly executed double homicides up here. This isn't *Murder She Wrote*, Mr. Duck. I pride myself on the rigor of my men, but we are slightly out of our depth."

"Her real name is Wendy Pulski, she had a juvenile arrest for soliciting in Las Vegas, and she has what appears to be an illegal credit card under her pseudonym. You can verify this with Daisy Mae, she did some checking for me."

"I will do that."

"Thank you for not laughing me out of here."

"You're welcome, Mr. Duck. Is there anything else you'd like me to hear from you?"

"I've slept with her."

"Ah. Now I feel better."

When I got home there were three messages on my machine. My grandmother: "Jon, I know about Emily. Even Jesus cast out demons. Do something quickly."

Faith: "Jonny, no need to come, Benjamin's home. There was no will and we've decided to cremate him in New York. Sari said he was absolutely terrified of coffins, so that's that. Benjamin's very upset, much more than I would have thought. I'm sorry we fought. I love you."

Pebble: "Uncle Jonny, hi! I know I've been a dork about writing. I've been having such a great time, and every day I say I will, and then I forget! Anyway, I just wanted you to know I'm really fine and you won't even recognize me. I'm like almost skinny! I tried to reach Momma but all I get is her machine, so tell her I love her and I love you, too. Gotta go, I'm meeting my friends for tennis. 'Bye."

I took a long hot shower, poured a big fat drink, and went to bed. I was on autopilot. All that I wanted was one night's worth of oblivion, a sleep cure, an escape from all conflict until morning.

* * *

Sleep allows you to run, but dreams have their own agendas and from the wonders of the unconscious there is nowhere to hide. I thrashed in semi-sleep, visions of detached doll heads, blank painted plastic faces floating across my mind's eye.

Her face, those dead mauve orbs, sightseers, thick-lashed obscurers of truth. Barbie Doll heads, whirling round and round, then Granny, Pebble, Faith, Sari, Rita, Emily, and her again, Jasmine head, figurine from the underworld. Kali head, blinkless, winkless, soulless creature from myth. "Jonny, I loved you. Jonny."

The phone was ringing. I jumped from my nightmares, drenched with sweat. It was morning. Light flooded my room.

"Hello?"

"Hello?" A creaky harsh voice, an old woman's tremble without the warmth and strength of my grandmother's. "Jon, Mrs. Callahan. Your grandmother's passed. Father Murphy is over there now. Better come home."

Receiver clattering down. The brusque stroke of the bottom line. Old people dealt with death that way because it surrounded them and lost its novelty and maybe even its power. I got up, still soaked with night sweat, and padded into the kitchen. I made coffee and stood at the sink, looking out the window at the peonies growing in the yard next to mine. Peonies as pink and fat as fists, like my grandmother's prize winners.

A feeling of emptiness enfolded me unlike anything I had ever known, not even after my mother's death, trapping me inside as if something had been taken that was so necessary for my ability to be alive there would simply be no way to climb out of it. Granny O had been the rock on which we balanced ourselves all our lives. We, unsteady; she, solid beneath us.

I held on to the sink, heaving with grief, and prayed only that she hadn't suffered, that she had gone back in peace to the Maker she so fervently worshiped. Death was swirling around me and my sister like quicksilver, sliding everywhere. In my dream the doll heads had all been shouting something at me, one word over and over. I remembered it then. "Why? Why? Why?"

The drive down from the Cape to Newport early on a summer morning was so lovely, so filled with merriment and the bright romantic crispness of possibility, that it was difficult to balance my pathos against it. I soon quit trying. One lesson my grandmother had taught us was that grief, like any other emotion, ebbed and flowed, blended with joy, whipped into anger, shifted about like the wind on the tides of change.

I allowed myself the pleasure of poignancy, memories of so many summers past. When I reached Easton's Beach, known to Newporters as First Beach, I turned off, paying the inflated seasonal parking fee just to stop for a moment and remember.

Easton's Beach was a nostalgia trip back to the days of boardwalks and bathing pavilions, when going to the beach was the main family summer outing of the week.

It had a long promenade, though it was now covered in cement, and a series of connected Victorian-style shingle buildings housing an aquarium, a snack bar, a children's carousel, amusement attractions, and cabanas available for rent.

From Memorial Day to Labor Day, the tall white lifeguard stands were manned with the hearty unisex young, and Rhode Islanders from near and not so near filled the deep sandy beach and splashed in the waves from dawn until sunset. Navy jocks jogged; toddlers, hands sticky with ice cream and ketchup, built castles in the grainy beige sand; and the summer girls with long strong legs and long strong hair strolled up and down, testing their charms.

There was almost a time warp quality about Easton's, which all of Newport still had. There seemed to be no menace, nothing to fear here. No gangs, no unsavory characters roaming about. It had none of the jaded self-involved aloofness of the West Coast city beaches or the uneasy, slightly malevolent quality of Jones Beach or the Jersey shore.

In the evenings there were free concerts, the sound carrying on the humid evening breeze for miles down Cliff Walk. Old people came with their grandchildren, teenagers came with one another, and the pavilion, which had been destroyed by Hurricane Bob but so exactly reconstructed that only experts could tell eighty-year-old photos from current ones, sat like a crown on the proud colonial head of the place, pond on one side, Atlantic on the other, and the sound of gulls and radios and people partaking of life's simple pleasures echoing through its walls, filling the summer nights.

It was the beach of my childhood, and sitting there in my borrowed car I could remember every single summer. Mr. Finnegan and my grandmother serving up chocolate milk as we sat, teeth chattering, lips purple with sea cold, so hungry, so engorged with the present. Nothing else I have eaten in my life has equaled those soggy beach-blanket lunches. No sleep I have ever slept has been as peaceful and trusting as those after-picnic naps next to my sister, the sun baking us brown on that hot summer sand.

I want to go back and do it again. The thought, the longing for the impossible, crept in beneath my defenses. I realized that my face was covered with tears. For a moment I saw my grandmother in her navy blue and white bathing costume, standing at the shoreline, doing her deep breathing before the plunge.

At age eighty she still swam there every fair day until October. Arms high over her head, the strap of her bathing cap tight under her chin, swimming out with even, steady strokes, fearless and sure of herself. *I don't know how to live without you. Come back so I can tell you how much I love you, just one minute more.*

The fifth ward is a community and my grandmother was the fifth ward, in spite of the fact that she was an outsider. No one whose family hadn't rooted before the Revolution was ever really considered a Newporter. The prejudice flared occasionally, fanned by those who had nothing besides bloodline with which to compete. The street was filled with neighbors coming to pay respects. The parlor and the hall were jammed with priests, nuns, tavern keeps, gardeners, countermen from Sig's Deli, and others I had never seen before.

I weaved my way to the kitchen, past condolences and greetings. The door was closed, probably for the first time, and I opened it carefully, not knowing what to expect. Faith, Benjamin, and Pebble were sitting at the table, talking to a portly pink-faced man wearing a cheap khaki suit.

"Hi," Faith said, reaching up for my eyes; her own seemed to be floating in panic. *She's not taking her medication.* The thought crossed over and I made a note to ask her, remembering that look in her eyes from long ago, preceding swamps of depression, the look of somebody who has just stepped into quicksand and cannot find a branch or a buddy to grab on to.

Benjamin got up and shook my hand, which touched me. He looked tired, his face drawn and pasty under his perennial golden glow.

I had never seen him look vincible before and it disturbed me, as if my opponent had surrendered while I was still sparring, cheating me of something.

Pebble slid out of her chair and grabbed hold, pushing hard against my side. She was thin and tan and beautiful and I wanted her gone, wanted her rewound to the seraphic gaiety of her phone message. How does a not quite ten-year-old absorb the loss of her uncle, her friend, and her great-grandmother in one parents-suddenly-appearing-at-camp conversation? I wanted to lift her and my sister up and carry them out, take them back to the beach, put them in a skiff, and head out to sea, to Japan or China or back in time, somewhere safer and easier to navigate.

"Jonny, this is Mr. Whitley. Mêmê Duckworth sent him. She's asked to have the wake at her house."

Sail away and never come back. This was what death did. It brought the past forward, untying all the dangling nerves, the coiled veins of old hurts, ripping all the delicate grafts and bypasses into newly damaged strands. I had no idea what to say because I was struck dumb by the thought. Neither Faith nor I had been back in that house since the night of our mother's death.

"That's very nice of her, but I think our grandmother would've wanted to have it here, in her own community and her own home."

The pink-faced flunky cleared his throat. No one returned to Mêmê Duckworth empty-handed. Even at ninety-seven, she ruled the Bellevue Avenue crowd with a silver-plated scepter. As far as I knew, she had not spoken to my grandmother in thirty-five years.

"Well, Mrs. Duckworth certainly respects that, but the thing is, your grandmother was so loved and revered in town—well, it looks like there may be hundreds of citizens who would like to pay their respects, and no offense but the house here just isn't adequate. Mrs. Duckworth felt that Mrs. O'Brien should have a proper laying out."

Flashback: my mother's body in the parlor, hardly more than a girl: a toy in a velvet-lined box. I looked at Faith. "What do you want to do?"

"Well, I don't quite—I mean, this is so unexpected."

Benjamin to the rescue, the executive doing what he did best, exerting power over the less powerful. "Let her do it. It lifts a burden, and it allows for a proper tribute—with a smack of irony she wouldn't have missed."

We all stayed over in the house, stumbling past one another, banging into our loss like crows against picture windows. We went through the after-death procedures, reading the will we never knew she had, that sounded so like her it made us laugh, pulling us back into her aura.

Jon and Faith. When I go, this is what I want: Tom Toole to bury me in the cheapest pine box he makes. Don't let him work one of those salesman numbers; no one but God matters, so I don't want one spare dime spent on any nonsense.

Put me in my white summer dress with the little roses embroidered around the collar, nice and cheerful, and don't let them put any paint on me; just comb my hair and use a bit of the pink lipstick on my dresser.

I want your grandfather's picture and the one of all of you in there with me, and my Bible and rosary. The house goes to both of you and all that's in it. Mr. Sullivan at the bank knows where my safety box key is. My savings go to the church. I want my stone to say my name and the dates and nothing else. No beloved this or that. I have a plot right next to your mother, and we'll be fine.

I want you to know that the wonder of my life was to have you both to care for. It has been an honor and the source of all my joy and strength, and Pebble was the Lord's love just pouring all over me. May his mercy bless your journeys as it's blessed mine and never doubt it. No moping. I've been lucky, so raise a glass for me and have a twinkle in your eyes when you think of your old granny. Now, get on with it!

The Duckworth mansion straddled almost a city block, a monument to the excesses of old, a gaudy limestone relic with a massive black wrought-iron and glass entrance.

There were other faux French monoliths as grand, but the Newport houses that really defined the WASP society who resided in them were the wooden "cottages," standing tall and white, facing the sea. Victorian dollhouses inflated to grand scale with vast polished verandas and thick green lawns.

The houses mirrored the inhabitants—polished and crisp on the outside, but cross the threshold and inside were dusty, dark, closed-in spaces reeking of the past. The dead stared out of yellowed photographs, stifling the living. Every room and heirloom creaked with fear of change.

Don't forget us! The eyes demanded. Don't move a chair, don't open a curtain; things must be as they were or our kind will perish and you will be nothing!

Ghosts were everywhere, tight, moribund, without the oxygen of the open heart.

Mêmê Duckworth's château-style palace was immaculately kept up, the long gravel drive raked, the potted trees rotated seasonally, the decorations lavish and appropriate to each holiday: huge polished pumpkins for Halloween, orchids and lilies at Easter, poinsettias and reams of tiny white lights for Christmas.

The motor court was lined with shiny black cars of various sizes and levels of pretension, and all the lights burned around the clock. Mêmê had a terror of the dark that had been heightened by a series of insider robberies, a decaying dowager's cross to bear.

Rumor had it that in fact all she had left of the Duckworth fortune was the house, and she used her remaining capital to keep it running. Whatever the truth, Mêmê still kept a full staff of servants and a live-in chauffeur, who also served as her frequent companion at the soporific dinner parties and galas that she attended. My father was the only heir of note. We had been allotted a small trust, which Granny used to raise and educate us. It had come with a codicil that basically disinherited us, our sin being that we were the issue of the woman who disgraced them. "The crazy gold digger" and "the whore from the fifth ward" were some of the descriptions we had heard as children.

From time to time, over the years, I'd run into guys from the Duckworth part of my childhood when I came home, and I'd think about what my life might have been if my father had stuck around or even if our paternal grandmother had been nice. Newport was sprinkled with men almost like me but with better

relatives, few of whom ever made anything of their opportunities. Most grew up to be well-bred, well-dressed, well-educated
losers drifting along on the current of apathy and appearances,
too afraid of failure—of sailing outside their ancestral bay—to
risk doing anything on their own.

The shadows of their forebears were long and dark, leaving no
wiggle room for zeal or individuality. The saddest of them were
the guest-house dwellers, with just enough in the waning trust
fund to get by, living free on the grounds of the family home.
Free rent is the surest wind-stiller of ambition, especially free
rent with an ocean view. Would I have had the character to say no
or say yes but still raise anchor and do something with my life? I
hope so. But I've honestly never felt bitter or resentful at not
sharing their privilege. I mourned the loss of my parents, one
final, one unresolved, but I never envied the lives of the guest-
cottage guys. Never.

Several years after my mother's suicide and my father's physical, financial, and emotional withdrawal from our lives, Mêmê
Duckworth had a horrifying accident at her hairdresser. The dryer
caught fire, igniting her head and neck. Her face was hideously
disfigured, and all the hair was broiled off her head. The muscles
and bones in her neck were also injured, leaving her bent almost
in half.

No one expected her to live, but live she did. In fact, it hardly
slowed her down. She showed up everywhere, with her entourage
of Eurotrash freeloaders and relatives from near and far in tow,
her clawlike hands weighted in jewels, clutching the arm of her
driver of the moment, her scarred, hawklike face fully made up,
her baldness covered with a large curly blond wig.

We would see her occasionally in the back of her Bentley or
Lincoln or Cadillac, on her way somewhere that required formal
clothes, whether day or night. Nothing stopped her. You had to
admire her fortitude, if not her values. Children were known to

burst into tears and run from her, and we probably would have too, but we were both cast out by then and so spared the stress of having to be brave.

Whatever had really happened on the day of my mother's death at Mêmê Duckworth's, I'd never known. It was Faith who found her and, as close as we were, it was the one topic we never discussed. She shut it out, locked irretrievably away.

If you tried to make her talk about it, as I had for years after, she would clasp her hands over her ears, squeeze her eyes shut, and shake her head, rocking back and forth until I stopped. Now she just looked at me with a closed, slightly addled look that said, I don't want to remember and I won't be pushed.

I often felt, though I had assumed the role of her protector, it was Faith who was protecting me from the horror of that afternoon and allowing me my unambiguous adoration of my mother. If this was true, it applied to Granny O as well.

We were the minstrels who carried the tale of our lost angel, wounded by the treachery of the Duckworths, driven to death. Faith held her secret as tightly as swaddling clothes. I'd always believed her depressions were emotional roadkill, the price she paid for shielding us from the devastation her memory held.

The day of the wake arrived and we prepared Pebble as best we could for her first meeting with this long-lost great-grandparent. I understood Mêmê's gesture. Two old warhorses, one from the upper crust and one from the town, both proud and uncompromising, standing guard over their territory in a siege of attrition that had suddenly ended.

My grandmother had lost the battle by dying first, but Mêmê Duckworth had lost the entire crusade by shrink-wrapping her heart under layers of snobbery and pettiness. Now, with the enemy gone, she could offer this public gesture to the poor orphans.

We got out of the car and stood looking up at the monolithic monstrosity as if a time machine had suddenly snapped us back forty years. I, Pebble's age, and Faith half that, two pug-nosed stick-skinny tykes, dwarfed by the magnitude of this other part of our lives.

It seemed hard to believe that this had once been our home, or rather the guest house was, where we were ensconced when my father began to stray, roaming the globe, gambling and womanizing, spending his trust fund in the way of those who have no concept of what work is or that money is tangible, finite, something that can run out.

My mother and Faith and I lived in a small Hansel and Gretel version of the big house, chauffeurs carting us to Saint Michael's School and back and forth between the mansion and Granny O's, where my mother went to sob and we went to be freed of our poor little rich kids chains.

We hated living there, hovered over, continually criticized and shushed, forced to obey arcane rules about everything; but mostly we hated what being there did to our mother: the damp-eyed distraction of her moods, the neglect of us as the inevitable result of her self-absorption. There we were, our paws up, our wet tongues eager to lick away her hurt, but she couldn't value us. Because we offered ourselves so freely, we had no worth. The only thing that was real to her was what she didn't have, our father's love and attention.

Inside, the place looked almost exactly as I remembered it, down to the silver bowl that held calling cards and social invitations.

Le Bal Rochambeau

The Colonel Commanding, Officers and Men of
The Artillery Company of Newport
request the honor of your presence at the
Company's 258th Anniversary Fête to celebrate
the alliance of America and Royal France

during the American Revolution
on the 212th Anniversary of the Treaty of Paris.

Military Uniform
White Tie
Black Tie
Evening Dress

It hushed you like church: the silence of stone, the vast stretch of empty space that formed the center hall, the soaring fan palms in the Chinese porcelain pots. Faith clung to me as if we were our child selves. Pebble hung on to her father's hand, understanding, without anyone's saying it, that this experience was between her mother and her uncle more than anyone else.

The butler approached, wearing white gloves and dressed in a white waistcoat with gold trim, and led us to the ballroom where Granny O now resided, her plain pine coffin a sore thumb in the midst of all the Empire splendor. I can only imagine Mêmê's reaction when they brought the pauper's bier into her grandeur.

Mêmê sat in her favorite Louis XIV throne chair just as she had all that time ago, except that she was very old now and grotesque, her head hanging over her chest, the wig slipping forward in a macabre parody of her former beauteous self. But what unnerved me and stopped my processional was who was standing behind her.

"Faith, that's Father!" I said, holding her back, wanting again to sweep her up and sail away.

The man standing there, whom we had last seen at ages twelve and seven, was as much a caricature of his former self as was Mêmê. My father, the handsome patrician rake, had been transformed by decades of excess into a prefab popinjay. He was close to seventy-five, but it was obvious even at a distance that hair dye and the surgeon's scalpel had been used to evade the toll of time.

I recognized the signs from information given to me by Rita: the unnatural bulges where cheek implants had been placed, the feminizing of the features that eye tucks and face lifts cause, the shiny iridescence of the braised skin. He had kept his Duck-worth form, with only a small paunch to show for all those fancy French meals and decanted burgundies, and this added to the absurdity. He looked old but unprocessed, waxy and artificial, like an overexposed Polaroid.

Faith leaned against me, and I could feel her body trilling like a meadow lark. "Oh, God, Jonny, I don't think I can do this."

I looked back and waved to Benjamin, who came at once, his command back in place, directing Pebble with a slight shift of his arm. "Is there a problem?" His eyes slid over our heads, scanning the room.

Faith's voice was as trembly as her body, pressed close against my arm. "It's our father, Benjamin. I don't think—I really don't want to do this now."

Benjamin took her arm from mine. "You don't have to. Let's all go sit somewhere for a while. Pebble, honey, come on."

Pebble pulled away. "It's okay, I'll stay with Uncle Jonny."

I looked down at her. "Are you sure?"

She grinned, radiant with her newfound confidence, "Sure. I mean, what can they do to me? Besides, they might be nicer if you have a child with you."

We took our place in the receiving line, surrounded by wheel-chairs holding shriveled women attended by bovine black girls, whose beatitude counterbalanced the irritability of their charges, still engaged in the games of society while waiting helplessly for the end of their pampered widowhood.

There were at least eight of these duos in line, interspersed with the still ambulatory array of crones, resplendent in almost identical paying-respects suits and diamond brooches, snatching the Spanish peanuts and Ritz cracker canapés with their gnarled arthritic hands.

Threaded between the fossils of the Gilded Age were their heirs and the summer-dwelling international fops, parading for one another amid smells of scotch before lunch and imported cigars and French perfume, making me queasy as tiny fragments of conversation drifted by, like a scanner search on the radio.

"No matter how desperate Grandmama got, she *never* sold the emeralds."

"Everyone thinks Oswald is stupid. But he's not, he's just over-bred."

"The only way to end this political mess is to stop permitting anyone who doesn't own land to vote!"

"The little kike faggot actually thought he could buy his way in here."

I turned, not quite believing my ears. I was in a human zoo. All the specimens seemed to be blond and tan, whether twenty or ninety. Most of the women were wearing large hats and dark glasses and pearls, ropes of fat shiny pearls. The people, stranded like the pearls, chattering away.

They were there to pay tribute to Mêmê, to partake of the notoriously stingy hors d'oeuvres and cheap booze, the glasses jiggling on the huge silver trays wobbling in the hands of the withered waitresses, less fortunate widows, who had served the rich in Newport for generations. It was hot. Pebble's hand was damp and light in mine. The gripping was back; the cat was try-ing to get my attention. The voices seemed louder now as more people arrived, nodding and greeting, viewers and viewed, creat-ing their post-event gossip as they passed.

Biff and Buffy, meet Miff and Muffy. Coco, meet Bobo. Puffy, here's Posie. Momsie, there's Popsie; Batsie, meet Topsie; Tinker, meet Taylor. What had we done?

And then came the moment that in a way I had been expecting every day since my twelfth year. The second of reckoning; all the fantasy revenge conversations, righteous indignation, martyr-dom, decades of compressed hurt, pushed up from the long-buried pile compacted to fit neatly into my unconscious. My father's eyes, trolling the room like any good angler worth his social sea legs, met mine and moved on. Moved on without a flicker of recognition, a flash of connection. If he had bolted across the receiving line and smote me, it couldn't have wounded more. I was nothing to him. There was no point in railing, accusing, holding him accountable. We had been expendable.

I turned, searching for someone from the fifth ward. Far across the room in the corner, almost cowering by the door, I saw Mr. Finnegan with his grandson. "Pebble, come on." I squeezed her hand, surrendering our place in line and dodging wheelchairs through the crowd to reach him.

"Where are we going?" Pebble stumbled next to me, trying to keep up.

"I want to talk to Mr. Finnegan."

Finnegan had his mouth wide in its usual Munch position, a cadaver that stood upright but a mind still sharply tuned. "Jonny, good ta see ya."

"Good to see you too, sir. Can you tell me why no other of Granny's friends are here?"

"Bunch of chicken hearts. Too scared, too anti this lot. You know, boy, you lived here long enough."

"I guess I'd forgotten."

"Couldn't even get Callahan to come."

"This is terrible."

"Heh. Your granny would have a thought or two, I bet.... Been wantin' to tell you somethin', to make you feel a little better about her final night. She wasn't all alone when she passed. She went out with comfort."

"What?" My cat hissed, poised for bedlam.

"Yep. I was looking over like I always do, one final check of my ladies with my binocs before bed, and I saw someone dressed in black in her room. Think it must have been one of the sisters from the convent."

"A woman?" Cold sweat covered my back, dripped down my forehead, beaded on my upper lip.

"Just a shadow across her bedroom window. Now if I had some of those infrared thingamabobs like Schwarzenegger used in that picture he made here, I coulda seen clearer, but I'd say so, because they was wearing something nunlike. Don't know who helped her, but she passed with mercy."

No, not mercy. I knew who it was. Who would question a ninety-year-old woman dying in her sleep? Granny's voice in my head: "Don't worry about me. I'm fine. The doctor says I can make a hundred." *She killed my grandmother!*

"Mr. Finnegan, I'll be back in a minute."

I held tight to Pebble, leading her across the vast stone hall to the sitting room where Benjamin and Faith had headed. Faith was pale and red-eyed and Benjamin looked tense and unsettled.

"Jonny, what?" She reached out for Pebble, who fell into her arms, surrendering to the child's need for comfort and relief from the hidden feelings that zoomed through grown-up activities like concept cars on cruise control.

"We've made a mistake. I have no idea what this setup is really for, having Father here and all, but this has nothing to do with Granny O. The room's filled with Mêmê's crowd; Finnegan said none of her friends would come. No one's even gone near her casket; they're all lined up to pay homage to the Duckworths. It's disgusting. We've got to stop it. I don't want to speak to either of them, especially in front of two hundred WASPs! What's the fucking point? We've got to get her out of here!"

Benjamin stood up. "Good idea."

"Jonny, yes!" Faith stopped crying.

I took the card out of my pocket, walked over to the phone, and dialed. Tom Toole answered.

"Mr. Toole, this is Jonny Duck. I am about to ask a unusual favor on behalf of my grandmother. I would like you to send a hearse over to the Duckworth mansion immediately to remove her and take her home." Three pairs of eyes were on me while I listened to his response.

"Thank you, very much."

Benjamin smiled. "What?"

"He said he'd be delighted."

Newport is a very small city, and even in the height of the tourist season it took only seven minutes for four of Tom Toole's beefy sons and nephews to arrive. We joined them, forming a sort of O'Brien and Company flank formation, marching into the ballroom like the liberators through Bayeux. The butler tried to stop us, but I darted forward, moving him firmly aside and holding his braided arm, local man to local man. "Trust me on this, pal. You're on our team."

People moved aside, stage-whispering in shock, and I could hear Mêmê's wispy cackle demanding information. "What is it? What? What? You fool, tell me what's happening!" The fool she referred to seemed to be our father, who looked meek and embarrassed, having probably been coerced into appearing, since he had no more to say to us than we did to him.

No one made any attempt to intervene, the Toole boys lifted her up, and we followed them out. She looked so peaceful, so serene in her embroidered summer dress, her wonderful white angel-dusted hair swept up off her handsome face. I was convinced her smile was approval and she was chuckling all the way.

Word had spread around the ward, and when we arrived the entire neighborhood seemed to be waiting, whistling and cheering, clapping their support. We marched in, setting her down in the parlor where our mother's coffin sat all those years ago, and someone put on Granny O's favorite jigs and someone else poured from a keg and bottles of Irish whiskey appeared and shouts of good cheer and toasts serenaded us.

Our tiny remaining family was flushed with the glory of a moment in life when a choice is made heedless of what others think. I watched Pebble awash in glee at the outrageousness of our behavior, a tyke's pure vision of death and life, joy and sorrow. We were united for a moment and we did what our grandmother had asked, we raised a glass together in her honor. Nothing, not even the horror of the information I now held, interfered.

I will always be grateful we didn't know then that it would be the last such moment we would ever have together.

CHAPTER SEVENTEEN

I slept in my grandmother's room that night, and in my dream she spoke to me. "Tell Benjamin," she said. I woke at dawn, remembering. I had never gone behind Faith's back, but then our family had never been infiltrated by a sociopathic murderer.

I got up from my grandmother's groaning old bed, which had held her peacefully all those nights but her last, and began to search the sanctity of her private space for signs of the beast. The smell was on a pillow, a small needlepoint cushion stitched with yellow tulips. I held it over my nose and sniffed, and I knew she had rammed it hard against my grandmother's face, smothering her and leaving no trace.

I dressed and went downstairs. A shadow against the parlor wall, my sister sat in the dawning light beside the coffin, hands folded in her lap, eyes closed. I waited in the doorway, seeing this as a sign, one last chance to convince her of the danger.

"Hi," I said. "Have you been here all night?"

She opened her eyes. She looked very young. "Mostly. Just saying good-bye."

"Any thoughts about yesterday?"

She smiled. "I adored it. Quite a story to tell our grandchildren. You were great."

"Are you sure you don't want to see him?"

"Yes. It's just what you said, What's the point? And I know Pebble doesn't want to. She told me last night she was absolutely terrified of having to talk to them, but she didn't want to leave you alone."

"Do you want me to drive her back to camp after the burial?"

"Yes, please. She really wants to finish her summer there. I can stay and settle things here and you can go back to the inn."

"All right. Is Sari coming?"

"Yes, but she's leaving right after for California, which is another issue. Jasmine wanted to come, but I really thought it best that someone trustworthy was in charge up there."

"Faith, I've got to talk to you—"

She jumped up so suddenly, I half expected Granny O to rise and see what the fuss was. "No! Don't you dare! I mean it, Jonny. I have enough to deal with now. Leave me alone! I won't hear any more about her. She's too important to me."

"Okay. I won't talk about her, but I must ask you a question. Have you stopped taking your medication?"

Her eyes narrowed. I could feel her resistance to the threat that I seemed to represent. "I'm trying something more holistic, so I've just changed, not stopped."

"Did she suggest this?" Rage overpowered my control.

"Stop it! If you won't, then I can't be around you!"

She ran from me, leaving me in the shadows with all that remained of our unifying principle. I looked down at my grandmother, waiting peacefully to be released from the needs of those remaining. *Do something,* was the last thing she had said to me, and so far I had failed her.

*   *   *

Faith avoided me at the cemetery, and Sari did too. I stood under a plum tree next to my mother's grave and mourned alone. My plan was to talk to Benjamin after the service and then drive Pebble immediately up to camp. I wanted to be on the Cape in time to see Ezra Clay before day's end.

The black cars with their flags waving waited for us, vehicles built for endings, escorting the bereaved in back seats filmed with tears of anguish and anger and relief. Driving back to Granny's, I wondered what the seats would say if they could talk. Pebble came with me and we patted our pain together. I held her and she cried and we talked about her puppy and Emily and Granny. I should have just kidnapped them when I had the chance.

Plans. Best-laid plans. Some other plan coming from elsewhere. Fool's dice, mocking my arrogance. Up the steps to the house, seeking Benjamin. Where was he? Gone, in his mourner's car; he was gone. Busy, busy man, only enough time to spare for freeze-dried mourning, microwavable loss. He was gone, taking Sari to the airport, both of them flying off away from us and Faith wanting no part of me, leaving both of us abandoned, stranded by our need. He was gone. What to do? Danger abounded. Rita, I had to warn Rita, some sort of plan was afoot, not my plan or maybe even God's, maybe the other guy's. Rita had the file first, would she be next? Got to get back, keep Faith away, warn Rita. Do something.

Driving Pebble. Driving too fast. She, sleeping, child-tired, exhausted from fully being, fully feeling, allowing the surrender. I would keep her from harm, I would deliver her from evil, I would protect her journey. Gulping container coffee from drive-through takeouts, not a moment to spare, got to get back and warn them, bring the message, like the runners of old, carry the news across the land. The plague is coming! Flee for your lives! Do something and do it quick; that was my legacy,

Got to find Rita. Driving again, too fast, Pebble's sapphire eyes in my mind. Children know, they are born knowing it all; growing up is trying to forget what we start out knowing. Knowing and accepting without doubt, without obstacle. Obstacles form later, denial forms at puberty. Does sex cause it? Maybe it's hormonal, the price for lost innocence. Pebble knew everything; it was in her eyes. Sari's mad at you, she said. Momma's got that look again, she said. I still think someone's out to get us, she said. No fear of the truth yet, no resistance.

We are lucky if at the end of our lives we have gotten somewhere close to what we began with. Releasing her back into the smells of mountains in summer, pine smells and lake water and oranges and chlorine. Children running to greet her, happy to see her, making me swallow hard. Pebble claiming her power, slenderness her badge of conquest.

Keep her safe. Got to keep them safe. Must find Rita, tell her to go. Was she next? Was I? Faith? Why? Why was she doing this to us? She was, though. That dead look in her eyes on the bed, my face slobbering between her legs. Drive, you fucker, drive.

Back at sunset. On the beach, Thomasina said. She was on the beach. Tide was low, sun going down, streaks of coral and lilac across the sky. Rita alone, throwing rocks into the water. Throwing hard, using all her might. Grunting and heaving bits of stone back into their birthplace. Millions of years old, re-forming endlessly but never ceasing, mountain to boulder to rock to pebble (must keep Pebble from harm) to sand, grinding down, pulverized by the forces of time, stages of the world pounding against you.

Rita turning, her face wet with tears and sweat. Why is it that women never throw rocks into the water? Only men, only boys? Isn't that strange? She asks, panting from the effort. We throw together, venting, pitching against our despair. She's right, never have seen a woman hurling stones into the sea. Feels so good. I don't want to stop, but I must tell her.

Go away. Go now. Something bad, the beast will harm you. I don't care. She throws, gasping now. She'd be doing me a favor. Tell the police. I have, I say. No proof. Nothing yet, but I will, I promise. Promises I may not keep. Go to Europe with Inga's uncle. Live for Emily, don't give up. Go. Mucus drips from her nose, black runs down her lashes like an African warrior. Jungle warriors, jungle beasts. Panthers are really leopards during their spotless phase. Almost perfect predators, I read somewhere.

Please, I beg. Go tomorrow. Stay tonight with Debbie and Inga, get out of here until I find something. She's not here, anyway, she says, picking up a big one, needing both hands, grunting as she heaves it. Sun now low, yellow and gray lines on the horizon. What do you mean? I ask, afraid of the answer, grown-up fear of truth.

She went down to Newport to comfort Faith, she says. Just for the night. Oh, God, please, not this. Would she dare? After telling someone where? Got to go back and do something, anything. No time for Clay now, have to wait.

Don't stop. Drive, you fucker, drive. Up the stairs, the house quiet and dark now. Granny gone for good. The smell of death, covered by stale beer and smoke. Faith? I call, running in and out. The house empty, no one there. Almost midnight, where, oh, where?

Out the door, looking across for Finnegan's light, sound of a radio, Letterman, sound of restless old people late at night. Jonny? Cranky voice next door. Mrs. Callahan, where's my sister? Went off with some tall black-haired lady. Heard her say the house was too sad, going to some hotel.

What to do? Where to begin? Phone books stacked in the pantry as always, begin with the obvious ones, call all night. Call until I slump forward on the battered old table where so much living has gone on, dazed with fear and fatigue. If she hurts Faith, I will kill her. Do it myself, no more waiting, no more patient fellow trying not to do harm. Nothing to do now but wait.

The beast had waited until we all left and Faith was alone. She appeared then, full of concern and compassion. "I've buried my own mother. I know how it feels; come with me. Let's get out of this house. I know a lovely little inn near Mystic. Let's just go, have a nice dinner, and not wallow."

Faith obeyed, setting off like Little Red Riding Hood following the wolf. And the price came higher than a few blisters and a long scary walk in the woods. She had chosen a fork in the road, one of those decisions that with a few footsteps can turn a life from growth and hope to tangled malevolence.

We are an egoistic, stubborn, and lazy genus; we do not like to admit we've been mistaken, easier just to keep skipping down the wrong road, hoping there's a way out without having to go all the way back to the point of confusion.

CHAPTER EIGHTEEN

*I*n the middle of the night of the day we buried our grand-mother, Jasmine went into my sister's unlocked room in the inn at Mystic. "What is it? I heard you crying."

Faith's teeth were chattering and she was wrapped in a blanket, although it was a densely humid summer night.

"May I tell you something? I have to tell a safe person.... I can't tell Jonny. I've never been able to tell Jonny, it would hurt him too much. Please, Jasmine, I have to."

Jasmine sat down in front of her on the floor, black silk kimono draped around her. "I'm right here, Faith, take your time. There's nothing you can't tell me." Jasmine reached for her hand.

Faith's fingers were icy, and the contact seemed to frighten her. She pulled her hand away, burrowing deeper into the rough mothball-smelling blanket that had warmed countless shivering travelers on cold or anxious nights.

"You can trust me with anything."

Faith lowered her head onto her knees, holding on, her fine hair soaked with sweat and tears.

"Wait," Jasmine said, and got up. She went into the bathroom and poured a glass of water, wet a washcloth, and carried them back, Faith's sobs and the rustle of her robe against the floor the only sounds. Faith accepted the offerings. She sipped the water and held the cloth over her face. When she took it away she was calmer, as if she had made peace with what she was going to reveal.

"I'm going to tell you what really happened the day my mother died." She folded the washcloth neatly and laid it down beside her on the bed.

"Jonny wasn't there, he was at school. We were living in Mêmê Duckworth's guest house but sometimes we stayed in the main house; there was this room they called the nursery, though I was five and Jonny was almost ten by then. I hated being there, the house was so enormous. I felt like a tiny little pea that might roll under some statue or something and never be found again. Going back today for the wake, I felt the same way.

"You know how they say when you return to childhood places as an adult you see them as smaller than you remembered? Well, it seemed exactly the same: those endless pink marble halls and that staircase winding around forever. I felt the same too.

"That day, I was asleep in the nursery. I must have come home from kindergarten and gone up to play and fallen asleep. I woke up and I remember being very cold, like tonight, and frightened by a dream. There were spiders in the dream.

"It was just turning into autumn and it was getting dark and the shadows looked like spiders and the butler hadn't put the lights on yet and I remember running down the hall looking for my mother or Edna, the maid who took care of us, but there was only one light on and it was in Pêpê Duckworth's room and that stopped me, because he was dead and no one *ever* went into that room. Jonny and I used to close our eyes, hold our breath, and race past it, because we were convinced his ghost was in there. But this time I was so scared by my dream that I put my ear against the door, and I heard my mother. It sounded like she was laughing, which was odd enough, and I opened the door and tiptoed in, more afraid of the dark and the spiders than of the strangeness of my mother's being in that forbidden place." She started to shake again, holding her knees tightly against herself.

"It's okay, I'm right here," Jasmine purred.

"I went in, and it was quite a sight. The room was just the way it must have been the day he died. His tuxedo was laid out on the chaise, complete with his gloves and satin bowler, even a pair of red silk boxer shorts. His pipe was on the table by his bed, and everything smelt of aftershave and tobacco, the way he had. My heart was beating so fast I could barely breathe. I was sure his ghost was going to pounce on me. I heard running water, and I ran and pushed open the bathroom door, looking for my mother."

She gulped air, searching for Jasmine's eyes. "Oh, God, it's like I'm there again! I can see everything! My mother was naked, and she was sitting in the tub, which was only about half filled, and there was a large glass of—I guess it was gin, next to her and a half-empty bottle on the tile floor.

"It was one of those old-fashioned tubs with claw legs, very ornate, with gold faucets shaped like swans. They were so lovely I remember staring at them and not seeing what was really there. Then I felt this—this terrible thing inside of me, not even fear but something almost alive with menace, and I saw that the tub was filled with blood. My mother's blood!

"She was holding my grandfather's ivory-handled razor and looking down at her wrist and blood was gushing out and she was laughing. She turned and looked right through me. She looked so beautiful. Her hair was golden, and she had put it up and ringlets were falling around her face and her skin was shiny and all the tension was gone from her eyes.

"I started screaming and I ran over and tried to take the razor out of her hand, but she pushed me back. 'Go away,' she said, and her voice was so mean, so icy, it cut me as deeply as if she'd slashed me with the blade. I was screaming, 'Mommy, Mommy! You're hurt! You're bleeding!' I ran and grabbed one of grandfather's towels. It was red, like the blood. It had his initials on it in black and gold braid, and I remember thinking how pretty it was, and I ran back and tried to cover her wrist.

"I was pulling on her arm and she was just watching me, laughing at me, and then she raised the other hand, the one with the razor, and she held it over me. 'Let go,' she said, as if she hated me, as if all the years of my life she had been pretending to care about me but now she didn't have to pretend anymore. I was nothing, and this was far more terrifying even than the blood. I started to understand that she wasn't hurt by accident, that she had done this to herself, and I was shrieking then, grabbing at her arm, and she was holding the razor up at me, keeping me away.

"I was screaming, 'Mommy, Mommy, please don't hurt yourself. I love you. I'll be so good. I'll do whatever you say! I'll stay with you forever! Please, Mommy, please! I need you! Jonny needs you! I love you, please don't! Please!'

"And she stopped laughing and slashing the air with the razor and she looked at me as if she loathed me, as if my anguish disgusted her, and she said in this stranger's voice, 'You're not enough,' and then she took the razor and ... and she—oh God, Jasmine—she ... slit her ... her throat! I can still hear the sound, a cracking sound, and then a gurgle, and I climbed into the tub and held her throat with my hands, screaming and screaming for someone to help me but no one came. No one.

"She died with me straddling her, trying to push the blood back in. I stayed there like that forever. It was night when I got out and I knew she was dead. I must have been in shock, because I was very calm. I was covered in her blood and I left tracks of it all down the hall and the stairs. The lights had been turned on, but no one had heard me.

"I walked down the stairs and I went into the kitchen and all the staff was in there drinking tea and gossiping. The kitchen was warm and cozy and it smelled of lamb roasting and something else—onions, I think, and fresh bread—and they all turned and I could see the horror on their faces and I said, 'My mommy's dead,' and I fainted dead away and I never told anyone. I just said that I found her. If I told I would have had to see her face, the meanness in her eyes, the words, 'You're not enough.' Oh, God, Jasmine, those words ruined me. They truly did."

Faith held her knees, rocking back and forth, rocky, rocky. Cradles falling, children falling, hurting, crying for comfort. The fickle protection of mother love. *Mommy, Mommy, I need you.*

Peace followed, the precious release that trails truth when a scuffle with the self has ended. Faith looked up, aware suddenly of the eerie silence surrounding them. Jasmine was leaning against the fake Victorian dresser, gazing at herself in the matching mirror.

"I burdened you, didn't I?"

Silence again. Too many spaces between. The beast staring at herself as if Faith were not present.

"Did you know that at six weeks embryos need to protect themselves from the immune systems of their own mothers?"

Faith uncrossed her legs and wiped her face, feeling a cloud of shame descend over her moment of grace. "No. I didn't know that."

Jasmine turned slowly, and retied the sash of her kimono, as graceful and methodical as a kabuki dancer. "Yes, well, I'm not surprised. You know so little. But it does say it all, doesn't it? They are our natural enemies. You are Pebble's and your mother was yours, so why you should be so whiny and neurotic about the obvious is frankly beyond me. More to the point, it's a bore."

"Jasmine, what are you doing?"

"Nothing. I'm not doing anything. I'm just giving you a little insight, long overdue, I'd say. I have tried to bring you along, Faith. But I'm afraid, now that you've revealed yourself, that it's really hopeless. Actually, though, it does speed everything up. I was beginning to think this was all going to go on for months."

"You're my friend."

"Oh, please. You really are such a silly little fool. Your friend! Why would I have a friend as easily manipulated as you? You weren't even a challenge. If you must know, I detest women like you. You have everything and you don't deserve any of it. I'm the one who would do great things, reach the stars. You can do whatever you want and you just creep around in your awful tacky clothes like all the other pathetic do-gooders. You make me sick."

Faith was back in Pêpê's bathroom, blood trickling, water sounds, her mother's look in the beast's eyes. She was slipping down into the blankness, the hingeing of past and present, red water washing over her, coating her with shame.

"Why are you doing this?"

"Ah, a decent question. Wouldn't you like to know. But why waste the energy? Let's just say I have what I came for and I can leave you now, knowing with some certainty what will happen. I'm counting on you, Faith, to carry out my plan."

"You did do all those horrible things, didn't you?"

"Oh, dear, don't be tedious. You know what Milton said. Better to reign in hell. I leave the value judgments to weaklings like you."

"Get out of here!"

"With pleasure. My puzzle is just about complete. Only a few small pieces left to fit. Just one last thought. Your mother was right, you know. You're not enough. You're nothing. Sweet dreams, dear." She moved to the door, silk sounds sliding over the hooked rugs.

* * *

I lifted my head off the kitchen table, pain shooting across my forehead and down my neck. My sister stood over me, looking punched in, battered.

"I've called every fucking hotel in Rhode Island. Where were you? What happened? You look—"

"Connecticut. Some fake Victorian spot." She slumped down next to me in Granny's seat.

"Why are you back now?"

Tears dripping, unattached to her feelings, like one of those crying dolls. "You were right about Jasmine, Jonny. God, I really did it this time."

My sister had been sucked into the past, swallowed by the unhealed child.

"Tell me." I reached for her hand, but she pulled away.

"I told her my secret about Mother and I don't—I can't talk about it again. It was dreadful. . . . Jonny, why couldn't I see?"

"You've got to talk to me. For chrissakes, it's time."

I had asked for a truth I wasn't really prepared for either. With it came memories, tearing my illusions of my mother, and anger and horror at my own cowardice. I'd let my sister carry this all alone. I'd sent the message that I didn't want the information and allowed her to shoulder the burden, and so had our grandmother. The lie was always between us, making a mockery of our bond. Undermining any real closeness, as secrets always do.

When she finished, she got up and poured two glasses of water, and we sat together and drank them down without speaking, sucked dry, dehydrated by the purge.

"She did just what you said, Jonny: the puppy and Pebble's weight and the rats. God, it's so evil."

My own rage at her delusiveness, the decades of tiptoeing around, always afraid to step on the baby chick, kicked in. "What the hell are you saying? If we're telling the truth here, then let's tell it. I've been protecting you too, you know. Puppies and rats! The woman has murdered three people! She killed Andy and Emily and our grandmother! She's a fucking monster, and God knows who's next. I thought it was going to be you! Why do you think I've been calling every hotel in the state?"

When I saw her face, I knew I'd gone too far. The consequence of my truth-telling seemed too great. She stood up and started for the door, then stopped, backing up like a wind-up toy that's bumped into a wall. Her entire being seemed to short-circuit, her nervous system desperately trying to absorb the sparks. She spun around suddenly, robotically, almost electric with shock. "God, Jonny. We've got to get Pebble! Jasmine said 'a few more pieces of the puzzle.' If she ... it's my fault they're dead, Jonny, but Pebble—"

She grabbed the phone and called the camp. It rang and rang and she held on, her hands white on the receiver. Finally someone answered.

"This is Faith Wise, Pebble's mother. You must go and get my daughter right away and keep her with you until I get there. She may be in danger and it's very important. . . . What? When? Oh, my God!"

She dropped the phone, streaks of red blotching her pallor.

"Jonny, she took Pebble. We've got to call the police and get back to the inn!"

We saw flames from a mile away, rocketing into the summer sky. We didn't say a word to each other, but we knew it was the inn. Faith was out of the car the moment I hit the brake, running back and forth, seeking a way in. I ran after, trying to pull her back. The force of the blaze was enormous, a hell fire, venom splashed as propellant.

Faith was screaming now. "My baby's in there! Help! Please help! Pebble! Pebble! Momma's here!"

I grabbed her and held on, afraid she would bolt into the

inferno. If Pebble was in there, she was gone. I moved toward the firefighters, dragging Faith with me.

"My sister's the owner. Her little girl may be in there! Who can help us? What's being done?"

"Jonny, it's okay."

We both turned back toward the ambulances in the driveway. Daisy Mae Dexter and Ezra Clay were standing in the debris. Daisy Mae had Pebble enfolded in her arms.

"Momma!" Pebble ran to Faith, ran toward the haven of mother love as we wish it to be.

Faith collapsed onto her knees, holding her. Answered prayers, thoughts in my head of all the stories I had covered, all the children sacrificed. Bits of babies flying through space. Pebble was babbling with the excitement of the experience, processing the way children do, outward bursts and inward trickles, pooling deep inside.

"She gave me drugs, Momma! I drank a soda she brought and I felt all creepy, and the next thing I knew I woke up in Jasmine's room and it was filled with smoke and I heard Daisy Mae yelling and glass breaking.

"She saved my life! Just like in a movie! She came up a ladder and pulled me out the window! 'Cause I'm thin now. Otherwise I would of burned to a crisp!

"Oh, my God, Momma, Jasmine tried to kill me! I was right. Someone was trying to get us! Really, totally amazing! Momma, are you okay? You look so sad. Be happy. We're all alive!"

I followed Ezra Clay and Daisy Mae back to the police car.

"What happened?"

Daisy Mae pulled coffee containers out of a huge bag and handed them around. Clay took his and winked at her. "She's fat but she's fast. Shoulda seen this woman climb that ladder. Put all these young turks to shame."

"We got lucky, Duckman. I was takin' a few days off, since you brought my old pal Big Foot here back into my lonely life, and we were tossin' a few at his office, so when you called we pedaled over here, seconds before the big kahuna really let fly.

"Seems like it was set, probably in the cottages, and the wind blew the embers onto the roof of the main house. But since Pebble says she was drugged—we'll know for sure when we get some blood—I'd say it's your Vegas pal and she knew what she was doin'. We got all the guests out safe. Some fucking vacation."

"Daisy Mae, I owe you one helluva dinner."

"You kidding? I told you, friends are few. Come on, Clay, I need a beer."

"Wait.... Detective, what about Jasmine? She said something to Faith earlier tonight about being part of her plan. If she's still loose, we're all in danger."

Ezra Clay crumpled up his coffee cup, which he had drained in what seemed to be a single long sip. "Where Pebble was, the first cottage—was that hers?"

"Yes."

"Well, like Daisy Mae said, those burned hot and quick. The only body we've found so far was in there. Can't tell much yet, the corpse is charred, but it's female, tall, with long black hair, so my calculated guess is, it's our gal. Pretty gruesome way to do yourself in, but as you suspected, too many barnacles on her anchor for sure. We'll let you know more when the forensics boys finish up."

"I told Big Foot, if they get stuck, maybe Theo could come up and help 'em out. He loves shit like this."

Faith and Pebble came over, and I turned away from the deeper uncertainty, choosing the immediate relief I felt at seeing that look gone from my sister's face. "It looks like Jasmine died in the fire."

Pebble's eyes, wide with wonder. "She's dead?" She paused, truth radar searching for its signal, "But why would she bother to kill me, if she was going to kill herself?"

Faith's eyes, the opposite of Pebble's, narrowing with uncertainty. "Maybe it was an accident. She got careless and made a mistake."

"Maybe." Neither of us really believed that, but we did believe she was dead. How or why we would never know, but fate had knocked her puzzle off the coffee table and given us our lives back. We turned and watched what was left of my sister's dream, her clapboard Shangri-La by the Sea, collapse in a bevel of cinders.

The phone woke me before seven.

"Jonny, it's Rita. Meet me at the fruiter's latte bench in fifteen minutes. Don't shave, I didn't."

She was there before me, all dressed up and holding our lattes on her lap. She handed me my container before I sat down. "I must be doing something right 'cause old Waldo actually sprinkled cinnamon on mine without a request."

I took my cup and sat next to her, amazed at the ability of the human spirit to sponge up so much pain and still sip coffee and make jokes. "You heard?"

"Everybody on the Cape's heard. We're talking about a town where the opening of a new supermarket is on the front page of the local paper; what would you expect? Possible arson and immolated centerfolds would certainly get some attention."

"How are you?"

She took a sip, leaving foam on her upper lip. "To steal one of your lines, how am I is a relative-type question. Compared to having my baby alive and sitting together poolside at the Cipriani in Venice sipping Bellinis, I'm fucked. But compared to being on a slab in the Provincetown morgue looking like a briquette, I'm fine. Having the bitch dead has done wonders, and having her die like a horror movie has put the pink back in my cheeks. I was going to do it myself, Jonny, I really was, and I can't even shoot a water pistol."

"Never worth it."

"Yeah, well, bullshit. Don't tell me you didn't think about it too."

"I won't."

"So, aren't you going to ask me why I'm here hours before my usual arousal time and all dressed up?"

"No."

"I'm taking your advice. I'm going to meet Inga's uncle in Switzerland. Funny, but as long as she was alive, I wouldn't have left. I would have stayed even if she had killed me. Didn't much care. But now she's gone, I can go. I decided to see what's left for me to live for, like you said, but really because it's what Emily wanted.

"She was always so worried about me, pretending she didn't want to go away to college even, when she just didn't want to leave me alone. I started to think about that, how she was always trying to prepare me for her leaving, like she was the mother in a way. One night last fall, she was on my case, trying to get me to tone myself down, clean up my mouth, so some desperate slob would take me off her hands and she could go off to school and not feel bad. We were in a restaurant downtown with this hunky bartender, and Emily was goading me about what I should do to attract a man. 'Mom, you haven't had a date since, like, the Reagan administration.' The bartender laughed, so Emily says to him, 'Give me one reason why you wouldn't date this woman.' I'm totally mortified. 'Too obstreperous,' he says. A regular rocket scientist. I didn't say anything because I didn't know what the damn word meant until I got home and looked it up, but the guy was right. My point is, she wanted me to be happy and find some love, so maybe I should try."

Her eyes filled, and I knew she was trying not to dissolve her perfectly prepared face, even before she said so.

"I am not going to cry and spoil forty-five minutes of hard work."

I reached out and took her free hand and kissed her knuckles. "Yeah. You too, pal. I'll be in touch."

She left, and I sat for a while, finishing both our coffees. It was the third week in August, but the summer was over for my sister and me. All I wanted to do now was sweep all the ashes into a nice round pile and go back to the city. And that's what we did.

CHAPTER NINETEEN

So the circle closed but it didn't end. Walking home from the morgue that fine spring day, the vision of the real body of the beast newly in my head, images began twirling in my mind. Nooses and wreaths, spirals of complexity, calamity, and confusion. Faith in one and Jasmine in another. And who was the woman in the ashes of the inn?

It had been almost eight months since we'd left the Cape and come back to Manhattan. We'd returned like all refugees, grateful but haunted by specters of failure. When you try the dream and it turns into *Nightmare on Elm Street*, there is a flattening of the orb of the future, the hope of change.

The joke was that we'd had change aplenty. An engorged piñata party of change. Change had fallen down all over us like fiesta favors, but that wasn't exactly what we'd had in mind. Or mainly what Faith had in mind.

I'd left the city for far less starry-eyed or formed reasons, more as a time-out than a life alteration; a moving of a button till I lost a few pounds rather than a recutting of my only suit. But running away from and running toward got all wrinkled up together; that was how we returned.

We were changed. Refugees after the war alighting at the village, our belongings tied up with the twine of our losses, the horror of what we'd seen. The villagers who hadn't fled, who hadn't borne witness to our disasters and awakenings, weren't changed in any concurrent way, which only spun the lasso faster, making the coils of reentry far too tricky. Faith and I waited outside the circle, mesmerized by the whirling rope but too unsteady to risk jumping back in. Pebble had the resilience of childhood and her newfound camp confidence, and she did far better. When we tried to talk about our experience in a chipper way, it was always Pebble we cited as the one positive that had come from the tragedies.

Pebble was in a new school downtown, and Benjamin had reordered his travel schedule to be in New York more. I was doing what guys tend to do in any situation where they have changed in spite of themselves, what Sari once called "male-pattern bonding": playing racquet ball obsessively and hanging out at my old haunts.

I finished my book proposal and tried to resume some pathetic and fainthearted attempt at a social life. I missed Sari constantly, her absence like a gash across my heart, hurting whenever I moved, whenever memory tottered in, staggering past my denial. I wrote, but she never answered.

On the surface, my sister seemed to be coping. Having Pebble thrive and Benjamin home helped immensely. She was taking yoga classes and seeing her therapist, and she was back on her antidepressant medication. Benjamin was coaxing her ever so gently but firmly into his business. There were certainly enough aspects she could work in, many events to plan and interiors to design. I thought it was a good idea, a way out of herself.

Our relationship had been breached by all that had happened.

The night of truth-telling had created unease, a barrier where a bond had been, but neither of us seemed to have the energy or the courage to address it. Months passed, and the refugees began to be reabsorbed into the community. The reasons for fleeing in the first place were still present, but muffled, blurred by the events of the journey.

Memories of the summer receded, fading like bathing attire left to dry too long in the sun: still wearable but different, changed (that word again) by time and the power of the elements. We'd survived and returned, and we carried back with us all the tattered baggage of survivors, guilt and loss and sadness and strength, all rolling around together in newly endless circles.

By the time I walked from the morgue to my apartment, I was physically dizzy from the spinning in my brain, like some demented geometry student with his compass on autopilot. What did this mean? If Jasmine hadn't died in the fire, if she had set that up too, maybe Faith's death wasn't a suicide. But then who had killed Jasmine?

The business cards the police had found in her drawer belonged to me, Rita, Sari, and the one I didn't know, someone called Hans Schmidt with an address in Geneva, possibly the mystery payer of the apartment rent. I'd tried to hold on to the card long enough to memorize the address, but as the revolutions and revelations escalated, the letters and numbers had flown out of my reach, rotating around, lost to me in my dervish condition.

The phone was ringing when I opened my door, a rare enough event in my refugee life to clear my head. It was Detective Clay. Good news may travel fast, but bad news is a veritable jet stream.

"Mr. Duck, I've heard about the interesting new tack in the case. It got me up and off my duff and I have uncovered something I think you will find most useful."

"Sounds very Jessica Fletcher in spite of yourself, sir."

"Well, I have to admit, I'm pretty keyed up about this. Pretty racy compared to our usual roster of DWIs and parking offenses."

"What is it? I don't mean to be abrupt, but I don't think I can handle many more guessing games today."

"I understand, but I think it best I bring this in person. I can be in the city for supper."

"Fine. Do you have a place in mind?"

"Anything but Cape fare."

"Gallagher's at seven?"

"Ah. Takes me back to times past."

I hung up, the anticipation of relief replacing the dizziness. Reflexively, I started to pick up the phone, but there was no one left to call. Rita off in Switzerland, Granny and Faith gone forever, Sari unavailable.

There hadn't been a ceremony for Faith, but Sari came anyway, and after the burial I followed her out of the cemetery. We tripped across the grass like drunks or blind people in a haze of anguish, and she let me take her arm. I didn't want to let go of her, would have tackled her, held her prisoner to stop her from leaving me. She must have sensed my desperation, because she freed herself. It started to rain, and when she faced me, drops fell on her hair, tracing the curls before sliding onto her shoulders.

"You really don't know very much about me, Jonny. The fact is, my childhood sucked. So what I did to get by was never trust anybody, ever. I guess that's what attracted me to Andy. I knew I'd never have to risk really trusting him. Tell me that isn't pathetic!"

She stopped, tears mingling with raindrops. My hand, having a will of its own, reached out to wipe them. She pulled her head back, leaving my fingers wet with need.

"Please, Jonny, don't touch me. It's too hard as it is. Faith and then you were the only people I ever trusted. It hurts bad. It throbs like holy hell."

I opened my mouth but nothing came out, and she reached

over and put her sweet gingery fingers on my lips. "I miss you too," she said, leaving me even more alone than I'd been a moment before.

I picked up the phone and dialed her New York number on the chance she was still in town. Her answering machine came on and I heard her throaty, lusty voice, beating against my hurt.

"Sari, Jasmine's dead. Someone murdered her here, in New York; the body at the Inn wasn't hers. Jesus, Sari, I need to see you. We're all that's left from this. Please, if you hear this, please call me ... I love you."

I hung up and lay down on my bed, falling into a thudded sleep. I regretted the call immediately. I'd been about as subtle as Hitler's art collection. I slept until it was time to meet Ezra Clay.

I was fifteen minutes early but he was there when I arrived, a Calvinist to the tips of his giant toes. He was sipping from a martini glass as big as a goldfish bowl. I was aware that my pulse was racing and the cat was back, climbing up and down the middle of my spine. My anticipation was a surf-and-turf of fear of and eagerness for the information waiting in the yellow folder on the seat beside him. Enlightenment comes with a price. I sat down and signaled the waiter to bring me a fishbowl of my own.

Clay smiled, making his slightly pointy Adam's apple pop up over his starched collar. "Can't drink these in New England, they think I'm putting on airs. But there's only so much beer a fellow can swallow."

"You don't seem to be a man who's swayed by the opinions of others. I'd have thought you'd take delight in shocking them."

"Ah, well, human nature being what it is, we must always disappoint one another eventually. I am weak about my heritage. I like to fit in. Not proud of it, though."

My drink came. "Well, let's toast disappointment in our fellow-man and the mixed bag of belonging to a group or to nothing like myself."

We sipped in silence. I relaxed a bit, steadied by the presence of a solid soul, however limited. One hunter-gatherer hoisting with another, instinctively sure that neither of us was likely to bonk the other with his club and make off with the winter's rations.

"What do you have, Ezra?" It was the first time I'd used his Christian name.

He seemed to sense my anxiety and gave me one of those man-of-the-sea steely-eyed stares that reminded me of my grandmother.

"Well now, like with most things of importance, there is the good news and there is the bad news. I think I'll tell you the good news and let you read through the other in privacy after dinner, so's not to upset the digestive enzymes."

"Okay, head me into the gale."

He picked up the folder. "This here is the mysteriously missing file that you were so nervous about after Emily Riley's car crash. When I got the call from Daisy Mae about the true identity of the body in the New York morgue as opposed to the body we had, it was like a straw in my craw: couldn't swallow it, wouldn't come up or go down. So on a hunch I drove up to the inn again to poke around.

"They haven't cleared the wreckage yet because the insurance people have taken so long to come to terms on the loss—lucky for us—so the part of the cottage we found the body in was still standing. The plumbing fixtures and the bathroom's bearing walls and tiled floor were intact. I had my scaling knife and I loosened some tiles; couldn't find anything, but I thought maybe she'd hidden something there. So I picked up the top of the toilet tank to use as a hammer, and what do you know! The file was in the tank in a rubber sleeve taped to the side. Felt just like one of those TV cops. Damn shame how things turn out. If we'd had it then, could of at least saved your grandmother and the inn, maybe even your poor sister. But, no use peeking in the pelican's beak."

He shoved a big hunk of buttered bread into his dentally challenged mouth. "It seems Miss Jasmine Jones had some history. Her mother and a new stepfather out in Lake Tahoe, Nevada, were both killed in—guess what?—a suspicious fire! Our girl, real name as you told me, Wendy Pulski, was suspected, but there was no proof. She was fifteen and I'm sure she razzle-dazzled the skivvies right off all those firemen and adjusters.

"She got some insurance money and ran off to Las Vegas. Now all those juvenile records were expunged, but Mrs. Riley's friends, who are most definitely of the organized crime persuasion, have their own sources. They knew this girl from her relationships with the men of the Mob.

"She made a career out of charming and disarming, but it's a small town and her bait passed over too many hooks, as it were, and eventually she made a couple of very dangerous fellows real mad. Not nice to splash around with the egos of the underworld. So I presume she got kinda panicky and was looking for a way out of town and found it. But that's the part for your private discourse."

I nodded, trying to sort through the whirling lassos of emotion and information. "So who was the girl in the fire?"

"Don't know. May never know. But my best guess is we'll discover some teenage runaway, the psychology of whom our lady was well acquainted with from her own past—probably gay or bisexual, probably on the street—who just happened to be unlucky enough to resemble Miss Jones and be in the proverbial wrong place.

"She knew you were charting her course. Quite a clever way of bailing out and leaving no ripples. By the way, did you know that three out of four serial killers live in the U.S. of A.? We spawn 'em like trout."

"Any thoughts about who killed her?"

"A few. One pretty obvious suspect. You'll see for yourself soon enough. Not something we should chat about before Daisy Mae has a gander, which I delivered before I came here.

"So let's eat and you can go home and figure the rest out. I want a steak as big as this beverage container, and I'd prefer your not ordering lobster. I don't want to see another of the red devils till I go home."

We ate and talked about sailing, both of us aware that I was really just readying myself for what awaited as dessert.

CHAPTER TWENTY

When I left Ezra Clay, both of us glutted with beef and booze, I walked home, hoping to burn off the effects and the muted but still present spinning above my head, but when I reached my building, I resisted. I didn't want to go back into the emptiness of that space to open this packet of potential devastation alone in a silent room. I kept walking until I was at a cop hangout I used to frequent near the Nineteenth Precinct.

It was quiet, only a few late-shift vice guys and a couple of desk jockeys nursing their exhaustion. No one paid any attention to me, and I ordered coffee and carried it to a booth in the back by the pool table.

A memory flashed by: Faith meeting me here as a lark and shooting pool with Daisy Mae, her gentility and loveliness like a fizz across the room, laughing her crackly startled laugh, surprising herself with joy. A wave of grief sickness hit, pulling me under. I ripped open the envelope and took out the file.

Whatever ego gratification I've allowed myself, in the illusion that I could see around the corners of human nature, psych out phonies and manipulators, and play the game as good as I got, dropped away with the first paragraph. A big fat hat pin popped my smug balloon. I hadn't had even a whiff of this. Well, maybe one.

It was almost eleven when I arrived at Benjamin and Faith's building and the night man was somewhat hesitant to buzz, given the probable lunatic glint in my eyes and the way I clutched at the coffee-stained documents in my hand.

The phone rang for a long time and the two of us avoided eye contact until my brother-in-law answered and I was granted entry. Up I went in the elevator I hated, thoughts of my sister's last journey down circling with the other spheres, wreaths and nooses now part of the lasso, rotating faster, just waiting for me to attempt a step inside.

Benjamin opened the door, wearing white satin pajamas under a black cashmere robe. His hair was sleek and his slippers were velvet. I had a moment of sheer awe at the sight of him. There really were human beings like Benjamin who slept in fancy pajamas and wore velvet slippers even when no one was around. This gave him a sort of magically sinister quality that made more sense now than ever before.

I hadn't seen him since Faith's burial and he'd been a different Benjamin that day: creased and slightly acrid, his hair unslicked and flying at angles, his suit damp with sweat. The force of his pain had startled me and frightened Pebble, so powerfully expressed that it pushed our own feelings aside and took precedence, which angered me, displacing my own rite and consuming the space we all needed to share.

One week later, alone at home, he was back on track. Gleaming and slick, the model moon man, primped for all stargazers who just might pass by. His huge eyes took me in, seeing, I knew, more than I would like. "Jonny?" My name was all the question he needed to ask.

"I know it's late, but I have to talk to you."

"Of course. I was in the study." He turned and I followed him across the huge hall of pretense, past all the decorator-chosen art, selected for image, revealing nothing of his sensibility or my sister's, sterile objects devoid of the transparency of personal choice.

A night-light switched on in my consciousness. My sister and I hated this apartment because it was a mini version of Mêmê Duckworth's house, the barren entry, the staircase curving dramatically up like a stage set, the coldness of form without passion beneath it. Possessions chosen by strangers, however tasteful, were like gourmet takeout, always lacking the smack of real food.

A fire was roaring in the carved marble fireplace, two hand-tooled leather settees flanking it, his cigar in a sterling dish, a brandy snifter beside it, Cuban smoke curling up, disappearing into the holes in my brain. This was the way he really lived all alone, in satin and velvet, Cuban cigars and French brandy by firelight, not a beer and a ball game and ham san on a napkin, no boxers beneath a threadbare terry. Poor Pebble, I thought.

"What can I get you?" He smiled and sat back down without waiting for my reply.

"Nothing, thanks. Where's Pebble?"

A slight raising of one feathery black brow. "She's staying the night with one of her new friends. Why?"

I dropped the file on top of one of his fancy Renaissance art books without answering. "I think you'll find this more interesting than whatever the fuck you read in here: *The Rise and Fall of the Third Reich,* or the complete works of the Marquis de Sade, or possibly something lighter, like Socrates, maybe the essays on irony."

He kept smiling and puffing on his cigar, but he picked up my crumpled folder and took out the file. Like me, he didn't have to read much. He put it down, and I witnessed something extraordinary and totally unexpected, fooling me again, punching into the certainty of my worldview.

He dropped the cigar and began to cry. He didn't cover his face or lower his head; in fact, he threw his head back, the moon man looking to the heavens, his mouth open wide in moaning despair. It was emotionally different from the funeral, and I understood the difference. As upset as he had been then, he had still been acting from within his image, under his own control. But now he was bared, shoved out from behind his facade by a blast of reality for which he had clearly not prepared.

"Oh, God help me, I killed my wife, my precious angel. It's all my fault. Jesus God, I'm so sorry!"

"Get a fucking grip and tell me. I need you to tell me!"

He took a handkerchief out of his pocket and blew his nose. His body shuddered. He jumped up, as if startled by his own thoughts, and reached out for the mantel, pushing forward against his own weight, then slumping back against the fireplace as if he'd been shoved.

"You've got it all there. Isn't that enough?"

"No. Tell me!"

"All right. I guess I owe you that much." He raised his arms, smoothing his hair, calming himself.

"I was in Vegas doing a deal with one of the big hotel syndicates, and Andy was helping me. He'd represented one of the studio chiefs on a couple of books and he knew some of the Hollywood people involved, and of course Andy liked the action as well as the money." He stopped, sighing deeply, the aging diver returning to the big board.

"He met her at a party. He'd just married Sari, but, you can imagine, this woman we knew as Madeline James, the effect she'd have on Andy. For her it was a way out of a mess she'd gotten herself into, playing two mobsters against each other. She was just using Andy until the next mark, but he didn't notice, he was besotted, and he took her with him to the south of France for a meeting we had scheduled. I met her there."

He put his hands over his eyes, as if squeezing the past into focus. "Jesus, Jonny, you knew her; you can understand. It was like she put a spell on me. She was the exact opposite of Faith. This was at one of those really low points. Faith was just out of the hospital, she'd been deeply depressed for months, and I was worn out by it, pulled down, and, I guess, angry at her and ashamed of it.

"We hadn't had any sex life for almost a year, and in walks this creature—Holy Christ—and on top of the whole sordid enchilada, she had fucked my brother! You know how we were with one another and she knew too. She knew everything about human frailty and she played us.

"Well, when she found out who I was, Andy was dumped so fast he hardly had time to wipe the leer off his face. And it began: seven years, on and off. I set her up in an apartment in Nice. Andy couldn't bear to be out of the loop even if she'd rejected him, so he became the middleman. He had an alias at a bank in Geneva, and I supported her that way.

"Hans Schmidt?"

"Yes. I'd try to end it periodically, and then she'd call or send a photo or a note or just a damn Kleenex with her scent on it, and I'd drop everything and run back. I was consumed with lust for her. The first time I made love to her she told me she had never come before, that no one had ever opened her, and something about that fed the darkest part of my ego. It was the biggest turn-on of my life; everything about her was like some movie from the fifties or something. The Barefoot fucking Contessa, all that style and mystery and beauty and intelligence—the unfathomableness of her!

"We'd walk into a room at some private club in Athens or Berlin and it would just stop. Fucking stop! People would hold their breath. I felt as if I were being eaten alive, as if my will had been sucked out of me, and I still couldn't stop. But then it started to escalate. She wanted more. She wanted me to leave Faith and marry her, and that I would never do. I know how this sounds, Jonny, but this obsession with Madeline had nothing to do with my love for Faith. It was almost as if I were two separate people, but when she crossed the invisible line I had drawn between her and my family, I knew I had to choose and I did. I ended it.

"I told Andy to take care of her, give her whatever she wanted within reason. I set up an account for her with a million dollars in it in stocks and prime mutual funds, and an allowance until she put her life back together.

"I told her the only condition was that she was not to contact me—if she did I would cut her off—and I told Andy I didn't want to know anything unless her requests became unreasonable. I just stopped, cold turkey.

"That was about six months before Faith decided to open the inn. My reluctance was partly because I was afraid of what would happen to me if I had too much time alone, one of the problems we had anyway, with me traveling so much. But as far as I knew, Madeline James was living in the south of France and out of my life forever. She was so fucking good at the game, too. When I first told her it was over, she just sat there, tears pouring out of those unreal violet eyes, like I had pierced her soul. 'I understand the words, Benjamin, but our hearts are attached and I don't believe this is possible,' she said.

"She never contacted me, no threats, no clinging; it was one perfect performance, the mistress role of the century. I had no idea she had leased an apartment in New York. When Faith started telling me about this incredible woman who had shown up, I didn't pay much attention. First of all, when I knew Madeline her hair was blond and very short, nothing like the woman Faith described. Also, I was so busy, so exhausted and preoccupied with work, that I wasn't tracking. I'd shut Madeline out of my consciousness in order to proceed, and I wasn't interested in looking for trouble. I didn't make any connections.

"But after a while, the way Faith described this woman started to make me nervous, so I called Andy. When he told me that Madeline had asked 'Mr. Schmidt' to spring for a year's lease on a condo in Manhattan, I asked him to go up to Truro and check it out, but we never talked again. God, Jonny, I never linked her to his death! I still saw her as a magnificent person! I had never seen beneath her facade; she was like seamless, you know?

"Even when I started to think that Madeline might be this Jasmine Jones my wife was so mad about, I just thought it was her way of staying in my life. Then, when Andy died, everything accelerated, but before I could sort it out this unknown woman was dead!

"Faith never said one word to me about anything traumatic happening between them, but I knew that something had changed by the way she reacted after the fire. It was Pebble who finally told me something about what really happened, the parts she knew, and what I did then was deny it to myself. No fucking way the woman that had consumed me with longing for all those years could be this madwoman who tried to kill my daughter!

"Faith never told me you suspected Jasmine of causing the other deaths, and neither did you, Jonny! If you thought that was being loyal to Faith, you were wrong. I didn't know anything until after Faith's death, when I found the tape."

"What tape?"

"I'll get to that in a minute. About a month before Faith killed herself, I got a call from Madeline. I hadn't heard from her since I'd left her in France, and since the woman who I'd thought might have been her was burned to death on the Cape, I completely split the two in my mind. She asked to see me for lunch, said she needed some business advice, and I agreed. I knew it was a mistake, but I did it anyway.

"I met her someplace way downtown, where I wouldn't run

into anyone, and when I saw her, it was exactly the same, like someone was pulling my brain out of my head, and lust like I was a fucking satyr. I guess she was wearing a blond wig—so she still looked totally unlike the woman Faith described.

"She wanted to know if something had happened to Andy. Someone from the bank had told her Mr. Schmidt had died, and since Andy had stopped contacting her she put two and two together, she said. She told me about a business opportunity she had—it was all very misty and charged—and then she cried and told me she loved me and couldn't live without me, and she took my hand in the restaurant under the table so I could feel how wet she was and we ended up at her apartment where, among other things, she made a videotape of our lovemaking."

"You knew this?"

"Of course I didn't know it! It was obviously part of her game. She taped us, and then she took the tape and went to see Faith.

"I checked the door log; she came here one night when I was out of town, two days before Faith killed herself. She must have done some real Verdi number on her, but she knew Faith wouldn't confront me. In fact Faith hid the tape where she obviously thought I'd never find it.

"Jasmine didn't know someone was going to murder her before she could retrieve it! She gave my wife the tape of us together, and she did it to trigger a suicidal depression.

"I guess she'd figured all the other losses and betrayals would have been enough to buckle Faith, but she was stronger than that, so Madeline played her ace, a Vegas girl to her frigid, bloodless heart. When I played the tape, I knew what was in Faith's head when she climbed down onto that subway track, and I'm as responsible as if I had flung her off the platform. Jesus Christ, Jonny! Why didn't anybody tell me the fucking truth? I never had a shot at stopping any of it! I could have done something! Faith didn't trust me and neither did you."

I was sick to my stomach again, images of my sister looking at a tape that I could only too well picture and one orchestrated for maximum injury, like a shrapnel bomb, created to wreck havoc, to maim rather than simply kill.

"Why should we have trusted you? It turns out you weren't so trustworthy, after all."

He stiffened as if all his joints had suddenly locked.

"You're right, of course. I can't expect you to have any empathy."

"Wrong again. I do have empathy! She seduced me too, Benjamin. I too got the 'no one's ever made me come' routine. I lost Sari because of her and I knew better, but I still kept wanting not to believe it. My ambivalance contributed to three deaths!

"Faith actually believed all the tragedy was *her* fault! We all took the guilt on, and none of us are really to blame. We were played by one of the masters of the form. The perfect sociopath. The Devil disguised as the fucking archangel.

"Look at this." I reached over and pulled a diagram from the folder Ezra Clay had delivered. "It's all here in flowing purple cursive. Jasmine, Madeline, Wendy—whoever she was—here's her plan to destroy my sister." The diagram had given me the why, reattaching the dolls heads from my dream.

"Her goal is printed at the top, in a big heart-shaped box. TO HAVE FAITH'S LIFE, BENJAMIN, AND THEIR WORLD. It's very clever ... like reading a highly efficient executive's takeover scheme. Probably a lot like charts you've done yourself.

"She did her homework. She knew everything about Faith's mental history and childhood. She had personal profiles on all of us. She understood that if she just killed Faith, it could backfire, and also this was a game to her, bigger than Vegas; using her wits to destroy her competition really turned her on. She needed to isolate Faith, stoke her longing for a strong, protective mother she could lean on and trust, and then remove all other support, one by one. She fed her demons, and when she was really frightened and dependent, she manipulated her off her medication.

"You made it easy, because you were gone all the time. I was one of the 'barriers,' and so were Sari and Granny. So she seduced me, rendering me helpless. Sari sold her screenplay, so the fates worked for her.

"When she came for Faith the night of Granny's burial, Faith told her what really happened the day our mother killed herself. The secret she never told you or me or her shrinks, a sacred trust that Jasmine used to rip her heart out. She took off her mask for one horrible moment and shattered Faith's spirit. It's all here, a map of human carnage, well-organized and without any crossouts.

"She planned to kill Pebble and burn the inn to finish destroying Faith, because Faith driven to suicide was how she could have you in what she saw as the purest way, and by faking her own death she covered her trail and became another victim. But like all sociopaths, she got too cocky and underestimated the forces outside her control.

"Pebble survived, and Faith found the will to fight back. See, here at the bottom of the chart, she's a little frazzled; her penmanship gets messy. Look, I missed this. It says, *Tape sex and show her. She'll never tell him.*

"Well, she was right about all of it; that did the trick like some miracle folk remedy. It led Faith right down onto the train tracks, cracked her will like a steel bar across the kneecaps, and if you hadn't found the tape and someone hadn't shot her face off, it might have worked.

"Of course, eventually she would have had to kill me and Pebble too, because the minute you appeared with her, it would have been over.

"In some perverse way, we got lucky. Someone stopped her."

Benjamin was staring at the diagram as if it held the answer to life itself. We were both quiet, the unsaid between us now part of the circle. Either of us could have killed her.

The buzzer rang and he moved stiffly, gracelessly. "Yes? ... All right, send them up."

He put down the phone and looked at me, his eyes swollen almost shut. "The police."

I sighed. "Daisy Mae must have read this. Give me your lawyer's number and I'll call him, but don't act defensive or arrogant, and for God's sake don't say anything; let them tell you first."

His face was as white as his pajamas. "Will you arrange for Pebble after school tomorrow, if they hold me?"

"Sure. I'll stay here if you want."

"I'd appreciate that, Jonny." The doorbell rang and he started to turn away, hesitating to say what was still unsaid.

"I didn't kill her, Jonny. I swear to fucking Christ."

Pacci and Dinelli took Benjamin away. I called his lawyer and left a note for Tilly, telling her I would be staying for a couple of days. I should have been wiped out but I was wired, a crackling restlessness moving me forward. I grabbed a flashlight from Tilly's supply drawer and one of Benjamin's baseball caps and his house keys and I went out. It was past one and there were no cabs in sight, so I began walking uptown in the chilly quiet of Upper East Side Manhattan, thinking my night thoughts.

The building where the beast had lived was one of those anonymous condo jobs geared to less affluent aspirers who wouldn't qualify before any tony co-op board but still had bucks enough for some cachet.

The doorman was slightly pugnacious but clearly bored out of his head and not too interested in the privacy of a dead former occupant no longer able to provide him with tips or a nice Christmas bonus. He barely glanced at my police credentials before handing me the passkey.

I slid the yellow crime-scene ribbon back and unlocked the door. The electricity had been shut off. I snapped on the flashlight and stood for a moment, adjusting to the darkness. Her aura was everywhere, the power of her presence so ferocious that even death hadn't stopped it. And the scent, tickling my senses, mocking me. It was a replica of her cottage on the Cape, the bare necessities of function, revealing nothing of the inhabitant, the rooms of a person without needs, compulsions, obsessions, desires or vices; without vanity or interests; without weakness or humanity.

There was something alarming and also pitiable about it, as if her entire existence had been put in limbo until she had taken over Faith's life. She would wait until then to leave her imprint on the world. And yet the energy still vibrating from her was so strong it seemed the untamable panther would spring forth and smite me with the sheer force of her depravity.

I followed my beam where it fell, looking for the unknown object seeking my light, a sign, a clue, something unclaimed, waiting in the shadows for someone to return. I opened the refrigerator. A bottle of expensive red wine, a bunch of shriveled purple grapes, and a moldy wedge of French cheese, a minimalist down to the last moment. I searched every drawer, the bedroom, the closet, the bath. I pointed my light under the sparse rented furniture, then followed the beam back to the hallway, the place of her last stand, the site of the kill, when her luck ran out, her insolence fouled her instincts, and she fell, outsmarted by one of the flawed lesser beings she so abhorred.

A sparkle behind the radiator. I knelt down on my knees and reached back, but my hand was too large. I pulled Benjamin's keys out of my pocket and pushed the longest one in, and the glimmer rolled forth onto the parquet floor, across the crime-scene cutout where she had fallen, making a small tumbling sound, like dice on a dining table.

I picked it up: a small silver cube with an initial, a remnant from the bracelets I'd bought Faith and Sari and Rita and Pebble when the inn opened. A cube that had been left behind in the killer's haste, one tiny sterling die. I staggered to my feet and lurched across the floor to the guest bath. The grief sickness gurgled through me, retching forth the unthinkable.

* * *

What to do, what to do? Rinsing my face, fumbling in my pocket for one of my father's hankies, like Benjamin's, silk with initials, sensual corruption, wet it down, cover my prints, backing out.

Down the elevator, a fifty for the doorman; I was never here, a phantom to him anyway. Where to go? Home, must go home, don't know why. No more lassos or wreaths or nooses, only me and a hula hoop, banging against my belly, try to keep my hips moving, keep it from falling, keep it twirling, keep it up.

In a cab, crazy-driving son of Islam, icons dangling, pictures of children, darkly curled, circles again, smiling children, refugees also, trying to fit in. Tipping lavishly, compassion for a comrade, up I went. Message light flashing, proof I exist. Press the button. Benjamin's law man, $500 per phone call, steady tone, delivering bad news, good at spin, like my hula hoop, my hips wiggling faster, straining to keep us from falling.

"Mr. Duck, bad news, I'm afraid. They've verified registration on a twenty-two automatic Benjamin owns, uses the same caliber bullets as the murder weapon. So even without the actual gun, now that they've established motive and opportunity, it's enough for them to hold him. He wants you to tell his daughter, and I need to talk with you as soon as possible. Call me any time day or night."

Day or night, sun or moon, light or dark no longer matters; in Australia this hasn't happened yet. What to do? Where to turn, whom to trust? So tired, maybe just sleep, can't lie down without dropping the hoop, keep moving, something will come. Walk till morning, only thing to do, wait, wait for her at school.

Hear her laugh, down the street she comes, with her friend, first laugh since Faith, blond hair bouncing, friend holding her arm. Forgot the hoop in my haste, stumbling over the rim, gravity taking it down. Uncle Jonny, what's the matter? Assumption now that a grown-up arriving unannounced means trouble, loss, skinning of innocence.

I lead her away, tell her teacher family emergency, walking fast, where to go? My place so grim, but safe. Quiet in cab, bouncing up Sixth Avenue, looking out at hustlers and drug dealers, garmentos *and Hassidim, skateboarders and roller bladers, daring the streets. Flower dealers pushing plant carts, women in black pumps and trench coats, freshly washed work hair swirling in the breeze, men in rack suits, carrying sample cases. Puerto Rican mothers at the bus stops, pretty little girls holding their hands. Kamikaze van drivers shouting at pedestrians: Fuck you, moron! Move your fucking ass, dickhead! Chants of early workday routes, intersection music, how we cope here, tribal rituals, part of the deal.*

Pebble solemn, pale under freckles. Me, griefstruck, now and forever, stomach churning, every pothole bringing bile, bringing fear. At the door, Pebble's first visit, seeing my straggly refugee life through her eyes. See she's sorry for me, wanting something better. Her eyes so big, Benjamin's shape and Granny O's color, children a stew, a mixture of all the love and everything else. Secret ingredients, things unknown.

Sit down, honey. Want a soda? It's only eight in the morning, she says, more grown up than I. Okay, how 'bout coffee? Face brightens, something illicit. Grand, she says, sounding like her mother. I make some, mostly milk and sugar for her, mostly black and bitter for me. What can I do? We sit on my only couch and sip, her eyes never leaving, knowing without knowing. I tell her about her father and she puts the cup down, curls in a ball, like an embryo, a trilobite, frozen in time by circumstances beyond her control. Small shoulders heaving, child's pain, ratcheting me, only one direction now, no way back.

Up she sits, freeing herself from the lava flow, truth her way out. Daddy didn't do it, Uncle Jonny. I know, I say, my lips trembling, eyes twitching in sorrow. I take out the silver cube, no gleam now, it lies tarnished, dull, and meaningless in my hand. I curse buying them, having to know this. Small soft hand, nails pink and shiny, takes it from me. Eyes clear now, no more tears, except the used ones sliding down her freckles.

It's mine, she says, sighing so deep, a woman's sigh.

I want her child sighs back, want for her what I never had, Faith never had. Damn Faith, doing the same thing, leaving her like this. Damn all of it. Pick her up and take her away. Easton's Beach, sleep in the summer sand, head out to sea.

"I killed her, Uncle Jonny," she said, new tears now, giant drops, like raindrops turning to hail.

"Jasmine came to our house, she wasn't dead! She looked all different. I hid behind the door. No one knew I was there. She made Momma cry, scared her, said bad things about her, but Momma was brave, she stood up, told her she'd kill her if she came near me, told her she was calling the police.

"Jasmine laughed, said she had a present for her. I ran and got Daddy's gun from his desk—I knew where the key was—.

"I waited outside. I heard noises, she was watching a tape, people having sex. I couldn't hear much, but I knew that. Momma was sobbing, saying, 'No! No! Not this, not this!' Things like that.

"I knew, though, I knew it was Daddy, so I ran out; I followed Jasmine home. It was so easy, Momma never even knew I'd gone. I went back the next day after school and I snuck in behind a delivery boy. I had the gun but I wasn't going to do anything. I just wanted to scare her, make her leave my father alone, make her stay away from my mother.

"I just wanted to warn her, but she laughed at me! She called me a 'pathetic little piglet.' She laughed, Uncle Jonny, so I shot her and she fell down, like on TV, and I freaked. I tripped and I dropped the gun and my bracelet popped open, but I was too scared, I ran away.

"I didn't know what to do! They'd blame Daddy or Momma! I ran all the way to your apartment, but I couldn't, you think I'm so nice, I couldn't, but I thought of someone else who could help me and I went there, and they did. They said, 'We'll take care of it,' and I kept waiting for the police, but they didn't come until now. They must have found the gun and now Daddy's in jail for what I did! Take me down there, Uncle Jonny. I have to tell them right away!"

Reaching out, holding her, breathing together, breathing deep, nausea gone, truth always better. Patting her, sorting through. Good news circling bad.

"You didn't kill her, Pebble, someone else did. You just wounded her and hardly that, and no one's found the gun. They just traced registration and connected the make to the bullet. It could have come from a thousand different guns. You didn't do it, Pebs. She was alive when you left. It's okay, sweetheart."

"But Daddy! They'll blame Daddy!"

What to do? So many choices. "I need to know who you went to see."

"I can't, I swore. I'll never tell, not ever."

"Just tell me, not the police."

"No, I swore. I can't be a traitor too! Never. I'll confess. I'm a kid, it won't be so bad for me."

"You don't even know how she died; only the killer does."

"Oh, no! I can't tell, Uncle Jonny!"

Up and out, moving too fast for me to stop her. Can't let her be alone, chasing after, too slow, child vanishing into the crowd. Call Daisy Mae, send a car, find her fast. Not there, message left.

Where would she go? What to do? In a cab, up and down, Tilly's eyes red behind her glasses, magnifying her turmoil, if she comes, hold her here. Out again, following her leads, checking child haunts, nowhere to be found, try the precinct. No little girl here. Where can she be?

Frantic now, hog-tied, choking on the noose, thrashing about, here and there, back to school, not wanting to alarm, waiting for the bell. Children pouring out. Downtown school, attitude, funny clothes, no mother's little miracles here; real kids, misfits maybe. Kids with grit, finding their way through school hell, learning the world as it is—savage and unfinished, petty and jealous and unfair and phony and mendacious, luck of the draw; pretty and ugly, short and tall, fat and slender, nice families and not, the way it is. Learning to cope, make do, survive, learning about the other things, joy and humor and the magic of kindness, friendship, and the shape of thought, snowflakes rushing out the door, no two alike, even with-

*out a magnifying glass, Pebble our snowflake, as precious as breath, where
would she go?*

*I cruise Sari's house, last guess. Ring the bell. Yes? Sari's there, Sari's
hair, smells in my head. I'm looking for Pebble. I don't know where else to
go. She's here, it's okay. Not okay, no way! I have to see her! Leave her be,
she's asleep. I'll bring her later. We're fine, go now, go! Go how? Go where?
What to do?*

*Back to Benjamin's to wait by the phone. Tilly hovering, making me eat,
rubber shoes squeaking on stone, French clock dinging, so quiet. Roaming
around. Faith's little room, pictures of us all, looking for something, like
after my mother died, must have left something for me. Hard to bear, left
like that, like Faith had said, like we were nothing, she and I, now Pebble
and I, hardly pausing to think of the wreckage they left behind.*

*The child rising to defend, child Pebble like child Faith, willing to die, to
kill to protect, children braver, more loyal than us, using the powerlessness
of their place to try and keep everyone safe, ironies piled high. Shit. Who?
Where was she now, Sari? Oh, no. Would Sari have done it? Would Sari
harm her now, if she told what I know? Harm her to save herself? Can't
believe it. What to do?*

*Phone ringing somewhere, Tilly squeaking, calling my name. Ben-
jamin's lawyer sounding proud, they've let him go, amazing turn of tide,
found a fingerprint. He's coming home! Whoopdy-do. What to do? Take
Pebble from Sari, just in case.*

I called Daisy Mae again.

"Hey, Duckman, did you hear?"

"Yes, what does it mean?"

"Well, this is very, very close to the vest; I'm trusting you here.
This is gonna be hard, pal. The print belonged to Faith. She was
the only other person with access to the weapon, motive, and
opportunity. It also explains the suicide. So I think we can wrap
this up now."

I can't speak. My mouth opens and closes like a puppet or a
Pez machine in a kid's hand, strangled sounds trying to form.

"No fucking way! If my sister was capable of doing what I saw, then there is no fucking way for me to live on this planet or to trust any human being enough to walk beside them on the streets of the earth. No fucking way."

"Hey, friend of mine. Anyone pushed that far and with that much to lose can do anything. She had to sever all traces to protect her family. We've got the prints, Benjamin's off the hook, and Pebble won't lose both her parents. Faith's gone, Jonny. Let it be her contrition."

"I can't accept this." My voice was cracking, breaking up like a weak cell signal, moving out of range.

"Hey, Duckster, it will pass, it all passes. Look, it's Theo's birthday, he's doing a barbecue, and I'm late already. Come see me before the people zoo heats up tomorrow. It's still quiet about seven-thirty; we'll go over everything then, okay?"

"No, but I haven't much choice." I hung up. I took a photo of Faith and myself when we were kids, and one of the two of us at the Inn just before it opened, and put them in my pocket, and I sat down at my sister's desk to wait for Benjamin. House sounds, small noises that go unnoticed, filtered through my thoughts.

"Hi." Benjamin, standing in the doorway, looking so tired, so unlike the vision in cashmere and velvet of the previous night.

"We've got to talk."

"Can't it wait?"

"No."

"Okay. Let's have a drink, then."

I followed him down the staircase to the kitchen. Tilly had left a tray of sandwiches and a bottle of wine. I sat while he opened the bottle, still the guest, the lonely uncle, passing by.

I listened to the house sounds, a radiator rattling, the hum of a fan, ice dropping into a tray.

"What did they tell you?"

He tried a smile. "Elvis did it."

"The print was Faith's."

Our eyes met, equals now, no more pissing contests. Tears clouded our view, moans blotted the house sounds.

"I don't believe this, Benjamin. I won't. My sister couldn't do what I saw in the morgue, not even to save Pebble."

"Pebble? What does Pebble have to do with this?"

I told him, holding his eyes through the journey, watching him change as I spoke, likening it to my grandmother's tale of her hair turning white.

"God, Jonny," he said, finally. "Who else knows about this?"

"No one."

"Where is she?"

"With Sari. Go get her now, just to be safe."

"Safe?" Moon man again, brows raising high. "Not Sari, not possible!"

"It's a fucking short list. Just go get her, she needs you."

He stood up slowly, a different man now, fallen to earth.

"Jonny, you're right. Faith couldn't have done it. Find out, please, for Faith and Pebble. Please."

"I'll try." *Do better.* My grandmother's voice in my head now forever.

I started toward home, then turned back uptown, aimless, wandering, the maze of random thoughts sprinting across my mind's eye. That word, sticking: *contrition.* Contrition for what?

And I knew. I went to an ATM machine, and got some cash, and hailed a cab. I'd spent more on cabs in the last twelve hours than the last twelve months, but this was not a subway sort of situation. I realized that all the frenzied, palsied anxiety and queasiness was gone. I was quiet, still at the center.

"Staten Island. I'll direct you when we get over the bridge."

While we rode, I put the pieces in place. I had the window open and I could smell Theo's barbecue before I saw the little red-brick row house, right across from the water. I paid and went around the back. The night was surprisingly warm, and it looked like the entire precinct was present.

Theo was holding court, explaining to the first-timers the superiority of Texas over Carolina barbecue. "We baste the meat; them idiots just smoke the meat and dump the sauce on after." Ribs were sizzling, and a whole pig was rotating on a spit above his in-ground pit. People waved, I heard a few scattered *Hey, Jonny, long times*, touching me like all refugees, reminding me I once had a life.

I found her in the kitchen sipping a long neck, as Theo called beer in bottles. If she was surprised to see me, it didn't show. "Hey, it's the Duckman! A little class for the unwashed! Get this man a brew. Get him two, he needs 'em."

I shook my head and stopped the eager party aide. "Can we talk somewhere?"

Her smile shortened, and I saw hardness closing off the back of her wise, weary eyes.

"Sure, just so long's I don't miss that first rack off the grill. I been savin' my fat calories for weeks."

"You won't miss a bone." I followed her through the throng and into Theo's bedroom, which she seemed quite at home in. She plopped down on his bed, making it moan under her weight, and took a long sip of her beer. "Still wrestling with the news?"

I stood in front of her, amazed at how relaxed I felt.

"Naw. No more wrestling. I know the truth. It was that word you used, *contrition*. I kept rolling it around. Contrition for what? Let me tell you what I think happened. Some I know for sure; the rest, you do.

"I think that when Pebble ran out of Jasmine's apartment, petrified and not knowing where to turn, she turned to the most likely person, the woman who had saved her life once already, someone who knew about crime, someone who loved her family. I know Pebble shot her, but we both know she didn't kill her. She wouldn't tell me who she talked to; she ran away from me. But it had to be you.

"So here comes Pebble, pouring out this nightmare, and you

made a choice. You crossed a line. You went back to the apartment, no problem getting past that baloney head at the door, or maybe you went in the back, used one of your cop keys. And you found her, one shot, kid's aim, must have been the surface one in her abdomen.

"She was stunned, hadn't been able to crawl over and call for help yet. You picked up the gun and blew the psychopathic filth back to the hell hole she crawled out of.

"The mutilations made it impossible to connect her to anyone, let alone us. You cleaned up everything, Pebble's bracelet, whatever. But one little cube got lost, and you missed the business cards with my name, Sari's, all of it. The fucking link. So when your guys found them, you had to do your job.

"You'd dumped the gun and I was easy enough at that interview, so you were able to punt. A blot on your record, not finding the perp, but there were your two detectives to catch the heat. Who could have figured that your old swain, Detective Big Foot, would get inspired and find that file?

"So then you're fucked. Can't let Benjamin take the fall. You're too good a cop for that, and even if you weren't, Pebble wouldn't have allowed it. She'd have spilled her heart and slipped up, and they'd have found out it was you.

"No way anyone would believe that kid was cold and cunning enough to do what was done to Jasmine. Besides, she couldn't have told them, because she didn't know. So you've got a major mother of a problem. What would a cop's cop do? Not too hard to lift one of Faith's prints and plant it in the apartment or even in the lab with the evidence. 'Just a hunch, guys, but dust that doorknob one more time.' Bingo. You had Faith's prints on file because of the suicide. Perfect, she's dead, anyway.

"So, it does become an act of contrition: Faith's repentance for committing a mortal sin and for leaving her daughter motherless. In a way, then, she's sacrificing herself to save Pebble and protecting you too, because you went all the way across the field for us with a very big ball under your arm. I just needed to know it wasn't my sister. I needed to know I couldn't have been that wrong about someone I thought I knew so well."

Daisy Mae put her bottle down on the floor, tossing her huge head of frizzy waves forward and back. Tears were gushing out of her eyes, pooling in pockets along the creases in her cheeks. I had never seen her cry before.

"Bravo, Duckman. Hit the little sucker right in the bull's-eye."

"No joy in it."

"Maybe just a little, the old male macho meat-beating, a little glee at getting it right, one over on the old pro."

"I'd rather have been wrong."

"Well, you weren't. So?"

"So?"

"What happens now? You've got all the barrels loaded. I'm the sitting duck now, pal o' mine. You're the fucking fowl hunter."

The tears were still gushing down her face and her body was shaking, all the vulnerability pushed down under her jolly-jelly take-no-prisoners facade, melting like fat on the grill outside.

I knelt down in front of her and took her damp hands in mine.

"Hey, lieutenant, remember what you told me? Friends are few. You saved Pebble twice. You put your life on the line for her. We know what Jasmine was, and God only knows what more she would have done and how many other people would have suffered and died.

"There still wasn't any proof to hook her to anything that happened on the Cape. Pebble would have gone to a state home, and Jasmine would have gone free, and probably nothing could have saved Faith by then anyway, but I'm sure you hoped killing Jasmine would help.

"All those years I covered the Mob, I picked up some of their coda. Faith would be proud of this; it *is* her contrition. You forgot who you were talking to."

She smiled and the hardness left her eyes. "Oh, Duckman, they for sure broke the mold with you."

"Thank God. Let's get a rack and suck some back."

And we did.

EPILOGUE

Summer came again and Pebble and I went home to Newport, to my grandmother's house. Benjamin and I have worked out a sort of dual custody plan. During the school year she's with him and a tutor, traveling where he travels. Summers she's with me in Newport.

At first I was going to clear everything out and refurbish and remodel, but Pebble convinced me otherwise and she was right. It's okay for some things to stay the same. So many memories, so close by, brings me joy and sorrow, pain and intense pleasure, connecting me every moment of the days here to myself, my life now, and my past. I guess because I've made peace with as many of the demons as I can see, it's okay. They are, after all, just feelings, not the bogeymen I thought they were.

So I'm back in the fifth ward for the summer, writing my book for quite a bit of money and taking my niece to Easton's Beach. The tuna sandwiches aren't as good and the naps have less surrender, but all in all, for both of us, healing together in our own way, it's pretty nice.

I wrote Sari at Pebble's urging and asked her to come up for a weekend and she wrote back saying she'd like that. I'd like it, too, but I don't want to get ahead of myself. I have no illusions about where the path will lead.

It all seems like footprints in the sand—life, that is. Every time you try and look back, nature's covered the trail. Forward it is, now, the sand deeper as I trudge, but warm and soft, and for that small gift I am grateful.

Gloria Nagy is a novelist and screenwriter. She is the author of eight novels including the best-selling *A House in the Hamptons* and the children's book *The Wizard Who Wanted to Be Santa*. Her latest novel, *The Beauty*, is set in Newport and Cape Cod. Critics have called her "the social chronicler of her time."

Her novels have been published around the world and translated into numerous languages, including German, Japanese, Hebrew, Russian, and Dutch.

Ms. Nagy lives in Newport, Rhode Island, with her husband, Richard Saul Wurman. They have four children, four grandchildren, and a dog named Max.

8/01   **FICTION**

DEMCO